THE EDGE OF
STRANGE HOLLOW

ALSO BY GABRIELLE K. BYRNE

Rise of the Dragon Moon

THE EDGE OF STRANGE HOLLOW

GABRIELLE K. BYRNE

[Imprint]
MAKE YOUR MARK
New York

[Imprint]
MAKE YOUR MARK

A part of Macmillan Publishing Group, LLC
120 Broadway, New York, NY 10271

THE EDGE OF STRANGE HOLLOW.
Copyright © 2021 by Gabrielle K. Byrne. All rights reserved.
Printed in the United States of America by
LSC Communications, Harrisonburg, Virginia.

Library of Congress Cataloging-in-Publication Data is available.
ISBN 978-1-250-62466-6 (hardcover) / ISBN 978-1-250-62467-3 (ebook)

Our books may be purchased in bulk for promotional, educational, or
business use. Please contact your local bookseller or the Macmillan Corporate
and Premium Sales Department at (800) 221-7945 ext. 5442
or by email at MacmillanSpecialMarkets@macmillan.com.

Book design by Jessica Lauren Chung

Imprint logo designed by Amanda Spielman

First edition, 2021

1   3   5   7   9   10   8   6   4   2

mackids.com

FOR ALTHEA AND ROWAN—
MY STORIES, MY HEART

This book is also dedicated to allll the many little
(or somewhat grown) denizens of my family forest,
including, but certainly not limited to:
Oliver R., Anjuli, Colin, Solveig, Aylin, Nicco, Etta,
Amanda, Olivia, Maya, Brooks, Raiel, Ava, Layla,
Lucas, Caden, Oliver B., Katie, Addie, Savanah,
Harmony, Cypress, Liam, Eleanor, Melanie, Malachi,
Mathias, Marcus, Breaunah, Natasha, Milla, Peja,
Bayla, Kiara, Jakobi, Taylia, and Zekai.

ONCE UPON A TIME

The twins—one boy and one girl—sat beneath the thick wooden table, listening. Rain pattered against the windows, and the fire crackled in front of their father as he carved a new ward to sit on Governor Gale's roof beam. The thin curls of wood flipped themselves neatly into the hearth as he worked. Their mother stood next to him in the firelight as they spoke in clipped whispers.

"They say he walked right out of his house last night," the girl heard her mother say.

Their father said nothing, but his mouth tightened and another curl of wood whipped itself into the fire.

"He was a good man—a good neighbor."

Their mother wiped her eyes on her sleeves. "He *never* went into the wood. He kept his wards strong."

The girl swallowed. She hadn't known Mr. Chaten well, but he had once brought a stew to share with them when her father was gone to Trader's Hollow.

"What was it?" their father asked, and the girl's heart quailed at the anger in his low voice.

"Governor Gale thinks the malediction took the shape of a fork. Just . . . just a plain fork."

Their father sighed and let the carving fall to his lap. He turned to their mother and took her hands. "Such a simple thing. Did he bring it inside? Did he use it?"

Her mother nodded, and the girl could feel the tickle of her brother's breath near her ear, listening with her.

"Uprooted it in his own field," their mother choked. "It could have been us, Rob. He thought it was his own. He laughed with Talon about it last night at the inn—how he'd grown careless in his old age."

"And—"

"And—this morning he was gone. Walked into the Grimwood on his own two feet in the night."

Their father turned back to his carving. Another flick of his knife. Another curl of wood hissing in the fire. "He won't be back."

"No. He won't be back."

"Any pickers?"

"Not that anyone saw. Only footprints."

The girl's brother shifted next to her. "I bet the pickers come tonight," the boy said in her ear, making the hair on her neck rise. His dark curls, a perfect match to hers, caught the light. "I bet you picked up a malediction and didn't even know it, just like Mr. Chaten—some little thing by the river—and tonight the pickers will walk through the Hollows with their stick bodies and their tiny heads, and their scrabbling legs. They'll tap at your window and call you out to follow them into the Grimwood."

"They will not!" The girl scowled as she sat up and crossed her arms. The two looked alike in every way—dark curls, dark eyes, and skin the color of gingerbread—the same shade as the pale brown earth under their fingernails. She was, perhaps, a bit smaller, a little thinner in the face—but perhaps not.

"Anyway, the pickers would never take me," she hissed at him. "Mother says I'm too ornery to feed to the thorn trees. But I bet the faeries *will* take *you* in the night." A gleam came into her eyes. "Their queen will come knocking. Mother won't even mind. She'll let them through the wards, and they'll take you away in chains."

The boy's face fell. Tears filled his eyes. A flash of remorse flew across the girl's face. Her brother was full of clever thoughts and bright plans, but the sharp edge of his imagination cut two ways. He was too quick to believe. She took his hand. "They won't really, Peter," she whispered, unable to meet his eyes.

They watched their mother's feet, silent in green wool house shoes, as she moved across the worn floor to open the front door of the cottage. The pensive blues of nightfall spilled into the room like the finest faery silk. "See," the girl insisted. "Mother's setting the wards now."

They peeked together out from under the table as their mother placed their protective ward gently on its post outside the door. The gruesome witch, with her twiggy carved hair and sharp teeth would keep away real witches—and other horrors they couldn't name. Then their mother sprinkled salt and iron shavings at their doorstep and held up the small bell, ringing it to set the wards. "Many are the roots," she sang. "Many are the eyes. Pass us by. Pass us by. Pass us by." Her words rang like the bell, over the top of their neighbors' voices as they did the same, their many voices and bells folding into a singsong. Pass us by. Pass us by.

The boy shivered, and grabbed his sister's other hand. "Say the rhyme with me, Mags."

Her smile could have warmed a stone. She turned to face him, both cross-legged, and met his eyes. Their voices pitched just over a whisper as the scent of warm bread filled the room.

Stay away from the Grimwood, child. Stay away from the fog. Stay away from the thorn trees, child. Stay away from the bog. Keep the promise. Rue the day. The Grimwood is no place to play. Close the shutters. Lock the doors. They come for you on twos and fours. They come for you on twos and fours.

CHAPTER ONE

There were terrible things in the Grimwood. Things that could, and would, try to kill her. This was why Poppy's parents didn't want her in the Grimwood at all. She understood that, and yet here she was, standing at the forest's edge.

Her heart raced, but not from fear. It wasn't likely she'd bump into a monster—not at high noon, so close to the town of Strange Hollow.

She peered into the wood's dappled shadows where the trees stretched away behind the cockeyed arches and towers of her house. Poppy could only manage one hundred paces into the wood before the ward her parents put on her became unbearable. They hoped it would curb her thirst to learn everything there was to know about the Grimwood, but it didn't. Trying to make her stay out only made the longing worse. Especially when her parents were always leaving on long, mysterious trips into the wood themselves.

She was nine when her parents stopped sharing

stories of their work. They must have realized that the light in Poppy's eyes was more than just a passing fancy. Instead they huddled together in the kitchen reviewing their plans when they thought she was asleep. Poppy, in turn, perfected the art of eavesdropping. She learned a lot that way, not just about the woods, but about the dangers her parents faced hunting maledictions. They risked their lives to bring the objects home and put them in stasis—making them powerless to lure the people of Strange Hollow into the wood.

Poppy tugged her long black hair into a ponytail and wiped her palms against her black jeans. She carried her small day pack, filled to bursting with her mother's old net gun, an extra knife (her favorite was holstered in her right boot), two apples, bug spray, and a water bottle. She slung the length of rope over her shoulder. Before she left the house, she'd swapped her own black T-shirt for one of her mother's from the laundry— decorated with a sea dragon and the words "They Might Be Giants," whatever that was supposed to mean. She lifted the neckline of the shirt and closed her eyes to take a deep breath. The bunched muscles of her shoulders eased as the warm green scent of her mother's vetiver oil washed over her.

Her parents had hunted maledictions in the Grimwood for the last three days. Jute told her they were back the moment she had woken up that morning. They'd arrived home when the sun was just a hint of green on the horizon, and they would sleep for most of the day. So Poppy was taking matters into her own hands.

It was time to prove they could make the Hollows safer *as a family*. She was tired of being alone. She was tired of hoping they would see she wasn't just another kid they had to protect, who had nothing to offer.

They had taught her a lot about the forest—more than they knew—but it wasn't enough. Poppy wanted to know *all* the Grimwood's secrets. Her questions itched under her skin, as numerous and irritating as the mosquitoes buzzing around her. Some of them were big . . . like whether the Alcyon sea was bottomless, or whether the Holly Oak could talk, or if unicorns were real. She wanted to know more about the maledictions—and how to tell the difference between a good witch and a bad one. Big or small, any question could keep her awake for hours—like, what did a thorn tree look like, or how many species of tentaculars were there?

Poppy wanted to see it all with her own eyes—was *going* to see it all. She was done starving for answers while her parents threw them out like bread crumbs.

She tugged on the fingerless leather gloves her uncle Jute had given her for her last birthday. The black leather made her skin look even paler than usual, but they beat the cuts and insect bites she used to come home with on her hands. Jute wasn't really her uncle. He was a hob her parents had rescued in the forest and invited home before she was even born.

Poppy finished pulling on her gloves, and straightened her spine. She would go in, get the Mogwen feather, and come straight out again. Alone, the Mogwen were no threat to a human—but they were rarely alone. A symphony of Mogwen, once angered, became merciless predators. But if she could get a Mogwen feather, her parents would see she was ready. She let herself imagine it—holding the long red and turquoise feather out as her mother's eyes widened in shock. Her father's mouth falling open . . . their faces full of resigned respect.

Poppy stared into the forest and considered. Yes, that would make them listen. It would prove she deserved to go all the way into the Grimwood—not just a hundred steps. She hoped that after today her parents would take their ward off her themselves.

Her parents were always going on about the town's useless obsession with wards. They carved statues of monsters and placed them on roof beams and posts outside their doors to keep the real monsters away. They put out bells to appease faeries. But they were just trinkets. They sang songs, too, and they were pretty—but *what good was a song*, her father would scoff.

No, there were only two kinds of wards that did any good at all. Rock salt mixed with iron shavings was one. The other was a blood ward, like the one her parents had put on her.

Poppy took a deep breath and stepped into the forest. Her ears buzzed with the warding, but she ignored it. The air was cool and smelled of sap and heat, and something else bitter-sharp, and like always—despite the ward, there was part of her that could breathe better here. It was as though she was a knot, drawn tight all the time, and only the air of the forest could untangle her. Ninety-eight steps left. Her boots sank a little in the summer soil, and her heart skipped a beat as she looked up into the canopy. There was no breeze, but the trees rustled and creaked.

Poppy paused to listen. In the distance she caught the Mogwen song—two birds, or maybe four—singing in two-part harmony. Mogwen weren't rare, but they were rarely caught. She moved quickly, holding tight to the loops of rope she'd slung over her shoulder and backpack. She stopped counting her steps. She had tested the ward with painstaking thoroughness, so she knew what would happen. First her skin would tingle, and then it would itch—and then, when she got close to her hundredth step, it would burn, and not in a pleasant way.

Poppy's breath rasped against her teeth as she hurried toward the birdsong. She hoped Mack would join her. He'd be angry at her if she "made bad choices" without him. Half a smile edged its way across her face at the thought of his stern expression. It was Mack who had told her about the Mogwen. He'd been her best and only friend ever since an afternoon two years ago when she found him picking mushrooms at the edge of the forest.

The song grew louder, and now the birds sang in three-part harmony. That meant there had to be at least six of them. Any more, and she'd have to come back another time; it would be too dangerous. Three more steps and her skin tingled everywhere with full-body pins and needles. Twenty steps left.

A flash of red feathers high above gave the Mogwen away. Poppy pressed herself against the sticky bark of a pine tree and looked up. The birds were in the highest branches of a white-barked birch—and beside it stood the first thorn tree she had ever seen.

Poppy's heart jumped. She knew what it was right away. Nothing else could have that shiny, smooth black bark. The tree almost glittered, as though it was draped in a fine sunlit layer of frost. The whip-like branches shifted, dancing in the nonexistent breeze, and she caught glimpses of the long thorns underneath. She hadn't expected them to be so . . . pretty. It was like a willow tree gone wrong.

Thorn trees grew from heavy black soil, watered in the blood of their prey, and littered with the skeletons of animals once wrapped in their thorny whips. In the Grimwood deep, whole groves of them grew. Her parents had stumbled on more than one that had caught a human. They spoke about the thorn trees in hushed voices, after they stumbled in from their death-defying missions. Young Poppy had loved the tiny shivers that ran down her spine when her parents told her about their work.

Seeing her first for-real thorn tree made Poppy's mouth go dry, but she resisted the urge to move closer for a better look. The trick with thorn trees was to see them before you got too close—before they sensed you were there. This one hadn't been there a few days ago. She'd heard they sprang out of the ground like springs, but did they always grow so fast, she wondered . . . and what was it doing here, so close to the edge?

The thorn trees defend the forest and feed its magic. Attack the forest, and a thorn tree would grow. Any creature that dared to cut down a tree in the Grimwood would soon find themselves looking at the world from high up, wrapped in the whips of a thorn tree. Had someone—besides her—gone into the forest and tried to, what? Cut down a tree?

The dark circle of soil around the thorn tree still held remnants of the shrubs and plants that had died when it rose. Poppy shivered. She didn't even want to imagine what had caused the huge groves in the deep wood to grow. Perhaps they had been there as long as the forest.

She peeled her gaze away from the tree, turning back toward the Mogwen. The birds were clever. They had perched just far enough away that the thorn-covered-whips couldn't reach to strike them down or wind them in a deadly embrace.

Poppy ignored the sparking sensations that fluttered over her skin and carefully reached back over her shoulder. Her fingers wrapped around the smooth cold barrel of the net gun as she lifted it free. She peered up at the nearest bird through the crosshairs and pressed her lips together. She'd forgotten how big they were. Easily two feet tall, with a pointed red crest and sharp black beak they used to pierce their prey.

Poppy paused and studied the trees. She'd have to choose one and climb to get close enough to nab the bird with her net gun. Her best option would be the pine just outside the circle of black soil that marked the thorn tree's territory. It was farther from the Mogwen than she liked, but she had the ward to consider—not to mention the thorn tree. The pine was just out of its range.

She wrapped the rope around the pine with a sharp exhale, coiling each end around one of her wrists. She gripped tight, leaned back, and gritting her teeth, began to climb.

Beams of sunlight pierced through the trees like arrows. The pine sap made the rope stick, and sweat burst out over Poppy's forehead as she quietly made her way up the tree. She tried not to step on the small purple and black tentaculars that scattered over the surface of the bark, each one waving its sticky arms in the air to gather pollen before bending them, one at a time, to the hole of its mouth.

Poppy's hands slicked, and she sent Jute silent thanks for the gloves.

The Mogwen song drifted over the forest, the three distinct patterns rising and falling together like a spell. Poppy pulled herself up to sit on a branch and caught her breath. The humming of the ward in her ears was starting to give her a headache, but she didn't care. She was almost as high as the Mogwen now—just below them, but close enough to see their round yellow eyes. One of them had cocked its head at her, watching.

She squeezed her hands into fists, gritting her teeth as she fought to push away the itching pinpricks of the ward. The pain was supposed to keep her out of the wood altogether. It was supposed to make her turn around and go home, but it only made her more determined.

She was shaking her hands out when a thump from below caught her attention. Mack scowled up at her. Her best friend's skin and chestnut curls were almost as dark as the pine bark, and for a moment all Poppy saw were his copper eyes looking up at her from the dappled shadows. Mack was an elf, but still growing and, for now, only a little taller than her. In addition to his many good qualities as a friend, Poppy had to admit that his forest savvy had been helpful on several occasions. From where she sat, high in the tree branches, he looked small. She gave a tiny wave.

"What are you doing?" he mouthed up at her.

She pointed across at the Mogwen.

Mack shook his head.

Poppy nodded and lifted her net gun from her lap.

She could hear his nose-sigh from all the way up the tree.

She scooted farther from the trunk to take aim, her body rocking as she balanced on the narrowing branch. She forced herself not to cringe as the buzzing of her ward grew louder in her ears. Slowly, she lifted the net gun to peer through the crosshairs and sighted a beautiful male Mogwen singing the bass line.

The gun gave a twang. The net careened toward the bird, and he squawked a deep cry, lifting into the air as it wrapped around his branch. Poppy let out a swear word as a single black whip, longer than the rest, looped up from the thorn tree, wrapped around Poppy's ankle, and yanked.

She toppled from the tree.

Mack dived to catch her, and she landed on him, knocking the wind out of both of them. Another whip struck the ground next to their faces, and Poppy rolled over, tugging to get her leg free as the thorn tree reeled her in.

Mack, choking and gasping for air, grabbed under her arms and scuttled backward, pulling until Poppy was suspended in the air, with Mack on one side and the thorn tree on the other.

"Lose the boot," Mack grunted.

Poppy tried to bend her knee, but her leg was pulled taut. "They're my . . . favorites," she ground out. Her knee-high leather boots had thick soles, and thick leather—and cute little skulls on the sides.

"By thorns, Poppy! Lose the boot!"

"I thought you were strong! Pull like you mean it, Mack!"

He gave her a yank that bent the thorn branch toward them. "Harder," Poppy hollered. "It's loosening."

Mack grunted again. "Your arms will come out of your sockets if I pull any harder."

"They'll heal! I'm not losing these boots! Wait! Move me forward."

Mack's heels skidded forward an inch. He tugged back again. "Forward? *Toward* the thorn tree? No way! You'll be killed!" He yanked again. "Thorns, Poppy! We'll *both* be killed!"

"My knife's in my boot. I can cut the whip."

Mack's grip loosened a little and Poppy stretched to just reach the wooden handle of her knife. She pulled it clear and swiped across the whip.

They fell back, but this time, Mack pulled them out of range of the thorn tree.

Poppy sat up and examined her boot. There were thorn scratches all over the leather, but no holes. She patted it with a smile, and returned her knife to the ankle holster inside. "Good boot."

She turned to look at Mack. He was lying on his back, staring up at the canopy and breathing hard. "You okay?"

"Uh-huh."

"Thanks for the help."

"Uh-huh."

"I mean . . . I could have dealt with it . . . but thanks."

Mack's gaze shifted to meet hers, then returned to the treetops. "You should have waited for me."

"I missed the Mogwen."

Mack scanned the trees. "You're lucky they flew away instead of attacking us."

Poppy pressed her lips tight. "They're faster than I expected." She hopped up and brushed herself off, then held out her hand to Mack to help him up.

He was barefoot, as always. The tight spirals of his hair—the same tawny brown as his skin, hung low over his coppery eyes. The points of his ears didn't give him better hearing, exactly, but they did pick up on vibrations that came through his feet. Today Mack had on a pair of jeans, and a green T-shirt with a hand holding a bunch of flowers on it.

He pointed at her T-shirt. "'They Might Be Giants'? What's that supposed to mean?"

Poppy shrugged. "I don't know. It's my mom's. I think she got it at the last solstice trade."

"So . . . it's a human thing—from outside the fog?"

"Probably," Poppy agreed, rolling her shoulders to work out the ache.

"It's a sea monster, though . . . not a giant." Mack shook his head, his eyebrows furrowed. "And there's only one. It should say, 'It might be a sea monster,' not 'They Might Be Giants.'"

Poppy waited. She knew where this was going.

"You don't think humans outside the fog think giants are . . . are sea monsters, do you?"

"No. I doubt it."

Finally, he got around to the point. "I wonder if my grandfather would have known about this."

Poppy put one hand up on Mack's shoulder in solidarity—united in their quest for the unknown. Ever since Mack had found out that one of his grandparents *might* have been human, he was as obsessed with learning about human things as Poppy was about the Grimwood. The grandparents in question had *apparently* had a whirlwind romance, then the grandfather had disappeared, and probably died, before the question could be resolved to Mack's family's satisfaction, *apparently*. The whole thing had been making his brain itch ever since.

"But there aren't even sea monsters or giants or elves . . . or any of the wood folk out there—past the fog, right?"

"Nope. Don't think so."

"So . . ."

"I don't get it either." Poppy frowned. "Things outside the fog are different from in the Hollows. It could mean anything."

The buzzing in her ears from the warding was starting to hurt. She squeezed her fists—open, closed, open, closed.

Mack caught sight of her hands and his expression turned stern. "You know what I don't get, Poppy? I don't get why we're hunting Mogwen."

She sighed, and looked back toward the thorn tree. A flash of red caught her eye. "No way," she said under her breath, then gave a little hop. "No! Way!"

"What?"

Poppy didn't answer.

Now was the time for action.

A single Mogwen feather lay at the base of the thorn tree. She'd have to cross the boundary of her ward, but she could do it. "Mack, take my pack." Poppy shrugged out of her backpack and pulled her knife again.

"Poppy . . . what are you . . ." He followed her gaze to the feather. "No way. Don't do it."

"I'm doing it."

"Poppy, that's a thorn tree. Seriously."

"It's already done." She launched herself forward. Two steps. Three.

She dived, grabbing the feather from the ground as she rolled back up to her feet, running. The whip cut the air behind her.

She dodged left, out of the tree's range as the pins and needles turned to burning. Pain lanced through her and she threw herself back across the boundary with a scream that was half anguish and half victory.

She lay on her back panting, the feather in her hand, as sweat rolled down her neck. A harsh laugh bubbled out of her. "See? No problem."

He crossed his arms. "I can't believe you just did that. That was really dangerous."

Poppy shot a smirk at him from the ground. Mack had never been a take-chances kind of guy. She understood that.

He scowled down at her. "It's just a feather, Poppy."

She couldn't stop her smile. "It's not just a feather. When my parents see this, it will change everything."

Poppy rose to her feet and gave him a friendly pat on the back as she shuffled past him. "Come on. Let's go see what Jute's got cooking."

CHAPTER TWO

They moved toward the edge of the forest, where the afternoon sunlight was beginning to turn gold. As they walked, Poppy told Mack about her plan to finally get her parents to listen to her. She knew Mack was mulling things over from the way his eyebrows knit together. Her best friend could be stodgy, and a worry-wart, but she still didn't like to upset him.

She cast an uncertain look at him as she rubbed at a scratch on the side of her neck. The thorn tree had been faster than she expected—almost wily, like it knew she couldn't resist the feather. Poppy stepped out of the trees and exhaled as the ward her parents placed on her fell away. She gave her body a shake, like a dog coming out of a cold river.

As they moved into the bright meadow that surrounded Poppy's house where it looked down over the village of Strange Hollow, Mack finally said what was on his mind.

He tugged her to a stop. "Just . . . if things don't go

your way with your parents . . . promise me you won't do anything reckless. Think first. And promise you'll listen, especially if I tell you something's dangerous. Promise me that, and whatever happens—as long as it doesn't put other people in danger, you can count me in."

She looked up into his guileless face and knew her relief showed. "Of course! I absolutely promise." The breeze shivered over her skin, and she tipped her chin up, sniffing the air.

"Because you're not always the best at—"

"Do you smell food?"

He scowled.

"Don't worry." She smiled. "This feather is going to work." She tried not to think too hard about what would happen if her parents didn't react the way she hoped. She had read in an older journal that blood wards could be broken, but that it would hurt. A lot. She pushed the thought away.

Her house stood waiting in all its contorted, twisted glory, confident of their return, and as proud of its odd beauty as a cat in the afternoon sun. The front of Poppy's home was the small cob cottage that her parents had built before she was born. It held the front door, and a small window of colored glass to either side. But above the door and around the cottage, stretching behind and three stories up, were all the rooms that the forest had grown for them. All of it—from the first floor up to the turret that was Poppy's bedroom, was made from thick tendrils of roots. It was as if the forest grew arms and hugged their home against its branches, clinging there like a dear friend.

The way her mother told it, as soon as her parents made the choice to enter the Grimwood and begin hunting the cursed objects that grew in the forest, the Grimwood had grown them a new house.

Understandably, her parents and Jute had slept in the meadow for a week before they decided to move back in and see what would come of it. They still had no idea, really, why it had happened, or who was responsible, but they had decided it was a thank-you, and moved in.

Not for the first time, Poppy wondered if the Holly Oak had something to do with making their house of roots. The Holly Oak was the oldest creature in the woods, and according to her parents' journals, revered by all the creatures of the wood.

Of course, after the house grew, everyone in the Hollows began avoiding her parents. They found it *suspicious* and *strange*. And when she was born, their fear stretched to include Poppy.

The smell of Jute's dinner made her stomach growl, and she was eager to show her parents the feather. She was just about to hurry Mack along when he caught a glimpse of some Strange Hollow kids setting up a game of capture the flag down across the mile of hilly meadow into the valley. He sent her a pleading look.

Poppy hesitated. Mack was fascinated by human games—well, by anything human. Of course, he wanted to watch them. She sighed and pulled out her ponytail. Her parents were safe at home now, and she could put off her victory a few more minutes for her best friend. Jute wouldn't mind if they were late for dinner. "Fine," she said.

Mack's grin was worth it. Without a word he flopped down on the grass to watch.

Poppy snorted, and flopped down next to him.

She didn't blame the people of Strange Hollow for being afraid of her family. Or, at least, she understood. The house growing overnight had jump-started the breach, but it wasn't the only thing. Everyone else avoided the forest, but Poppy's home was made of it. Most families had lost someone to the Grimwood over the generations, but her parents went in and out of the forest all the time. It was practically their morning commute. Naturally, people assumed her parents were in league with the wood. It didn't matter how many times they tried to explain that their work was in service to the Hollows.

Poppy had given up on the idea of ever having the Grimwood *and* being accepted in the Hollows.

The Grimwood was in her blood, somehow, just as Mack's mysterious human grandfather was in his.

Mack watched, spellbound, as the kids ran around the worn, man-high standing stones that dotted the landscape. Poppy could hear their laughter echoing across the valley, as one team made a break for the other's flag.

She pulled out her journal. She had copied her parents' more intriguing notes, and tried to keep track of what she saw in the Grimwood herself. So far, she'd drawn pictures of seven different species of tentaculars, seventeen different birds, and three mammals. She hadn't gotten to the insects yet, though she had caught a glimpse of a picker a few weeks ago, ambling through the wood. The huge insects were like person-size stick bugs, but with strange human eyes and sad green faces.

In the middle of the notebook were the notes on maledictions. **MALEDICTIONS YEARN TO BE USED**, she had copied in her father's bold capitals.

- Maledictions grow out of the soil in a thorn grove as ordinary-looking human objects—a jar, a pen, a fork, a book.
- We aren't sure how the maledictions get into the Hollows. The pickers might move them from the thorn groves to the Hollows, but this is unconfirmed.

- The thorn trees DO appear to have a symbiotic relationship with the pickers. We know it is the pickers that lead the victims of maledictions from the Hollows into the thorn tree groves where the trees will eat them.
- In return, the thorn trees do not seem to eat the pickers—though they eat every other living thing that comes within reach.
- We have also observed the pickers eating the soil at the base of the thorn trees.

Her father's notebook, which she'd snuck a peek at just before her parents left, had held some new intriguing hypotheses.

Can a powerful creature change a malediction for its own purposes? What is the Soul Jar?

Poppy rubbed at the words "Soul Jar" where she'd copied them into her own journal. She wished she could ask her dad more about this.

Her thoughts flashed to the one time she had asked her parents her truest question. She had been almost ten. It was late—the sound of crickets so loud in the summer heat that it was even hard to hear her own thoughts. She'd lain awake listening for more than an hour, and finally got up to steal another look at one of her parents' journals.

She had been shocked to see the light on. They were back from their latest adventure, and hard at work, each of them hunched over their desks in companionable silence. She had stood watching them from the doorway for some time before her mother looked up and saw her.

"Why, Poppy Sunshine! Why are you awake at this hour? Didn't Jute put you to bed?"

Her father looked up, curious perhaps, to hear her answer.

"No—I mean, yes. He did. I just couldn't sleep."

"I see," said her mother, the lamp light so bright against her dark hair that it cast shadows over the desk.

Poppy moved closer. "What . . . what are you doing?"

The corner of her mother's mouth had lifted. "Putting a malediction in stasis. Come and see."

"Jasmine."

"It's all right, David. She should know how to protect herself."

Poppy had hurried to her mother's side, her heart fluttering like a moth in a jar. Her mother held up her hands so that Poppy could see the long-sleeved black gloves. "Never touch an active malediction with bare skin."

"It will have you in a blink," her father called, unbending his long legs from under his desk and moving to stand behind Poppy.

"Now," her mother said, reaching into a box to hold up a comb—pretty, but simple. She glanced at Poppy's father. "If you'd be so kind, dear."

He rose and picked up the silver sewing needle on her

mother's desk. Poppy watched, barely daring to breathe as he pricked his finger and let three drops of blood fall onto the comb.

She wasn't sure what she had expected. Steam, or black smoke, maybe. Something. Instead the comb just sat there looking somewhat revolting. Her parents shared a look.

Her father cleared his throat and reached out to pick up the comb with his bare hand. Poppy stifled a gasp, snatching at her mother's cool hand.

"Shhh," she whispered. "It's your father's blood. The malediction can't hurt him now."

Her dad held the malediction and spoke clearly, so that the breath of his words swept across the comb's teeth. "You will harm none. You will harm none. You will harm none." He turned and deftly threw the comb, end over end, into another open wooden box at the end of his desk. A soft glow throbbed from the depths of the box.

Poppy frowned. "That . . . that's it?"

Her mom let go of her hand. "It's in stasis! Undone! That's it, my blue-eyed girl. It's finding them that's difficult."

"Nothing more powerful than blood in the Grimwood." Her father grinned. "Whatever you say takes hold. Salt and iron will help keep some things away of course, but a blood ward is the only other type of ward that actually works."

"Plenty of creatures know it too." Her mom stared past

Poppy, her thoughts lost in the wood. "Nasty witches—and the good ones too, of course. Faeries. Some of the smarter monsters."

Her father shook his head, and her mother let out a delicate snort. "We told people years ago that their so-called wards were just codswallup, not that they listened to us."

Pinching the bridge of his nose, her dad sighed. "Their wards make them feel better. That's what they do best. Actually keeping them safe? That's up to us."

David and Jasmine looked at each other again and something mysterious passed between them. Poppy could swear that sometimes her parents had whole conversations without saying a word.

Her father ruffled Poppy's hair before he moved to drop back into his chair, his face vanishing into his book. Her mother blinked, and Poppy could see she was about to return to hers as well.

She hadn't seen them in nearly a week and, desperate to hear her mother's voice again—to keep either of them talking to her—she had asked the first thing that popped into her head.

"Will you ever let me come with you?"

She didn't understand her dad's sudden burst of laughter, but a thrill ran through Poppy at the thought he might answer.

"What a question," was all he said.

Her mouth went dry. She hadn't meant to ask it. Some

part of her knew, perhaps, that she might not like the answer. She trembled in the chill night air.

A gentle smile played over her mother's face. "It's a good question. You're clever, and have noticed, I suppose, that we're not suited to . . . well, a lot of things." She threw out her hands, palms open, to take in the room of jars and herbs and papers, and the box of maledictions giving off the soft glow of stasis.

Her father crossed his arms, tipping back in his chair. "What your mother is trying to say is . . . we're not really suited to be parents," he chuckled.

Her mother joined him. "Not at all really."

Poppy stood very still.

"Our job is to keep you safe. That's the main thing. And to love you, of course," her father said as his expression grew serious. "That too."

A bitter taste worked up the back of Poppy's throat.

"Yes," her mother proclaimed. "You're our little Pandora Sunshine, and we love you with all our hearts."

"Just Poppy," Poppy muttered.

Her father tipped farther back in his chair, light filling his eyes as he smiled at her mother. "Our brightest light on the darkest day." Usually when her parents said this, it made her feel better. It was one small advantage of having an interesting birthday—born right at midnight on the winter solstice. This time the words just felt like words.

Her mother smiled back at him, then turned to Poppy

with a sigh. "The Grimwood is not safe. Your father and I have spent years learning the wood . . . watching each other's backs." She paused, her face clouding. "And we've had our fair share of close calls, Poppy."

Her father's expression was apologetic. He held up his hands. "You understand, right, sweetie?"

Poppy couldn't move. Her feet had turned to stone. Her whole body had turned to stone.

She didn't remember if she'd answered. She didn't even remember leaving the lab, or returning to her tower. All she could remember about the rest of that night was that she'd been cold. Cold from the inside, as though every thought and feeling had frozen solid in an instant. She'd lain awake until morning, not thinking at all.

Ever since then, she had made her own notebooks . . . though it hadn't stopped her from stealing a copy of the key and sneaking into the lab to read theirs. That was how she'd learned blood wards *could* be broken.

She slapped her journal shut and shoved it back into her bag.

She turned back to Mack. He had a goofy look on his face as several of the kids in the valley executed an impressive tackle. Laughter rang out as one team declared victory. Their happy shouts made her chest ache, so she yanked a handful of tiny daisies to catapult at Mack's face. Unfortunately, several clumps of dirt went with them.

"Ready to go?"

He shot her a look and threw a flower back at her, but didn't say anything. When one of his eyebrows lifted, Poppy knew they were thinking the same thing. He and Poppy could kick all their butts at that game if they ever had the chance.

"Come on." She frowned, pushing herself up before melancholy could take hold of them both. "I'm officially starving! Let's go tell Jute we're still alive."

Mack rose slowly, trailing behind her as Poppy hurried to her front door and ducked inside. The low frame made the soaring ceilings, open front room, and wide curving banister all the more surprising.

Poppy almost walked into Jute's stomach. The tall, thin hob had come to meet them at the door, and stood looking down his long nose at her with a question in his eyes. Poppy had always thought of them as quail-egg eyes, because even though Jute had dark brown pupils ringed in black, the whites of his eyes were freckled with little brown spots.

Jute, like all hobs, had hatched from a tree alone in the forest. And like all hobs, he had then gone in search of a home. Jute once told her that hobs were the heart of their tree, broken free, born to wander in search of a home to protect and a hearth to tend. Her parents had found him as a teenager, jammed into the back of a troll cave. He was miserable and shedding, his hair drifting off his head one red leaf at a time, leaving him with bald patches.

They'd invited him home for breakfast, and he'd never left. In fact, he rarely left the house at all—and claimed that, barring emergency, he would never set foot in the forest again. He said hobs wandered to find the home of their heart, and he had found his. Her parents had Poppy a short time later, and he offered to look after her in their absence—tutor her when she got older—if only they would let him stay.

"Hi, Uncle Jute! Where are Mom and Dad?"

The hob sneezed and brushed the dusty red leaves of his hair out of his eyes. "Where have you been?"

Something in his voice brought Poppy up short. His whole body was tense—angry. Before he could say another word, she wrapped her arms around him and held him tight. "I'm sorry. I know I haven't finished my essay assignment, and . . . and I should have left a note that I might be home a bit late. I didn't mean to make you worry." The last thing she wanted was for him to get angry, or worse, clingy and worried.

After a moment, Jute patted her hair and sighed. "I'm not angry at you, Poppy. There's cocoa for you and Mack. And mac and cheese."

Relief washed through her. Jute wasn't angry. And he made food. Conjuring ingredients was one of the hob's special skills. Another benefit of having a hob for an uncle—they apparently had all sorts of unique talents that appeared as they matured, and when they were needed. He was a great cook too . . . but maybe that was just practice.

Mack's face had brightened. "Those little hollow noodles with yellow sauce?"

"It's ch—"

She hadn't finished her sentence before Eta-Two-Brutus knocked her to the ground.

Dog, as Poppy affectionately called them when she was in a hurry, was a cerberus—a dog with three heads. They were rare, even in the Grimwood, according to her parents. They'd brought Dog out of the forest for Poppy as a gift for her tenth birthday three years ago, and she had insisted that each head get its own name.

Eta, the head on the left, had all Dog's smarts, and was more refined in her greeting. Brutus, the head on the right, controlled Dog's body, and now stood on her chest, smothering her with slobbery kisses. Two was the head in the middle, and had gotten everything left over, which wasn't much. All three of them had short caramel-colored fur and keenly pointed ears, but Eta and Brutus both had brown eyes, while Two had one brown and one blue, that often shifted outward while keeping track of his siblings.

"Okay, okay. Go bug Mack," Poppy laughed, shoving Brutus off and giving Eta and Two quick pats. They leaped into his arms without a second thought. Dog wasn't small, but Mack caught them as if they were a bouquet of flowers. "Good boy, Brutus. Good girl, Eta. You too, Two. Yes, Two. You too. Good dog."

Poppy wiped the slobber off her face and pushed herself up. Jute hadn't moved a muscle, except that the long fingers of his left hand had begun to drum against his forearm, his burled knuckles rising and falling in a small brown wave. "Poppy—" he began as she struggled to her feet.

The quiet of the house settled over her in an instant. It was too quiet, and the thought sent a twinge of fear shuddering over her skin. Jute was upset, tense. Something was wrong. Her gaze flicked away from him to the pictures of her on the wall, her heart's frantic thumps filling her chest. There was one picture for every year of her life, and in each one she stood straight and tall, by herself, looking out as if to challenge anyone who suggested it should be otherwise. She lifted her chin. "Where are they?"

Jute sneezed again, then placed one hand on her shoulder. "Poppy, I—"

"Where. Are. They?"

Jute sniffed the air like Dog on a hunt, and let out a violent sneeze. His eyes widened. "Did you—you didn't bring home a Mogwen feather, did you?"

Poppy frowned and took the feather from her pack, holding it up for him to see. "Yeah, I did. I—I got it myself. From the forest. I want to show Mom and Dad. Where are they, Jute?"

Jute wiped at his eyes. "Put that thing out. Get rid of it!"

"But—why? What's the matter?"

"I'm allergic to it, Poppy. I won't be able to speak in a moment." He sneezed again to punctuate his words. "Poppy." Jute sneezed and took her hand in his long knobby fingers. "Your parents—I'm sorry. They—your father had a hunch he wanted to follow. They left. On an urgent—"

Poppy's throat tightened. She sensed Mack at her side, but a thin veil had fallen over her vision. She blinked rapidly.

"Again?" Poppy shouted. Her voice sounded too high, too tight. Even Dog startled. The veil in front of her eyes washed red. "They're gone again?" The words were heavy and rotten in her mouth—as though she had pulled them up from a deep old well inside of her.

"Poppy—" Mack warned, no doubt sensing imminent destruction.

"I'm sorry, sweetling. I asked them to wait, but . . ." Jute trailed off.

"But they wouldn't. It was *too important*." Fury ripped through her veins. In a hot second, Poppy knew what she had to do. There would be no victory. Things didn't go her way. Things would *never* go her way. Her parents were gone. *Again*. Fine! They'd left her with no choice. She would have to show them what she was made of—that they couldn't just go off and leave her anymore.

With certainty born of rage, Poppy let out a growl and threw open the front door. Jute and Mack wore matching openmouthed expressions that would have given her the giggles in any other circumstance. Now, they just made her madder.

"Where should I put it?" she growled, holding the feather out away from her body.

Jute came out to stand by her side. "Just set it on the ground there, dear."

Poppy spoke through gritted teeth. "Where? Show me."

He patted her arm, and moved into the meadow to point at a patch of soil under the nearby lilac. "Here will be fine."

Poppy dropped the feather on the porch, spun away, and slammed the door behind her, sliding the bolt. Jute was locked out.

"What are you doing? Why did you do that?" Mack asked.

The hob began to rap his knuckles on the door. "Poppy? Poppy, dear—I know you're upset."

Poppy didn't wait to hear Jute coaxing her to open the door. If she was fast—and lucky—she wouldn't need long. She dashed through the kitchen and locked the back door too.

"What are you doing?" Mack asked again as Dog hopped out of his arms, Eta moving to sniff at Jute behind the door.

She slid to a stop and looked Mack in the eyes. "I'm done waiting."

Then she spun to race up the stairs.

CHAPTER
THREE

Jute was knocking harder now, calling for her to let him in. "I'm sorry, Jute!" Poppy called over her shoulder. Brutus was barking at the hob now, and she fought off a surge of guilt that made her want to run back down and let him in. Instead, she continued her run up the curving stairwell.

She heard Mack's footsteps behind her. They had reached the second-story landing when Jute called from outside. "Pandora Sunshine! Poppy! Whatever you're up to, it's not worth it! It's a bad idea! It's trouble!"

She pretended not to hear, and continued up the stairs, her heart pounding. She was going to figure out which malediction her mom and dad were going after. Jute wouldn't have to be out long. She racked her brain. They didn't keep their expedition plans in their journals anymore. She'd asked one too many questions.

The strongbox had to be in one of her parents' usual hiding places. Jute had told her about it one night after a particularly bad nightmare. She'd been worried about them never coming back, and he had wanted to comfort her. "They have a plan," he'd said. If there was ever an emergency, he was to check the strongbox, and take the contents to the Holly Oak. She'd found it several times, of course. It was just an old metal box with a padlock. Unfortunately, Jute had hidden the key well. Still, there were other ways to break a lock.

Jute's voice drifted through a window. "Dog, hush! Stop barking!"

"We have to hurry," Poppy said as Mack caught up.

"What are we doing? We should help Jute. You shouldn't have locked him out."

Poppy swallowed. Mack thought less of her for what she was doing to Jute—she did too. "I'll let him back in in a few minutes. I promise."

"What are we doing up here, Poppy? What are you planning?"

"We're looking for Mom and Dad's strongbox."

Mack stopped. Poppy didn't. "The sooner we find it," she called over her shoulder, "the sooner we can open the doors."

Mack nose-sighed. "Why are we looking for their strongbox?"

"You don't want to know." She paused. "In fact." She met his eyes. "If you don't want to help me, you can just go let Jute in. I understand. Just give me a five-minute head start."

Mack bristled, blinking. Poppy turned her back on him.

His breath huffed behind her. "Let's just hurry up. I'll check their closet."

Poppy knelt at the top of the stairs and bent to lift a loose board, crouching to see what was inside. She pulled out a curved knife, a fountain pen (a former malediction that her parents had undone), a feather duster, half of a rock-hard brownie, two bent nails, and a copy of *Grimm's Fairy Tales*. She peered into the hole. No strongbox.

Quickly she put everything back and ran into her parents' bedroom. "Find anything?" she called to Mack.

"Not yet," he called from deep in the closet. "Why does your mom have so many boots?"

Poppy gave an un-Poppy-like giggle as she jumped up onto their brass bed. "Never underestimate practical footwear." She took hold of the painting on the wall—a barn in the countryside, with a shaggy-haired cow that looked mildly affronted to be watched eating dinner. The picture swung open to reveal small shelves behind it.

Empty, except for an extra toothbrush and a pile of white pebbles.

Poppy moved to her mother's elegant mirror, scrolled all around with gold curls and loops. It was enchanted, of course, as was almost every mirror from the wood. She pushed up her sleeve and jammed her hand through, gasping as the cold gripped back. The glass rippled like water. She felt around carefully, but only got hold of a small silk bookmark with mold stains, a half-burned candle, and a dead spider. She yanked her hand back out and shook it until the feeling came back. "Don't worry, Mack! We'll find it."

Mack must have been at the very back of the closet. His voice sounded muffled and far off. "Not worried," he called. "I wouldn't know where to start."

Poppy thought. She'd checked all the usual places. Maybe they'd put it somewhere so obvious they thought she wouldn't bother looking. Her gaze fell on the bed. Before the thought had fully formed, she was on the floor, peering underneath. There was a rectangular shape tucked into the shadows. "Gotcha."

She pushed herself into the dusty darkness under the bed to grasp the strongbox. When she had crept out again, she only had time to brush herself off before another round of knocks from below propelled her into action.

"Mack! I got it! Come on!" Poppy raced down the stairs with Mack on her heels. Brutus was still jumping up and down and barking like Jute was under attack by an unseen assailant, which was almost true. Eta looked back at Poppy as if she knew her girl was up to something, but there was nothing she could do. Brutus was keeping them at the door. He barked and barked.

"Mack." Poppy gripped her friend's arm. "Get the dog

biscuits from on top of the cupboard. At least we can shut Dog up." Mack nodded.

Poppy grimaced. She hated locking Jute out, but she hated that her parents had left her again even more. She couldn't allow it. She had to do something. Poppy took the small strongbox to the kitchen and set it on top of the already hot stove, lock down. The kitchen filled with the smell of hot metal. She was certain her parents' latest expedition notes were inside.

The metal lock cracked open with a pop. Poppy shoved her hand into Jute's oven mitt, pulled off the red-hot lock, and flipped open the box. A small scroll lay inside.

Mack appeared back in the kitchen. "I can't stand it, Poppy. I've got to let him in." His face froze when he saw the scroll in her hand. He looked at her once with resignation and turned toward the front hall. Poppy's hand shook as she unrolled the scroll. Her father's handwriting curled over the page in pale black ink.

Malediction: The Soul Jar

Severity: Order 1-malevolent intent, in malevolent hands

Case Notes: When this malediction was first observed at the thorn grove at N:47, W: 123, it was just beginning its rise—too early for collection. We believe someone else took it, early, from the grove. We have not been able to determine who, but have heard rumors from a reliable source about the existence of a malediction with an altered function. We believe the so-called Soul Jar may be that malediction. If so, this would be the first such (known) malediction, and the first (known) malediction with its own name.

Altered Function: Trapping souls for consumption (or other usage)?

Current Location: Unknown

Current Owner: Unknown

Task: Find the jar, return it to the lab, and place the malediction in stasis.

Poppy shoved the scroll into her pocket and threw the box into the cupboard under the kitchen sink.

Poppy's thoughts bubbled like a boiling potion as she considered her father's words, a plan forming in her mind. Mack swung the door open to let Jute back in. She tried to catch Jute's eye as he walked past, just to tell him she was sorry . . . but he didn't look at her.

Her mind went blank.

The hob dropped to a seat in front of the tiny hearth fire. The flames hovered in the empty fireplace, burning nothing. Other folk collected windfall or harvested peat, but fire without fuel was one of Jute's special skills. This was just as well since cutting down trees was forbidden—and for good reason. Hurting any tree in the Grimwood would grow a thorn tree at your back, quicker than quick. The house always smelled nice too—like fruit and sunshine. But that might not be Jute's special powers. It might just be good habits.

The fire sputtered in the grate as Jute drew up his legs. His chin dropped to rest on top of his narrow knees, and after a moment he turned his cheek to face her. His eyes were bright green—a sure sign that he was upset and angry. Poppy's heart dropped into the toes of her boots. She had never seen him look so disappointed.

With a lump in her throat, she spun around and ran back into the kitchen to scoop up a bowl of mac and cheese, then poured a large cup of cocoa. "Here, Jute," she said, slipping them forward onto the small side table next to the hob. "I'm sorry . . . I'm sorry about that."

Mack did a nose-sigh from across the room.

Jute steepled his long fingers. "You know how much I love you, Poppy?"

She swallowed. "I do."

He paused, then reached out to wrap his long fingers around hers. "Why don't you tell me how you managed to get a Mogwen feather?"

Poppy withdrew her hand gently, staring down to rub at a hangnail. "I tracked them by their song, climbed a pine tree, and . . . and used Mom's extra net gun."

The green slowly shifted from Jute's eyes as he considered her words, leaving them their normal quail-egg colors again. "Oh, Poppy." His voice hitched. "I hate for you to be in danger. You know that."

"It was only a little danger—not much really," she said, rushing to put him at ease. "Nothing I can't handle. You worry too much, Jute."

"Perhaps. But someone must."

Poppy swallowed hard. Jute was the last person she wanted to upset. He was always there for her. When she was little, he was the one that told her stories every night, and he was the one who held her hand—sometimes until dawn—when she had nightmares about something happening to her parents, or about them deciding never to come back.

"I—I was careful," she insisted. "And Mack was there."

"I was, Jute. It's true," Mack added. "She was in . . . no . . . danger."

Poppy couldn't help her tiny eye roll. Mack couldn't fib to save his life.

Poppy moved closer to Jute. "I just . . . I just lost my temper when I realized Mom and Dad were gone again. I took it out on you. I'm sorry."

"I'm on your side, you know. I'm supposed to be taking care of you," he protested, lifting the cocoa.

"You do," Poppy said. "You do take care of me! You make sure I eat good food, and you check on me, and . . . and talk to me. It's not your fault I'm stubborn and have a mind of my own."

Jute slurped from his cup. "Yet, I can't help feeling that you're up to something."

Poppy looked down quickly. "You . . . You worry too much, Jute."

Jute lifted his sad freckled eyes and pursed his lips. "Oh, I do worry. You can count on that. And as to what you might be up to, just promise me you won't do anything rash. I know your feelings are hurt that they left again."

"I'm not hurt. I'm angry."

"Angry, then. But making important decisions when emotions are running strong is never in your best interest. Better to sit with things a little while. You'll understand what's in the pot when it's not boiling over."

"I know. It's just—" Poppy studied her torn, dirty fingernails. "Don't they . . . Don't they miss me at all?" Her voice hitched. "Don't they *want* to see me?"

Jute made a tutting sound and reached out to take her hand. "Of course they do, sweetling. Of course they do. Do you know the reason their work is so important?"

Poppy pulled her hand away with a scowl. "I know what they *say*. It's—"

"To keep *you* safe. It's not just the Hollows your parents are protecting . . . and it isn't just to understand the Grimwood either."

"They do it because they love their work more than anything else. That's all."

"They do it because if the maledictions aren't restrained, *you* will be in more danger. And you told me about the whispers in the market—all the gossip from Strange Hollow . . . there have been more maledictions born than ever before. Just last week, a man was taken. Ever since the new governor's election . . ."

"I wasn't even born when they started going into the wood. Their work has nothing to do with me."

"Yes, they started long ago, but now . . . they do it to protect you."

"Along with everyone else."

"Along with everyone else." Jute wore a sad expression as he turned to the fire. "You're very quiet back there, Mack. Why don't you pull your chair up?"

Mack dragged his chair across the room. "I tried to talk her out of—whatever it is—too, sir."

Jute gave the young elf a gentle smile. "Well, we both know how difficult it is to talk Poppy out of anything, once she's made up her mind." The hob studied Mack. "Tell you what, Mack. You can do something for me— something that would ease my mind a great deal."

Mack's eyebrows rose. "Sure! I mean, if I can."

"Whatever my Poppy gets up to, it would ease my mind to know that her good friend Mack was on her side. Can I count on you?"

"I—I am on her side, Jute. We watch each other's backs. You know that. I promise."

Jute nodded, draining the last of his cocoa. "Well, this day has been quite exciting enough. It's time to settle in for the evening."

Mack cleared his throat. "I—"

"No." Jute held up his hand. "I won't hear of it, Mackintosh. It's already getting dark, and your parents would not be pleased if I sent you home at this hour. You'll stay the night in your usual room. Poppy, bring me the penny whistle."

Poppy smirked at Mack and hopped up to get the slender silver whistle from its hook by the door. She handed it to Jute, who rose wearily from the chair.

They followed him up to the third floor, and Mack waited on the landing as Poppy followed Jute up the spiral stairs to her bedroom. The round turret room that was Poppy's looked out over the valley, Strange Hollow, and the Grimwood through a half-wall of windows that circled the room.

Jute walked past Poppy's mattress on the floor (she preferred it there, beneath the drafts), and stepped carefully over the piles of dirty clothes, open books, and broken weapons to the forest side of the room. He lifted the latch on one of the windows and leaned out to pipe a five-note refrain. It drifted toward the trees like light. Three more times, Jute blew the tune before the refrain came back to them with an extra note at the end. Jute gave a satisfied nod, then shut the window and waved Poppy along.

"Your parents have been notified that you will spend the night here," he told Mack as he passed, ushering them back downstairs to eat their dinners.

"Thank you, sir."

"It's my pleasure, young man. And as for you, Poppy,

given the circumstances of our evening, I hope you'll understand that I must attempt to send word out to your parents too."

Poppy swallowed, but gave a stiff nod. It was only fair.

CHAPTER FOUR

The morning came with its usual persistence, but Poppy jumped out of bed with *un*usual excitement. There was a lot to do. She threw on black jeans, her "They Must Be Giants" T-shirt, and a bulky black hoodie with zipper pockets. She grabbed the larger of her two backpacks—it was bigger than her daypack, but still smaller than the bulky monstrosities her parents used when they expected to have to travel in the Grimwood deep. She took the net gun and a spare roll of netting. She packed an extra knife, a change of clothes—and one of her dad's old shirts for Mack. They didn't have time for him to go home and pack his own bag.

She had a plan, and it was even better than the Mogwen feather.

Poppy took her canteen off the small corner desk, and paused to open a drawer. After a moment's hesitation, she snapped up her small iron bell—another gift from Jute—and shoved it in too. If she and Mack got separated, she could use it to signal him. She considered the small handful of gold coins gleaming from the corner of the drawer, then scooped them into a side pocket of her pack. Finally, she scraped together the loose change left over from her birthday money this year and put it in her jeans pocket—just in case.

Her hand hovered over the tiny gold locket her parents had given her with their pictures inside. She had gotten it on her ninth birthday, and although she'd worn it for a while, it had never comforted her after a nightmare the way Jute did. Instead, wearing it made her feel conspicuous, as if it were meant for someone else. The locket was shiny and heart-shaped, and happy in ways she never quite found comfortable. She'd taken it off and put it in her drawer, only taking it out now and then just to look at it.

She jammed the necklace in a pocket of her pack and went downstairs. Who knew how long they would be gone?

Mack was already awake and playing with Eta-Two-Brutus in the meadow. She could see him through the kitchen window. There was no sign of Jute.

Quickly, she made a batch of boar sandwiches with mustard and greens and tomatoes, on thick homemade bread. She threw in some slices of cheese and wrapped it all in waxed paper. She perused their stores. Jute would notice if she took everything . . . and who knew how much they would end up needing. She'd need something for Dog to eat too. They also didn't have any apples. She couldn't ask Mack to go along with her plan without apples. She gritted her teeth. Asking Jute to summon food was out of the question—he'd be too suspicious. No, she'd have to go through the village market and get some herself. She tightened up her boot strings and ran outside.

The meadow was sunlit and fragrant. The air hummed with bees as Eta-Two-Brutus kicked through the grass and wildflowers, dragging a huge stick back to Mack. Brutus held the biggest section, and kept yanking it away from his siblings. Then he'd get overexcited, and whack them in the face with it.

Poppy hitched her backpack over her shoulders. "Hey, Mack! I'm going into Strange Hollow for some food and a bone for Dog. Want anything else?"

Mack grinned at her. He was always happy playing with Dog in the meadow. Once, he'd dug his bare toes into the ground and told her the soil was joyful out here. "Nah. I'm good," he began. Then his smile faded. "Should I . . . come with you? I wouldn't mind."

She did consider it for a moment. Mack could almost pass as human, and it would almost be worth it just to see his face. Seeing Strange Hollow up close was on his life list.

Still, it was broad daylight, and there was no telling what might happen if people noticed his eyes, or his elven ears, which was likely. And in her experience, it was rarely a good thing to draw the eye of Strange Hollow folk. Poppy and her family had learned that lesson well. It was lucky none of the town folk had ever set eyes close-up on Jute, or Dog. Neither could ever pass for "normal," and who knows what people would do if they found out there were Grimwood creatures living so close. As it was, Poppy was content to be ignored.

"No thanks," she said at last. "You stay here with Dog."

"You sure?"

"Yeah. I'm sure. Thanks for the offer though."

She could feel Mack's eyes on her back as she strode down toward the valley. Honestly, he was as bad as Jute sometimes. "I'll be fine!" she called.

He didn't answer for a moment, but then, from the corner of her eye, she saw Dog's stick hurtle past, and thought she heard Mack say, "Just watch your back."

Poppy adjusted her pack as she walked down the slope of the hill toward Strange Hollow. The town was small, though it was the biggest of the seven Hollows that ringed the Grimwood. It was also the home of the new governor.

Poppy had never explored the Hollows themselves. What was the point? She couldn't even make a place for herself in her own Hollow—and the Grimwood held more excitement in its pinkie finger . . . not that it had a pinkie finger. She knew the Hollows were each a day's walk or so from one another. To the west of Strange Hollow was Golden Hollow, and then No Good Hollow and

Blue Hollow. To the east were Dark Hollow and Broken Hollow. Trader's Hollow stood a little apart, on the far side of the forest. For some reason no one really understood, people could only pass through the fog in Trader's Hollow. Perhaps because it was the Hollow farthest from the wood.

Once she knew the Grimwood's secrets, maybe she would try to learn about the fog, too, or travel to the human world beyond the fog. Mack would like that. Though exploring the fog would be just as dangerous as exploring the Grimwood. There were rumors that the fog itself was a monster too, and whether that was true or not, everyone knew that those who went in didn't come back out.

The fog wrapped around the outside of the Hollows and bound them to the wood, safe from the outside world. All the wood's magic—both good and bad—was trapped inside the fog's thick boundaries. It held the Grimwood and the Hollows wrapped tight the way fear can sometimes hold people together, even when they don't really like one another. The fog formed a looming wall at the outer edge of every Hollow. People kept their distance, though Poppy had seen some of the more adventurous children daring one another to get close. None of them were ever brave—or reckless enough—to come nearer than a few feet.

But inside the mile-thick walls of the fog, the Hollows

thrived well enough. They enjoyed a long growing season. It never snowed, and the air was always sweet, even in winter. Technology didn't work in the Hollows, but everyone seemed to get along fine without it. No one seemed to mind that the rest of the world—outside the fog lines—could talk to one another using tiny devices, or drive metal boxes around, or thought that killing monsters was a game. Poppy supposed the people found the benefits of living so close to the Grimwood worth the risk. As long as you didn't get caught by a malediction and lured into the forest, life was good.

Most people had no interest in the outside world anyway. They had their families and friends—and their warding customs, however useless they might be. And people who lived in the Hollows stayed healthy. They lived at least twice as long as people outside the fog. It wasn't unusual to celebrate your two hundredth birthday in the Hollows. Maybe it was because of the fog. Or maybe it was something in the water. Or maybe it was the soil. Mack was always going on about the soil.

And if you did want to see beyond the fog, you could try. Twice a year on the solstice, the governor would select a special few to pass through the fog lines from Trader's Hollow into the outside world. They would return with what the Hollows needed or requested—jeans and other clothing, new foods to try, tools . . . even furniture from towns with strange names like "Ikea."

Poppy's family didn't get to make requests. People that would trade with them were few and far between. Mostly her family would trade for whatever was left over to be sold at the market. They were lucky to have Jute to conjure food.

The fog rose beyond the rooftops of Strange Hollow as Poppy entered the town. It was bustling. Kids played on the cobbled road and in the alleys between the houses, kicking balls, playing tag, and helping with chores. People moved through the streets chatting and working. Voices stilled as she passed—as they usually did, but Poppy kept her chin held high and made her way toward the market.

Halfway down the street she noticed something was off. It wasn't until she was almost at the market that she figured out what. There were wards . . . everywhere. New waist-high monster carvings decked out almost every street corner. She *had* heard there had been more male-dictions lately.

A shiver ran across her skin like a breeze.

Poppy turned and made her way toward Beth's stall. The old woman was always kind, and still worked in the market every day, even though her son was the new governor of the Hollows, the highest-ranking person in all seven towns. It didn't help that he apparently didn't approve of Beth having a stand in the market. "But I prefer to stand on my own two feet," she'd explained.

Poppy swallowed as the sharp gaze of several boys her age followed her from the alleyways. Two of them fell in behind her, whispering. At first, she couldn't make out what they were saying, but the hair along the back of her neck stood up, so she knew it was about her. After a short distance, they got close enough for her to hear them.

"Do it," one said.

"You do it," said the other, with laughter in his voice.

"No, you."

Poppy stopped walking, but didn't turn. She spoke in a loud voice. "Somebody better do it, or I'm going to have to do it for you." Slowly, she spun to face them.

The two boys—one dirty blond and dirty in general, and one a redhead with a sprout of hair that stood straight up above his forehead, stared back.

The redhead laughed. "Ask her."

"You ask her."

The red-haired boy rolled his eyes. "Are you a witch?"

Poppy's eye roll made the boy look like an amateur. "Can't you think of something more creative than that?"

"Well, what are you, then? Not normal. Not like us."

Poppy swallowed. She refused to give them the satisfaction of upsetting her. "I'm a human girl . . . not a witch, or any other kind of creature. And you know my name just fine—but I'll tell you what. You can just call me Boss."

The blond tipped his head, reminding her a little of

Eta when she saw something she wanted to dig out of a hole. "Your name isn't Boss. It's Poppy."

"If you know it, why are you asking?"

The redhead lunged forward and poked her hard in the ribs.

Poppy gasped, doubling up.

"See," the kid said. "I told you she was just like a regular girl."

Poppy gritted her teeth, took two fast steps forward, and kicked him hard in the shin.

"OWW!" he hollered, and the blond kid scooted behind him fast.

"Is that *regular girl* enough for you?" she growled, spinning on her heel and marching away.

From behind her the red-haired boy called, "Pop-py Sun-shine ne-ver smiles."

"Looks just like a croc-o-dile," the other boy finished.

Poppy kept walking, but couldn't keep her shoulders from sagging just a little. "Shocking news," she gritted out. "I've read the encyclopedia too, you know. We don't even have crocodiles here."

The main road opened up onto the square and the market. She might have avoided the insults completely, not to mention the poke in the ribs, if she'd stuck to the back streets, but this way was faster, and she was eager to get back to Mack. She made straight for Beth's stall. The old woman's stand stood all the way at the far end of the market, and so, was one of the last to get people's business.

Beth wore a patchwork dress and her white hair was piled up like a bird nest. Poppy had no idea why, but Beth had always liked her.

"Hi, Beth. How's business?" Poppy smiled.

"Why, Poppy Sunshine! What a surprise. How are you, lightning bug?"

Poppy's cheeks heated. She hated pet names at the best of times, but she didn't have the heart to snap at Beth about it.

"Fine, thank you. How are you?"

"Oh, you know. I'm a hundred and twenty-six. My knees ache a bit. And my back aches a bit. My teeth aren't so good, and my eye is acting up again—but mostly I'm fine . . . just fine."

Poppy let a smile slip. "Want me to ask my mom to make you some more poplar salve for your aches?"

"Oh, that's sweet of you, dear. Yes. Do. With my thanks. Now! What can I get you? I've got some lovely asparagus." Beth turned to gather up her latest, and as she did, something caught Poppy's eye. A huge mouse the size of her palm perched on the edge of a bin, nibbling a snap pea.

Aside from being where it shouldn't be, there was something about it that didn't sit right with Poppy. Maybe it was the tufted ears, or the strangely long tail, but she hadn't even given it a conscious thought when her hand shot out and grabbed it.

She held the mouse firmly, but not too tight, intending to tuck it in her pocket and set it loose back in the meadow. Before she had moved though, the mouse turned into a long green snake, writhing and hissing as it coiled its tail around her hand and wrist. Poppy yelped, but managed to hang on to it so it couldn't bite, tucking her hand behind her back as Beth turned her head.

"What's wrong?"

"Oh! Nothing! Um. Just a spider. Startled me."

As soon as Poppy said "spider" she felt the snake change—and now her hand was cupped around something cold and hairy, with lots of legs.

Sweat burst out on Poppy's forehead. Spider bites were no joke, especially if the spider wasn't really a spider and was really something else. She racked her brain trying to think of creatures that could change form as she jammed the spider into a pocket of her hoodie, zipping it shut. She wiped her palm off on her chest as goose bumps traveled up and down her arms.

She took a few deep breaths to make her heart stop racing, and stared down at her pocket like it had grown a head, which maybe wasn't too far off. Whatever the creature was, it changed again. A faint growling came from inside her pocket.

Poppy cleared her throat. "Uh. A bag of apples, please,

Beth, and a loaf of bread and some cheese, please. Oh—
and a meat bone for my Dog, if you've got one. I—I'm in
a bit of a hurry."

More growling, and her pocket looked like it was trying to turn itself inside out.

Beth turned with a loose woven bag of apples in one
hand, and an ox bone in the other. "I'd like to see this dog
of yours someday, Poppy." Beth chuckled.

"Sure." Poppy clapped her hand down on her pocket.
The snarling stopped. "Sure . . . someday." She reached
out and tucked the bone under her arm, fishing in her
jeans for coins to pay Beth.

Beth patted her cheek and handed over the rest of the
supplies. "Never mind about that. You just bring some
more salve when you can, and be a good girl, lightning
bug. Come back and see me soon."

Poppy let her trademark smirk edge up into a smile,
and gave Beth a nod, shoving the food into her backpack.
When Beth was out of sight, Poppy headed back across
town. She ran like something was chasing her—until she
turned a corner and plowed into Governor Gale. Poppy
stumbled back, but he didn't try to catch her. Instead he
stared down at her, sneering as she tried to keep from
falling. When she caught her balance, she lifted her eyes
to his. They flashed darkly at her, and she took another
step back.

The new governor was tall, with skin white as paper,

and pale blond hair. It was hard to tell how old he was—though that was true of most people in the Hollows. She'd never seen him up close, but there was something familiar about him nonetheless. He wore straight brown pants, and a brown shirt, buttoned all the way to the top of his neck. It was so tight Poppy wondered if he had to keep his chin lifted to swallow. In fact, all of his features were pinched and tight, as though the governor needed to fart . . . but wouldn't allow it.

His face was long and pale, like he spent all his time indoors. As he stared down at Poppy, the corners of his mouth drew down until they looked as if they might fall right off his face. He didn't look much like his mother. In fact, it was hard to believe he was related to Beth at all.

"Miss Pandora Sunshine, I believe," he said, accentuating every word as though he didn't want them to touch his mouth. "I heard you were here . . . and I see you are as strange and wild as the rest of your family."

Poppy tamped down her instinct to skitter away from him, crossing her arms. "Thank you."

His eyes flickered as he pressed his words through his teeth. "It is *not* a compliment. *If* you are wise . . . you will cease running about like a wild thing." He motioned to the ward next to him—a carving of a bear standing on its hind legs. "The new wards I commissioned will keep the Grimwood at bay. Unlike your family, I have found the way to *actually* keep us safe." He narrowed his eyes at her, his chin lifting even higher to avoid the pinch of his collar. "I will make life in the Hollows fair again, *and* be remembered for it." He strode past her then, each stride an exclamation point.

The creature stirred in her pocket as Poppy watched him go. His message was clear enough.

Whatever, jerk.

She remembered the first time she had seen the governor, before his rise to power. He'd come to their house when she was . . . maybe eleven or so. She was on the way to the kitchen to ask Jute for a snack when she heard a strange man talking to her parents in the kitchen. She peered through the doorway. Jute was nowhere to be seen. Gale stood there stiff-limbed as his eyes darted all over their home—probably afraid something might jump out at him. His clothes had been the same mud brown then too, his shirt so tight she could see his Adam's apple bob when he swallowed.

He'd gripped their countertop as he spoke. "Once the house is empty, you'll of course stop this nonsense and move into the Strange Hollow right away."

"Certainly not," her mother had snapped, causing Poppy to shift quickly out of the kitchen door before they noticed her. She'd pressed herself on the far side against the wall where she could still hear every word.

"We have every right to live here," her mother finished.

"We've told you before." Her father's voice was steady. "We're not working for the Grimwood. Far from it. We find maledictions and put them in stasis so they can't harm—"

"*Stasis*," Gale sneered. "No one believes you. Look at this place! *I* don't believe you! And why should I? You come and go from that cursed wood without a scratch. You don't even have any wards that I can see. You. Show. No. Fear. If you expect *anyone* to trade with you, your only choice is to move into the Hollow and start acting like everyone else. Put up wards—"

Her father laughed. "Those carvings do as much good as your fear."

"One day you won't be so smug," Gale snarled. "One day someone will teach you a lesson."

Her father's face softened. "Knowledge is what we need most. Knowledge is the way to fight—"

"Nonsense. That's an excuse to do nothing. Knowing helps no one. Only action has value." Gale's voice seemed strained. "We already know the maledictions are evil— how could they be otherwise? They come from the wood. Knowing it doesn't keep them from taking—" He swallowed.

Her mother's voice was so soft, Poppy had to press her ear hard against the door. "I remember how much you cared for Miranda, Rupert," she said. "She was your best friend."

Poppy's throat had tightened, and she tiptoed away

from the door then, turning to creep back up the stairs to her room. She hadn't wanted to hear her parents try to comfort another adult. Adults weren't supposed to need comfort.

Another snarl from her hoodie snapped her out of her stupor. She spun around and ran for the house. She didn't have time to worry about Governor Gale. She had a monster in her pocket.

This time she didn't stop until she was back in the meadow. Mack saw her running toward him and came to meet her. Eta-Two-Brutus sat panting in the grass, all three smiling, worn out from playing. "What happened?" Mack asked. "What'd they do this time?"

Poppy held up her hand and bent double as she tried to catch her breath. After a few seconds she stood, and met Mack's eyes. "I need to show you . . . something in my pocket."

Mack smirked, but it faded fast as Poppy took a fighting stance and pulled the cloth of her sweatshirt out away from her body. His expression went from bemused to wary, his shoulders tensing. "What's in there, Pop?"

She shook her head. "No idea . . . but whatever it is sounds like it has teeth."

Mack cast around for a weapon, and spotted Dog's stick. He reached over and hauled it off the ground, letting go of Dog's collar long enough to snap a piece off. He held up the thick end like a club.

"Get ready," Poppy said as she slowly unzipped the pocket. She reached in and pulled the creature out.

It went still in her hand—soft. Was it dead? Had she killed it? She brought her hand close and uncurled her fingers.

Mack's shoulders relaxed. "It's just a mouse, Poppy."

"It isn't."

"It is. Look at it."

"I'm seeing it. But I'm telling you—"

She brought the mouse up to her face. "Listen, I can stand in this meadow all day. You don't know me, so I'm telling you. I'm as stubborn as the day is long."

The mouse peered back at her with shiny black eyes.

"Poppy . . ."

"Shhh!" Poppy cocked her head at the mouse. "Just show yourself and get it over with already."

There was a popping sound.

The mouse was gone.

Mack and Poppy both startled, and Eta gave a single bark as a petite girl with bluish skin appeared in the mouse's place. She had on gray leggings and a long dark blue tunic, but Poppy hadn't noticed what she was wearing. She was staring at the girl's long tufted tail, and the two-pointed cat ears that rose out of her close-cropped hair. The girl's ears were furry and tufted too, just like the mouse's, and both—ears and tail—were the same warm brown as her hair, but had bluish stripes, like water through sand.

"There," the girl snapped, moving her hands to her hips. "Happy?"

Mack drew himself up. "Who are you and why are you in Poppy's pocket?"

"Why am I in Poppy's pocket?" the girl shrilled, her tail whipping the air. "Why am I in Poppy's pocket? Because she grabbed me and trapped me in there! And you—" She whirled around.

Poppy stepped back.

"You must be Poppy, then. Well, thank you *very* much. I haven't had a snap pea in an age."

"I—" Poppy swallowed. "I'm . . . I'm sorry. I just thought you were . . . up to no good."

The girl sniffed and twitched an ear.

Poppy looked at Mack, who rolled his eyes. Poppy frowned. "I mean, you *were* up to no good."

The girl cringed. "It was only a pea."

"That's . . . true." Poppy scratched her head.

The girl held out her hand. "I'll take an apple."

"What?"

Her ears flattened. "I'll take an apple, I said—as an apology. I know you got some."

Poppy pulled a face, but she opened the bag of apples and dropped one into the girl's palm. "Sorry about—"

"Kidnapping me?"

"Yeah. I guess."

Mack tugged at a curl. "So . . . who are you?"

The girl's tail had slowed to a leisurely flip-flop. "Fionnula. But I prefer Nula. Please."

"Mack," said Mack, holding out his hand.

Nula paused, then grabbed his hand and shook. "And you're Poppy."

"Yup. And you are?"

Her ear twitched. "I told you. I'm Nula."

Poppy scratched her cheek. "I heard you, but . . . I don't mean to be . . . uh . . . rude or anything, but what I mean is . . . I'm asking *what* you are."

"Pooka," she and Mack said at the same time. Nula gave Poppy an exaggerated look of shock, then tipped her head. "What else would I be? Oh, come on," she added at Poppy's blank look. "Shape-shifter? One of the so-called lesser Fae? Don't tell me you've never met one of the pooka-kind? Well, imagine that. And you living so close to the forest," she added, looking around the meadow. "Why *are* you all the way over here . . . wrong neighborhood for a human, isn't it?"

"Why were you in Strange Hollow stealing from Beth?"

Nula blushed. "It *was* a bit risky with all the people about." She bit at one torn fingernail. "Obviously, since you caught me! But I couldn't help it. It's too early for decent veggies in the forest, and I thought . . ."

Poppy gave her a begrudging nod. She knew that look. She owned it. "You thought, why not have an adventure?"

Nula smiled back. "Exactly. No harm done." She eyed

Poppy's backpack. "Looks like you're off somewhere your-self. Where are you headed?"

Poppy looked hard at Mack, and he raised one eyebrow. She supposed it was as good a time as any to tell him.

"Bringing the cerberus?" Nula interrogated, not wait-ing for an answer to her first question. She tipped her chin at Eta-Two-Brutus.

Poppy thought the girl might be afraid of Dog, what with her catlike qualities, but she seemed more . . . curi-ous. "I would never leave Dog behind, so yeah, definitely bringing them."

The pooka seemed to consider this as she bent to pat their heads. "I totally get it. Anyone would love their com-pany."

But Poppy kept her eyes locked on Mack as she answered the pooka's first question. She had been wait-ing to tell him all day. "We're . . . We're going into the Grimwood to hunt down a malediction."

Poppy wasn't just going to beat her parents at their own game. She was going to break her blood ward, once and for all, no matter what it took.

CHAPTER FIVE

Mack's mouth fell open. "We're what now?"

Poppy stilled. "I'm going to beat them to it, Mack. We're going to find the Soul Jar—the one Mom and Dad are looking for—before they do. Then they'll see that they need me on their team."

"That's . . ."

"Brilliant," Nula chimed in. "Soul Jar, huh? I bet the Fae know all about it."

Poppy shrugged. Her plan was to head into the deeps to the Holly Oak—see if she would let them in. With luck, the tree would be impressed with her audacity. Impressed enough, at least, to point her in the right direction. She had always wanted to meet the Oak, and this was a perfect opportunity—maybe her only opportunity.

There was just the small matter of the ward her parents put on her to keep her out of the woods. She'd searched their lab, looking for anything that might point to a way to break it. The only thing she'd ever found was a hint that distance *might* snap it like a cord stretched too tight. The pain would be unbearable but . . . the ward should break. *It had to.* She shook off the thought of what might happen to her if it didn't.

"So—what do you say?" Nula asked, her tail curling back and forth in graceful arcs. "Why don't I show you the way to the faeries and you can ask them what they know about this Soul Jar thingie."

"No!" Mack said. "No way are we going to the Fae."

Nula flicked an ear. "I'm asking her. She's the one in charge, isn't she?"

Mack opened his mouth to retort, but Poppy gave Mack a tiny shake of her head, keeping her eyes on the pooka. It wasn't that she didn't appreciate the thought, but they didn't know Nula from a field mouse. What Poppy did know was that the pooka wasn't in charge of her expedition. "We've already got a plan," she said. "But thanks anyway."

"Right," Mack interjected. "There's nothing the faeries have that we need."

Nula's gold eyes narrowed. "The Fae are the most amazing creatures in the forest. They know everything, and they *love* telling you all about it. And I'm practically one of them—so I should know," she added as some emotion Poppy couldn't decode flitted across her face.

"Sure—they know lots," Mack said, raising a hand in surrender. "But I agree with Poppy. They're dangerous."

"I didn't say *that*," Poppy said.

Nula smiled, but it didn't quite reach her eyes.

"Everyone worth knowing is a little dangerous. Don't you think?" She flicked her tail. "Besides, they'll love the novelty of a human in the Grimwood. They love anything that's rare—anything new or unexpected—and that's the two of you together, for certain."

Poppy put a hand on her hip. "Maybe later. We're going to the Holly Oak."

The tension left the meadow like water draining from a tub, and Nula stretched her arms up, arching her back. "Suit yourselves." She moved to pet Dog's heads again, their tail wagging. "How much does your cerberus eat anyway? I mean—do you feed all three of them, or . . . do they take turns eating?"

Mack cast a look at Nula and moved to Poppy's side. "What about your parents' ward?"

Poppy grimaced. "I'll walk till it breaks."

Mack's mouth dropped open. "That is not a good—"

"A ward?" Nula interrupted.

Poppy turned to face the pooka. Her head had begun to ache just thinking about how bad this was going to hurt. "Blood ward," she grumbled.

Nula's eyes pinched. "On you?"

Poppy nodded.

Nula cringed. "Yeah, the elf is right. You could walk off the ward . . . and it *might* work. But it's more likely to just kill you outright."

Poppy felt her cheeks go pale.

The pooka smiled and leaned forward to confide in Poppy's ear. "But you know . . . the faeries like me way better than most pooka-kind, so I've picked up a few things."

"Like what?" Poppy asked. Mack was shaking his head and giving her hand signals that they should talk in private. But Poppy wanted to hear what the pooka had to say.

Nula's smile was so bright it made Poppy blink. "Like . . . how to break a blood ward," she said as Mack dropped his forehead into his palm and did a nose-sigh.

Poppy had to try it . . . but of course Mack was grumpy about it. It took two apples and an apology to cheer him up, and even then he kept kicking at the dirt with his toes as they walked the first hundred steps into the Grimwood, following a short distance behind the pooka.

Poppy stopped walking when they got close enough to see the thorn tree up ahead. Her head was pounding. Pins and needles raced over her body in waves. Dog shifted their weight to lean against her leg.

Nula studied the thorn tree. "Let's move west. That thing makes me nervous and I don't want to give it any ideas." She chuckled, but it sounded hollow.

Mack caught Poppy's arm. "Can we talk about this?"

"Not now, Mack. Maybe later."

"I'm really not sure about this, Pop."

"I know. But I am."

They walked west until they were out of sight of the thorn tree. This time it was Nula that called a halt. She whipped a tiny silver sickle out of her sleeve.

Mack moved to block her way.

"Take it easy!" Nula rolled her eyes. "It's just my herb knife. Now"—she turned to Poppy—"give me your hand."

"Uh . . ."

"Do you want me to help you break the blood ward or not? Blood for blood. It's the only way in the Grimwood."

Poppy swallowed and held out her hand.

"You don't have to do this," Mack said. "We can go back—see if Jute will make cookies."

Poppy didn't need to consider. Another few steps and she'd be in the forbidden part of the Grimwood. Farther than she'd ever been. Free.

Nula must have seen the decision in her eyes because she gave Poppy a nod and took her hand in a firm grip. Poppy gasped as Nula swiped the sickle across her hand. It was a small cut, but blood bloomed to the surface, pooling in her palm.

"Sorry," Nula said, not sounding the least bit sorry. She brushed away the leaves and twigs with her foot. "Now. Squeeze your hand tight and let the blood fall onto the Grimwood soil."

Mack groaned as Poppy stared at her palm. She shook off a wave of dizziness, and did what the pooka said.

Nula gripped her elbow and gave her a reassuring smile. "Repeat after me, okay?"

Poppy nodded and met the pooka's bright gold eyes.

"Let. Me. In."

Poppy blinked, then repeated after Nula. "Let. Me. In."

"Now, twice more. Everything is thrice in this bloody wood."

Poppy grinned. "Let. Me. In. Let. Me. In."

Nula let go and looked up. "Right. That's done. Got a bandage?"

Poppy stared. "Wait, what? That . . . that's it?"

Mack's face was full of storm clouds as he handed Poppy a roll of self-sticking bandages.

Nula snatched it out of her hand, wound Poppy's palm. "Blood wards on people can only take root with consent . . . or on those who aren't strong enough to give permission. Your parents probably did it when you were little, right?"

Poppy nodded.

"So. You've taken back your consent. Done."

Poppy turned her attention to her body. Nula was right. Although her hand was throbbing, the buzzing in her head had stopped . . . the pins and needles were . . . gone! All that was left was the pain where her hand had been cut. She let out a peal of laughter and ran across the invisible boundary. Dog leaped after her with a bark.

"Poppy, wait!" Mack shouted.

She skidded to a stop and tipped her head back to look up into the trees. The air was soft on her skin, as familiar as the touch of a friend.

Everything smelled sharp and golden—promising, like the scent of apples, and crushed pine needles under her feet, and of the heat rising off her skin. She was in the Grimwood! She could go as far as she wanted. Nothing could stop her. She spun in a circle until the dizziness came back, as Dog frolicked and barked around her, giddy and joyful.

She fell to the ground, looking up at the sky through the trees with her arms spread wide, as if she could hug the world.

Nula stood back, watching with an expression of startled bewilderment.

"Feel better?" Mack chuckled, snatching Poppy's injured hand from where she waved it in a sunbeam. He checked Nula's wrapping and gave a grim nod.

"I feel great!" Poppy shouted. "Mack!" She jumped to her feet and gripped his arms, shaking him. "We did it! I'm in the Grimwood. I'm really here."

He flushed, and his smile twitched. "Yup. You, me, and Pooka McStabby, over there." He rolled his eyes. "Really though," he said as he turned back to Poppy. "I'm glad you're happy."

"Now we just have to find a way to get you into Strange Hollow. Then we'll both have our wishes!"

Mack's cheeks grew redder.

Nula grimaced. "You're welcome, by the way. Why do you want to be in here so bad anyway?"

Poppy shook her head. "I—I can't explain."

How *could* she explain what the Grimwood meant to her? She had been hearing stories about it all her life . . . had held it up as the someday answer to every question. How could she tell a stranger that even though she'd never been past the edge of the wood, it was like family to her. The Grimwood had given her everything she loved. Mack! And Jute! And Dog! Even their home!

And now she could pursue things to the fullest, all her questions . . . every single one—even the ones she hadn't thought of yet—would be resolved and explored. She couldn't wait to write down how to break a blood ward in her journal.

Everything was perfect.

The Grimwood was perfect.

Mack let out a low grumble that she'd never heard before.

"What is it?" Poppy stared at her friend as the tips of his ears twitched.

"Something's coming." He turned to her, his copper eyes wide. "Something big."

As if echoing his words, she felt a strange drumming sound rise through the soles of her feet.

She looked up, but there was no storm—only a canopy of green and shadow.

"Hide, Poppy." Mack scoured the wood. He grabbed hold of Dog's collar. "Whatever it is, it's huge! Hide now."

"What is it?" Nula flattened herself into a low crouch.

Poppy could hear the drumming now—growing louder with every passing moment.

The ground began to shake and even the trees shivered in place. Poppy's stomach dropped. She pulled her knife from her boot.

Nula met Poppy's eyes and *poofed* into a small blue bird, rising to a high tree branch above Poppy.

"Shouldn't we run?" Poppy called to Mack, holding out one arm for balance.

He shook his head. "It's too late for that. And some things it's best not to run from. Just please—hide, like I said. Get behind a tree and try not to move. Hold on to it if you have to." He picked up Dog and slung them over his shoulder.

Poppy's pulse leaped as she leaned her back into an enormous beech tree and waited. Its leaves quaked and rustled all around her.

They stared into the forest—waiting as the drumming grew louder and louder. Dog whined, only to be hushed by Mack.

The flashes of light were the first thing she saw. A whole flock of sparkles that shifted through the forest like a dream. The drumming was loud in Poppy's head, echoing the throbbing of her pulse—faster. Faster. It sounded like . . . hoofbeats.

The sparkles shifted, resolved into shimmering forms. Poppy stared.

Unicorns! A whole herd of them. Their fur was thick and smooth—like mirrored silver, reflecting the sunlight and refracting rainbows as they ran. Their wide sides cast blurred reflections of the trees as they passed. Poppy gasped as one galloped so near that for a sharp moment she could see her own face reflected in its fur. It lifted its head and the light gleamed off its glass-like horn. Even their eyes seemed to catch the light and throw it back again.

A moment, maybe two, and the herd was gone. The drumbeat of their hooves faded away to nothing, and the forest stilled in their wake, as if shocked into silence. It took a few minutes for Poppy to stop shaking, but she knew she'd been given a gift, and she promised herself she would never forget it. The Grimwood was magical. She had always known it, but she had never imagined anything so beautiful.

"I wonder what they were running from," Mack said in a low, awestruck voice.

Nula, the bird, fluttered down from the tree to land between Poppy and Mack. A soft pop and she was a pooka again. "Wow," she breathed. "Glad I didn't miss that."

"Me too." Poppy swallowed as she turned to the pooka. "Thank you, Nula. Really."

Surprise flashed across Nula's face. Her cheeks flushed as she gave Poppy a small nod. "It was . . . It was no trouble."

On a whim, Poppy threw her arms around Mack's neck and squeezed. Her reward was his fleeting look of shock and a red stain that spread up his neck.

Poppy laughed and rolled her shoulders a few times until her neck cracked. Everything was perfect. She patted her leg to bring Dog to her side, relaxing as Eta leaned in to lick the back of her hand. "By the way, Nula. I've been meaning to ask you . . . When you change forms like that . . . what . . . happens to your clothes? I mean . . . they come right back again, but . . . where do you put them?"

Nula stopped walking and turned a blank face to Poppy. "I never thought about that." She laughed. "I don't *put* them anywhere. When I shift, I guess the magic just knows what things are mine—the same way it knows the rest of *me* belongs to me." She shrugged. "I don't need to know how, as long as everything comes back again."

A mystery for another day, Poppy thought, turning to look over her shoulder at Mack. Sure enough, his blush had deepened. She put him out of his misery and changed the subject.

"Let's go to the Holly Oak. If anyone can tell us where to start looking for an altered malediction, it's her."

Mack was still recovering from their conversation and Poppy's burst of exuberance. His voice was softer than normal. "I know the unicorns were amazing, but the Grimwood's not everything you think it is, Poppy."

"It's more than I even hoped it would be. We'll be fine—this is the right thing. Can't you feel it?"

"Well . . ."

"Come on, Mack! This might be my only chance to explore. And anyway, what's the worst that could happen?"

He frowned. "Seriously?" He met Nula's eyes, looking for backup, but the pooka's gaze slid away.

Poppy grinned at him. "We'll be careful," she amended. "I promise."

He huffed a breath. "Well, we'll have to be."

They moved into the forest at a good pace. As they moved through the wood, the trees grew denser. Here and there, they saw thorn trees and avoided the darker circles of soil that marked their reach.

Poppy was surprised how many there were . . . just on their own. Her parents' journals spoke of the thorn groves in the Grimwood deep on the far side of the Holly Oak, but she hadn't expected there to be so many thorn trees on the way. Dog kept their distance too. For the first time, Poppy could smell the iron-tinged scent of blood coming off the soil like a warning.

The wood was quieter than she expected too. A breeze rustled through the canopy from time to time. But besides that, the occasional Mogwen song in the distance, and the thumping of a woodpecker, the only sounds were their footsteps, and Dog, panting. Maybe she had just grown so used to the constant buzzing of the blood ward that once it was gone everything seemed quiet.

Dog was alert, except for Two, who kept falling asleep, his head lolling. Brutus trotted along next to Poppy, while Eta kept her ears cocked forward, listening.

Ahead of them Nula slowed as she passed a tall moss-covered stone. She dropped down into the form of a small lynx and prowled around it—sniffing.

"Mack?"

"Yeah. I see her."

"What's she doing? That looks almost like . . . a grave-stone."

Brutus's knees locked straight at the sight of the cat, but Poppy put her hand on his head. "Leave it, Brutus." He gave her a baleful look, checked to see whether Eta was interested (she wasn't), and huffed a breath.

Poppy slipped forward to examine the stone too. It sat under a hawthorn tree—yet another plant covered in two-inch-long thorns—but at least the hawthorn trees didn't try to eat you like thorn trees did. It had to be a really old grave. The stone crumbled at the corners, and the writing was so worn and covered in moss it was impossible to read.

Mack stiffened. His voice was wary. "Poppy, does it seem . . . darker to you?"

She looked up. A pall had fallen over the woods. "No . . . it's just fog."

As if naming it gave permission, the fog began to

sift up out of the ground. Nula appeared out of nowhere behind them and even Dog jumped. Brutus gave an offended woof.

"We should go now," Nula whined, herself again. She lay her ears flat into her thick brown hair. "I don't like it here."

Poppy nodded, just as a piercing scream rattled through the fog. Dog tucked their tail and took off running.

"Go!" Mack said.

They ran.

Nula was a lynx again, streaking through the trees like a ribbon. She passed Dog, and the cerberus raced forward, following Nula's every zig and zag. Mack ran straight ahead, and although his stride outpaced Poppy's, he stayed with her. They leaped over a fallen tree as behind them another wail rose.

Poppy risked a look back.

A woman made of fog and darkness swept toward them with wide blank eyes and open mouth. Her hair didn't move at all. She had no feet.

Poppy stumbled. "What is it?" she rasped as Mack hauled her up.

"Banshee," he said, panting. "I think it's a banshee! Run for the river!"

Poppy put on a burst of speed. She could feel the cold behind her like a wind at her back.

Mack's voice was ragged. "If an angry banshee catches us, we're done. It'll suck the life right out of us."

"Which way's the river?"

Mack pointed west and they cut to the left. Nula and Dog were way ahead, and Poppy hoped they were okay as she and Mack crashed through the undergrowth behind them. She tacked right to avoid a thorn tree and regretted letting go of Dog. What if they ran under one of the trees and the banshee grabbed them?

"I hear the river," Mack gasped.

The sound of water rushing was like a beacon. They half ran, half fell down a steep slope. Dirt cascaded into Poppy's boots. The river was fast and wide but didn't look too deep. There was no time to consider it further as she stumbled in, Mack right behind her. The fog rolled down the hill and stopped abruptly a few feet from the water. It rose into a wall that danced and swirled as something unseen paced back and forth inside.

Poppy leaned forward to catch her breath. The water was ice cold but thankfully didn't penetrate her boots. She looked upstream and saw Nula and Dog hurrying down the river toward them. Her lungs filled. *Thank goodness.* As soon as they were in reach, she pulled all three of Dog's heads close, rubbing her forehead against Two. "Good dog," she murmured as Eta kissed her cheek.

Poppy looked back up at the wall of fog, wondering how long the banshee would wait.

Next to her, Nula was wide-eyed and twitchy. Her skin had gone a deeper shade of blue. "Banshees aren't usually so aggressive," she said, wiping blue beads of sweat from her brow. "But I'm sure it will leave soon," she added in a whisper as if she had heard Poppy's thoughts and was trying to convince them both.

Mack cast a look at her. "Banshees are tied, either to their graves or to their families. They aren't meant to be aggressive at all . . . unless they're disturbed . . . which, I guess, this one was." He frowned. "Anyway, they can't go too far, so we should be out of her territory soon."

Poppy pressed her lips together. "We'll cross to the shore on the other side."

Poppy spun and marched toward the opposite bank, trying not to splash water over the tops of her boots. The river stayed shallow. She felt a rush of gratitude for practical footwear as she reached the other side and let her pack drop to the ground. She yanked out her journal.

Nula leaned toward Mack. "What's she doing?"

Mack snorted. "If I had to guess, I'd say she's making a little map showing the banshee grave . . . maybe taking a few notes?"

Poppy nodded, but otherwise ignored them.

"Now?"

Mack shrugged. "The banshee won't cross the river. Poppy doesn't want to forget."

Nula cast a hopeful look at Poppy. "You did bring lunch though, right?"

Poppy lifted her face to Nula's and pulled a face, aiming her thumb at her pack. "Of course I did. I want to get a little farther first though."

Nula frowned. "Oh. Of course you thought of that. I should have known. You're smarter than me, probably," she added. Something flickered through Nula's eyes, but it was gone before Poppy could even be sure she'd seen it.

The fog had faded back, but Poppy still felt as though something watched them from inside the white billows on the other side of the river. She wouldn't pass this way again if she could help it. "Right," she said. "I think all we need to do is follow the river upstream to reach the Holly Oak."

"Agreed," Mack said.

Nula paused. "The Fae are west."

Poppy scowled.

Nula held up her hands in defeat. "Okay, okay," she muttered, and proceeded to chat at Dog.

By the time the thin rays of early afternoon sun trickled through the forest canopy, all Poppy could hear was the sound of Mack's stomach growling. She stopped under a giant oak. The ground below it was littered with acorns.

"Perfect!" The pooka let out a little squeal and set to gathering them, while Dog trotted behind her hoping for a game of fetch.

Mack let out a groan and sank to sit with his back against the tree. He tipped his head back and looked up into the tree. "I'm famished."

Poppy's mouth twitched. "Hard to argue with that," she replied, pausing to look around for anything that might be lurking in the shadows before she dropped her pack off her shoulders. She collapsed to the ground and let herself lie back next to Mack, brushing away the acorns from underneath her. Above them, the branches shifted in the slight breeze, light shaking down through the leaves as they danced. She pushed the pack toward Mack. "Sandwiches."

He grinned at her and sat up to dig inside, fishing out three of the wrapped boar sandwiches she'd piled inside. He handed one to Nula who took it and sniffed at the mustard.

Poppy watched. "Homemade," she explained, with a pang. She loved Jute's mustard. Where had he been that morning? Sending word to her parents about what she'd done, most likely. What was he doing now? Pacing the floor, and worrying, if she had to guess.

"Careful," Mack told Nula. "It's a little spicy."

Nula scoffed and took a big bite. Her eyes widened. "This is good," she said in a muffled voice, through the sandwich.

Mack wiggled his eyebrows.

"So . . . can you change into other things . . . besides a mouse, snake, spider . . . and bird?" Poppy asked, needing to turn her thoughts away from Jute.

Nula dropped down to sit on the other side of Mack. "Sure. I can turn into pretty much anything," she said around another bite of sandwich. "Till I'm old enough to decide what my permanent form will be."

"Huh," Poppy said. "So, the mouse, and the snake . . . and the spider are regulars or . . ."

Nula smiled tightly. "Small things are easiest, and I like them—except for moths." She shuddered. "The lynx is the biggest creature I've done so far."

"Really?" Poppy smiled. "If I could change into animals, I'd change into . . . I don't know . . . a lion, or something huge and scary like that."

Another flicker crossed Nula's face. "Yeah, well. Small things can move fast," she explained. "And they can hide almost anywhere."

Poppy cocked her head at the pooka. "Makes sense."

"Anyway," Nula added, "you don't need to turn into anything. You're already scary enough."

Mack choked on his sandwich.

"What does that mean?" Poppy snapped.

Nula's eyes widened. "Oh! Sorry. I wasn't . . . I didn't . . . You just have, you know . . ." She halfway pointed at Poppy's face. "Resting witch face."

Poppy's mouth fell open as Mack barked a laugh. Nula flushed and turned to pick up Dog's bone with two fingers. She dropped it into Poppy's backpack. "How old are they anyway?" she asked, patting Two.

"Changing the subject." Mack grinned at her. "Good idea."

"About three," Poppy answered and gave Nula one last glare before she turned her attention to stroking Eta's face. Eta's eyes closed.

Nula looked at Dog sadly. "They're really special, Poppy. I . . . I wish—"

"Yeah. They were the best present ever. Well," she added, rising to brush herself off. "We should get going." She paused and met Nula's eyes. "Thanks." She held out her hand. "It was good to meet you."

Nula's face fell. "Oh. Oh . . . sure. Um . . . I'm really sorry if I insulted you earlier."

Poppy shook her head. "No problem. I'm sure you've got other stuff to do, and now that the banshee thing is over, we don't want to keep you. I think we're good from here."

It wasn't that she didn't like the pooka. She seemed okay. It was just that part of her wanted to explore the forest with Mack—just the two of them against all obstacles— like she'd always imagined. Besides, she was sure Nula needed to get back to her friends and family.

Nula looked away. "Um, okay, then. Good . . . Good to meet you."

Poppy and Mack waved and turned to keep following the river. The pooka stood under the oak, her pockets full of acorns, and watched them go.

Now that it was just them again, Mack's shoulders seemed to ease a little and he sent her a small nod of acknowledgment. The scent of pine and something darker wafted up from the forest floor as they moved past patches of trillium and around huckleberry hedges. Poppy forced herself to take a deep breath. She had an elf and a cerberus by her side. She was going to find the Soul Jar before her parents and show them once and for all that she was ready to be a family—to hunt maledictions by their side.

Despite her excitement, she had to admit that nothing here was really how she had imagined it. She hadn't expected it to be so quiet, for one thing. She hadn't expected to see so many thorn trees . . . or be attacked by a banshee . . . or to be followed by a pooka. Doubt chewed at the edges of her confidence, like a mouse nibbling a pea. What if she was wrong about the tree? What if the Holly Oak didn't know anything? What if she got her parents in trouble somehow, for going after maledictions? What if the tree laughed at her and told her she was acting like a child? Worse, what if she *was*—acting like a child?

Mack's steady footfalls fell beside her. A surge of warmth rolled over Poppy. The truth was that if Mack was there, she couldn't be doing the *wrong* thing. Her best friend would never have gone along with her—he wouldn't have stood for it.

Her ideas might not be the exact *right* thing . . . doubtless Mack would say staying home and listening to the grown-ups was the *right* thing . . . but at least it wasn't *wrong*. As long as her best friend was still at her side, things would be okay.

She shook off her doubts. They had a plan, and with a plan, and friends like Mack and Dog, she didn't need anything else. Nothing could go wrong.

CHAPTER SIX

The Holly Oak was at the very center of the forest. There was no way for them to get there in one day . . . at least, not on foot. A ripple of excitement fizzed along Poppy's spine. She was going to meet the Holly Oak, for real—not just in her imagination. Not just in some dream. She wanted to know everything there was to know about the tree, and then . . . she wanted to know more.

She pulled her journal out and checked the notes she'd copied from her parents one more time. "It should be right up here," she muttered.

Mack didn't ask questions, but he let out a long sigh, and Poppy sent him an apologetic smirk. Of course he wanted to know what she was planning—what *it* was—but she wasn't quite ready to share yet. She just had to make sure she was on the right track first.

Mack knew her scraps of knowledge about the Grimwood had never added up to enough. Not even close. Knowledge is the enemy of fear, her father liked to say, but to Poppy, knowledge meant more than the power to fight her fears. It meant belonging.

Two's head tipped sideways as Poppy stroked his ear. Mack stood patiently next to her, patting Eta's head, and then Brutus's. His mouth twitched into a half smile. "You have the funniest look on your face, Poppy. What are you thinking about?"

"Hm? Oh . . . I was thinking about this story my parents told me about the Holly Oak one time."

Mack's smile cracked wider. "What'd they say?"

"Well . . ." She reached up to yank her ponytail tight. "They had gone into the wood—into the deeps to one of the big thorn groves. And I guess they passed through a Hyphae village without realizing it." She watched his face for a reaction.

Mack cringed. "The fungus folk don't like anything to touch their soil without their permission."

Poppy smirked. "Right, well, my parents didn't know that at the time. The Hyphae mother tangled them in these long fungal ropes. Mom said they were so tight it was hard to breathe."

Mack shivered. "They're lucky they didn't get spored. How did they escape?"

"They didn't. The Hyphae took them to the Holly Oak." Poppy smirked. "It was the first time they met her. The Hyphae mother asked the Oak for justice."

Mack scrubbed one hand over his face. "Thorns! What happened?"

"The Holly Oak told Mom and Dad that ignorance was not an excuse. She said if they insisted on being in the Grimwood, then it was their task to learn about it and understand it. She told them how to watch for the Hyphae boundary."

"The ring of red mushrooms."

"And then she told them they had to make amends."

Mack pulled a face. "Make amends . . . how?"

Poppy grinned, holding back a laugh. "Mom told that part . . . and you should have seen the look she gave Dad."

Mack raised both brows. "What—"

"They had to carry these huge . . ." She snickered. "These huge backpacks full of fresh manure from Strange Hollow, back to the outskirts of the Hyphae village."

Mack barked a laugh. "I bet your mom loved that!"

Poppy couldn't hold back her laughter. "They had to . . . make two trips," she wheezed.

Poppy turned to the page in her journal where she'd had her dad draw one of the red mushrooms that signaled a Hyphae village, lifting it to show Mack. "Don't worry. I know what they look like now," she added.

Mack chuckled. "I know them. I'm sure we can make plenty of our own mistakes." He stretched his arms over his head, reaching for the lowest branch of a tall ash tree. "Speaking of which . . . you know the Holly Oak is way too far for one day's travel, right? I know you have *plans* and all, but we should set up camp for the night." He paused. "Please tell me you brought salt and iron."

"I did. But we're not camping."

"But—"

"We won't be in the wood for the night at all. Really," she added when he pulled a face. She shoved her journal back in her bag. "I have a plan."

"But Poppy—"

"Trust me, Mack. Now, come on. There's no time to waste." Poppy called Dog to her side and traipsed through the brush, following the riverbank upstream.

"Okay, so where *are* we going to spend the night?"

"Shush. I'm looking for the dock."

She heard him stop walking. "You mean . . . a dock for the Boatman? That kind of dock?"

She reached into her hoodie pocket and tossed an apple over her shoulder. "Yup."

Mack caught it and took a bite, jogging to catch up to her. "How are you going to pay him?"

"My gold coins are burning a hole in my pocket." Poppy had been young when her mother, speaking where Poppy could hear her, let it slip that three gold coins would buy a ride with the Boatman to anywhere in the Grimwood. She'd fallen asleep with more questions on her lips, but she remembered that much.

Mack rolled his eyes. "Your birthday money?"

Poppy winked. "It's weighing down my pocket."

"I thought you wanted to buy books at next solstice."

She lifted a shoulder. "This is better."

"Right. Well, I suppose I should be grateful. At least you're not running around looking for old ladies to trust and give your gold to," he muttered. "That never goes well in the wood."

Poppy looked up at him. "Well, I wasn't even considering *that* option . . . but why doesn't it?"

"When is an old lady in the Grimwood *ever* just an old lady? Answer . . . never! They always turn out to be witches."

Poppy laughed but quickly smothered it at the sight of Mack's earnest expression. "Huh. But witches help you sometimes if you help them first, don't they?"

"I mean, there are good ones and bad ones, sure. If you help an old woman in need, theoretically they *might* owe you something."

"Like information?"

"Sure, or, they might give you a poison apple that puts you to sleep for years, or steal your voice, or make you an old lady too." He punctuated the comment by biting his own apple. "Point is, you never know what you're going to get with old ladies in the wood. Unreliable."

His eyes followed Poppy as she moved ahead, searching the river. She was just beginning to doubt her parents' notes when they came around a bend and Poppy spotted an old dock, twisted and rotting. It stuck out into a deep part of the river and looked more likely to collapse than to hold their weight. What would the Boatman be like, she wondered. He was a strange creature, she had gleaned that much—a creature, not a human. Her mother's notes said he looked like a man, but . . . wrong. Whatever that meant.

Regardless, he might be the only creature who had access to the entire wood. His docks sprang up here and there all along the river Veena inside the forest, like fingers pointing. There were none of the Boatman's docks in any of the Hollows.

She had asked her father once how the Boatman got through the shallow parts of the river in his boat. Her father had laughed and told her he didn't think the actual river made much difference one way or another. She'd tried to get him to say more, but he only shuddered, and added that he sometimes wondered if, once you were in the Boatman's boat, the whole river might be a passage to somewhere else, other worlds . . . maybe the land of the dead, where the Boatman was said to travel.

Poppy stepped onto the dock first. An old iron bell hung from a pole at the far end. Once she rang it, *in theory*, the Boatman should arrive to take them where they wanted to go. As long as they paid him, *in theory*, they were safe. He wouldn't harm them, or take them anywhere else. *In theory*.

She wasn't sure she believed the Boatman could go between the Grimwood and the land of the dead, but she also didn't see any point in finding out if it was true. Dog came and stood by her side, watchful and quiet. Mack stood farther back, trying to distribute their weight along the rotting boards of the dock.

Poppy was reaching for the bell when a huge green and purple dragonfly landed between her and Mack, then turned into Nula.

"You were really going to leave me?" Her long tail whipped the air behind her.

Poppy jumped, but Mack just stared.

"What are you doing here, Nula?" Poppy blurted.

"You never asked where I was headed next," the pooka said, not meeting their eyes.

"Don't tell me . . ." Mack crossed his arms. "You're—"

"I'm going to the Holly Oak."

Poppy laughed out loud. "You are not."

"I am too. Don't tell me where I'm going." She turned to Poppy. "Could I—I mean . . . do you mind . . . if I go with you?"

Poppy considered. The pooka had helped them twice now, once with her blood ward, and once with the banshee. If Nula wanted their company, why should she argue?

Two friends, she thought, letting the idea roll around in her mind. "If you really want to," she said, and gave Nula a smirk. "I guess that's fine." She glanced back at Mack. "That's okay with you, right, Mack?"

Mack nose-sighed as Nula beamed at both of them,

and Poppy took the mallet off its peg and hit the bell. The deep tone rang out. It raced along Poppy's arm, leaving goose bumps behind, and seemed to ripple out over the river and into the trees. A hush fell over the forest.

The sound of an oar in the water made Poppy's heart beat faster. Nula moved to stand behind Mack, looking like she wasn't sure whether to hide behind him, or bolt. She and Dog both had their ears back. Everyone stared upstream, waiting. Even the woods seemed to be holding its breath.

And then, the Boatman appeared.

He was a wide, round man with pale white skin. His black beard and hair wrapped around his head like a mane, and looked singed at the edges, all of it sticking out as if he had been struck by lightning. His black eyes were fever-bright. He pulled the shallow boat up to the end of the dock, and held out his hand, palm up.

Poppy swallowed. "Can you take us to the Holly Oak?" she asked, her voice faltering.

He studied them for a moment, his gaze flickering over each of them as if weighing them, or perhaps, judging them. He didn't answer but moved his open hand nearer to Poppy.

She looked back at Mack. He just tipped his chin. Poppy's throat went dry as she reached into her pocket.

She pulled out three of her gold coins and dropped them into the Boatman's waiting palm. His thick fingers closed around them, and they hurried aboard. The boat rocked wildly as Dog jumped on, sending up the thick wet smell of the river. The murky scent seemed to rise from the Boatman himself as he stared at Eta-Two-Brutus with gleaming eyes. For a moment Poppy thought he might speak. She shuddered as he turned away to dip his oar in the water.

They shot upstream at a dizzying pace, the trees blurring on either side. Poppy clung to the edge of the boat with one arm around Dog, hoping she hadn't made a terrible mistake. Her breath clung in her throat as if it were afraid to leave. Mack sat in the back with wide eyes, while Nula hunched low in the middle looking around as if something might pop out at her at any moment.

The water grew rough. Cold foam splashed over the edge, gathering in the bottom of the boat where they huddled.

The trees blurred faster.

Nula leaned forward and threw her arms over her head, as Brutus began to whimper.

Poppy's heart faltered.

The Boatman began to laugh.

He laughed and laughed, a booming echo that swirled around them like a storm. Poppy squeezed her eyes shut. She could hear water raging beneath them now, but she was too afraid to look. Nula was crying behind her and Eta-Two-Brutus huddled by her feet.

They were moving so fast, Poppy couldn't lift her

head against the force of their movement. She turned it instead, and from the corner of her eye could see a tunnel of branches creaking and swaying above them.

The boat lurched to a stop. At the back, Mack leaned over the edge and threw up. They were at another dock. Poppy might have believed they had come right back to where they started except for two things. They were surrounded by water—and the only shore was the white cliffs gleaming, far away, in the last of the afternoon sun.

"It's the Alcyon," Mack announced, sounding more excited than Poppy expected. "I've always wanted to see this."

"The bottomless salt sea," Nula intoned.

The dock was attached to a huge island made of roots, and those roots rose up into the largest tree Poppy had ever seen. Its bark was a deep red-brown, streaked in black, and its trunk took up the entire island, except for a thin band of sand and rocky shore around it. She looked up, and up, into the thick branches stretching high above them. Shining green holly leaves with spiked black edges rattled in the breeze.

Her hands were clammy as she clambered out onto the dock, half dragging Dog with her. "The Holly Oak—we made it."

Mack, still recovering from his bout of nausea, stumbled out of the boat behind her.

Nula scrambled out onto the dock. Poppy looked back

in time to see the Boatman and his boat tip straight up and sink behind her, stern first, into the Alcyon sea without a sound or even a ripple to show their passage.

Dog whined, and Poppy wet her lips. "It's okay, Dog," she said, patting Eta's head. "This is the Holly Oak. Sacred ground. Nothing on this island can hurt us, right?"

Nula scoffed. "Whoever told you that must not be very creative."

"But—"

"Where there's a will there's a way, isn't that what you humans say?" Her ear flicked. "Honestly, for someone who breaks rules as a hobby, you're a little . . ."

Poppy drew back. "A little what?"

Nula shrugged. "I'm just saying—you should always watch your back. Tell her I'm right, Mack."

Mack's face was thoughtful. "I've always heard the island is the safest place in the wood, but she has a point, Poppy. It doesn't hurt to be careful."

Nula nibbled one clawlike nail. "Unless we *need* to be reckless. Then it might."

Poppy raised an eyebrow.

"Hurt to be careful, I mean," Nula clarified.

Mack shook his head.

"You're confusing, Nula," Poppy said, her lips quirking.

"Don't blame the messenger! It's not me that's confusing. It's the world." She looked around and lifted her blue hands to take it all in. "What now?"

Poppy looked up at the tree. It stretched into the sky as if it could pierce straight through, as if it were the center pole of the whole world, and everything revolved around it. She felt dizzy, staring up, and her pulse skipped a giddy beat that made it worse. She took a deep breath. "Now, we go see what the Oak knows about the Soul Jar."

Mack and Nula followed Poppy as they made the slow climb up the slope, scrambling over boulders clutched in the grip of the Holly Oak's roots.

"So," Nula called over. "A pooka, a human, an elf, and a cerberus walk into a tree . . ."

Mack laughed. "It does sound like the start of a bad joke," he admitted.

"Right?" Nula muttered. "I just hope we're not the punch line."

Mack laughed again, but Poppy didn't. Her hands shook. She couldn't make them stop. There was no telling if the Oak would welcome them or not—would welcome *her*, or not. She tipped her head back again to look up into its branches. What if the Oak sent her home? Could she do that? Poppy frowned. Well . . . there was only one way to find out.

She kept climbing.

CHAPTER SEVEN

They picked their way over the cobbles, stumbling over root and stone. Dog kept falling behind, and when Two let out a plaintive whine, Mack turned back to pick them up, slinging them over his shoulder.

Poppy was out of breath by the time the roots leveled out into a wide plateau. Rotted leaves and bark had turned into a thick layer of soil, and the ground from the top of the slope to the base of the tree bloomed with wildflowers and meadow grasses. Two large pavilions were staked out at the base of the tree. Beneath their shade, creatures milled around—waiting, Poppy supposed, to talk to the Holly Oak.

There were three werewolves, standing around chatting over small plates of raw meat. She also spotted several old women. One held a tentacular in her huge clawed hand. She gave Poppy a sharp-toothed grin as they passed by, forcing a shiver along her spine.

"Keep going," Nula hissed as they moved past another

old woman, dripping as though she'd just come out of a pond. The other creatures gave her patch of wet ground a wide berth—all except for a large flaming salamander, who lingered close, watching her with undisguised hatred in its black eyes.

Under the second pavilion a large winged serpent was curled up, sleeping. A species of wyvern, perhaps. Next to it, a small herd of boar-like creatures snuffled through piles of mushrooms. Poppy thought they were boar-like rather than actual boars, because though they were on all fours, they muttered among themselves, spraying bits of their food around. She spotted a Hyphae—one of the fungal folk— watching the boars from a shady corner. She slowed. He was tall, and his body was so thin he could slip through a crack if it weren't for his bulbous head. He was completely white— except for his round pinkish eyes, and a thin line of pink around his neck—all of him covered in downy white fuzz.

Mack started to move toward the pavilion and Poppy grabbed his sleeve, forcing herself to keep walking. Mack gave her a startled look.

It wasn't that she wasn't interested in the pavilions. Any other time she would have rushed under either of the canopies to learn as much as she could. But now . . . she didn't want to wait another moment to talk to the Holly Oak. She had already waited thirteen years. She wouldn't wait another day. Besides, there was no telling what harm the Soul Jar could do. They needed to find it fast—especially if she wanted to get to it before her parents. It was practically an emergency!

She looked toward the trunk of the tree and glimpsed a shadow curling along the trunk. She slowed, squinting to see what cast it.

"Stairs," Nula hissed in her ear, as if the pooka could read her mind. Like magic, once she knew what they were, Poppy could make them out. Spiraling around the trunk was a set of steps.

After that, she didn't think. She ran.

Mack called out from behind her, and Brutus gave an offended bark, but she didn't slow. This was the time for action. She was surprised to hear Nula running behind her—urging her forward. "Go," the pooka said. "Before they try and stop us. Hurry."

The stairs were wide enough for someone twice her size, but open, and there was no railing on the outside. She hesitated. It wasn't that she was afraid of heights, exactly. She just wasn't *not* afraid of heights. You can do it, she told herself. She didn't want anyone stopping her, and she didn't want Mack to try to talk her out of it either. He wouldn't like this one bit. She looked over her shoulder at him.

Mack had slowed, hanging on to Dog's collar to keep them out of trouble as they passed the far end of the pavilion. If she gave him time to catch up, he would try to stop her, for certain. She began to climb—then almost lost her balance still staring upward.

"If we're really doing this, you better move it," Nula said, giving her a shove.

"Poppy, wait!" Mack called.

Poppy dashed up the stairs, risking a glance back. Her best friend had skidded to a stop at the base of the stairs and was looking up at her with such a hurt expression that she almost turned back.

Almost.

She sped up, trailing one hand along the rough brown and black bark to keep her balance. The black streaks glittered like the sky at night. Poppy chanced a peek over the side. Her heart lurched, and she shot back, clinging to the tree. A moment later, she pushed onward again, higher and higher.

By the time she and Nula made it around the back side of the tree, Poppy's knees had begun to shake. She stopped, pausing to catch her breath, and closed her eyes as she leaned back against the trunk. If she looked down again she'd fall. Mack was definitely upset with her. He could have come too, she argued with herself—Nula did.

The pooka wasn't even out of breath. She stood at the outer edge of the steps, looking down the hundred feet or more to the ground as if she were looking for a place to have a picnic.

Poppy gave herself a mental shake. This was the right thing, even if it stressed Mack out. They had no time to waste. *Can it be the right thing if it feels terrible?* a part of her argued. She squeezed her eyes tighter and let her head thump back against the bark. She could feel Nula watching her. "Why are you staring at me?"

The pooka gave a bright laugh. "Sorry. I guess . . . I didn't realize how interesting humans are. You wear all your feelings on your face. Did you know that? I mean . . . Do you do it on purpose?"

"What are you talking about?" Poppy asked, opening her eyes. When she did, a strange spinning sensation took hold. Nula felt it too, because her gold eyes got even wider as she gripped the bark next to Poppy.

It was like riding on a corkscrew. The stairs spun backward. There was a strong breeze, and Mack came back into view. The entire stairway had coiled back to the ground.

Poppy's jaw dropped. "Thorns!"

Nula looked back up to where they had been standing a moment before. "Maybe if we ask nice, this thing will go the other direction," she muttered, crossing her arms.

As predicted, Mack was angry. "You just ran off!"

"Then again, maybe not," Nula muttered, ignoring him.

Poppy met Mack's eyes. "Come with us!" There was a moment of stillness between them; then she spun to dash back up the steps. This time Eta barked too.

Poppy ignored all of it. She wasn't going to be outsmarted by a tree, and she wasn't going to give up. If she had to pass some high-flying stair-climbing test, so be it.

She'd pass them all. Whatever the Holly Oak threw at her. She was getting in there.

She would wear it down.

She would go faster.

She took the stairs two at a time, with Nula's cascade of laughter at her heels.

This time, Mack came too. "Poppy!" he shouted past Nula. "You can't push your way in—the Holly Oak doesn't work like that!"

"We'll see!"

"Poppy's right, you know," Nula panted. "Sometimes you have to take matters into your own hands."

Poppy could almost hear Mack's scowl. "We should wait with the others," he called defiantly. "Things work better in the wood when you follow the rules."

Poppy's answer came in harsh breaths. "The Soul Jar is loose, Mack! Someone might be in real danger." As she said the words, she suddenly realized they were true. Whether she got to the malediction herself, or her parents did, *someone* was counting on them. But she still wanted to get there first. Her thighs were burning now, almost as much as her throat.

Mack's silence was ominous. She hoped he was just thinking over what she'd said. "If anyone can help," she added, "it's the Oak."

"Hey, look," Nula said, pointing up into the thin branches above them. "There's a little door up there."

Poppy reeled back so fast she bumped into Nula and lost her balance. The ground spun up at her from below. Nula gasped and Mack lurched past her to yank Poppy back to safety.

"Let me go in front," Nula said. "I have an idea."

Poppy stood shaking and let the pooka by. "Thanks, Mack," she managed to whisper.

He didn't say anything, but his warm skin was a shade paler, and he stayed at her back the rest of the way up.

Poppy's legs hurt, and her hand had gotten scraped on the bark. Also, her nose was running and she had no tissue. Sniffing, she slowed to a trudge. The stairs seemed to have gotten steeper.

Ahead of them, Nula's pace was so steady it was almost a drumbeat. Behind Poppy, Mack was quiet, lost in his own thoughts. Dog brought up the rear, tongues lolling.

They had to stop and catch their breath twice. The second time, Poppy lifted her face to look out across the landscape. She stayed back from the edge, but beneath them the island fell away, and beyond it, the wide open Alcyon sea lay sparkling, the waters dark and still. She could see smoke rising from Strange Hollow chimneys in the distance beyond the trees, and farther still—the fog.

Poppy wondered how deep the sea was. She wondered how the Holly Oak survived here, surrounded by a fathomless salt sea . . . and if it was—fathomless—where did the roots go? They entered the water. She had seen that for herself. Did it drink the salt water? Did it just make all its own soil and . . . float here?

She turned to Mack. "See? Aren't you glad I ran ahead?"

"It is quite a view." He gave her an uncertain smile. "I guess we better keep climbing."

Nula had gotten farther ahead with her drumbeat steps, and Poppy hurried to catch up, watching her feet as she climbed. Mack stayed close.

"There," she heard the pooka whisper, and Poppy's head shot up to see a small green door, narrow, with gilded hinges and a small round knob over a gold-plated keyhole. The whole door jutted forward slightly from a bump in the trunk. Poppy chewed her lip and tried to ignore the surge of hope. "How did you spot this from way down there? You're amazing, Nula!"

Nula hid a smile and the blue stripes in her ears darkened with pleasure. "I've had a lot of practice finding doors into places where I'm not wanted."

Poppy watched her friend jiggle the knob and wondered why she'd say something so sad.

"Locked," Nula confirmed.

Mack was looking around nervously, as though he expected the Oak to scold them.

"Now what?" Poppy said.

Nula grinned at her. She wrapped her fingers around the knob, and then she was gone.

A slender green snake disappeared through the keyhole. Poppy and Mack exchanged glances.

There was a creaking sound, and the door swung open.

CHAPTER EIGHT

Poppy stepped into a small, dark alcove—empty except for a bucket, a broom, and a small shelf above the door, filled with bottles and books, and several large spiders. The air was dusty. Was this . . . a closet?

The walls were the soft warm wood of the tree, as was the floor. She moved closer to Mack. "Nula?" she hissed.

"I'm right here," Nula said, tapping Poppy's shoulder with the tuft of her tail. She laughed when Poppy and Mack jumped. A tapestry curtain hung in front of them, completely blocking whatever was on the other side. Eta let out a low growl, Brutus and Two following her lead. Poppy lay one hand on Eta's head, and reached out to pull back the curtain.

Her mouth went dry.

The alcove opened into a huge chamber with soaring ceilings. Arched buttresses of smooth wood stretched away above them. Copper lanterns hung on the walls of the chamber, glowing with warm light that shifted and moved, but didn't flicker like fire.

"It's so quiet," Nula murmured.

"It's a sacred place," Mack replied. And then, as though he couldn't help himself, he added, "We really shouldn't be here without an invitation."

"It let us in, didn't it?" Poppy breathed.

"Did it?" Mack hedged.

She caught movement to her right as her vision adjusted in the dim glow. A picker paced along the wall. The hair on her neck rose at the sight of its long stick-insect body—twice as long as Dog and just as tall. She stared as it made a clumsy turn, making its way back the other way along the edge of the hall. She caught a glimpse of humanlike eyes in its triangular face and shuddered.

The floor of the chamber was wood, soft and worn along a center aisle from years, perhaps centuries, of visitors. They walked toward a tall column at the end of the chamber. As they got closer, Poppy realized it was a tree—another tree. A tree within a tree, rising so high that Poppy had to stop walking and stretch her neck to look up. It was as though the inner tree was holding up—or forming—the chamber. Its branches curved across the ceiling, smaller branches weaving together to form panels, extending them-selves into the buttressed arches. The only impressions of leaves were the ones carved into the curves of the room.

With a jolt, Poppy realized she'd fallen behind. Mack and Nula both had their heads tipped back too and hadn't noticed. Poppy wondered how many people tripped and fell on their faces the first time they came here.

They came to a platform in front of the tree and stopped.

Nula looked around. "Now what?"

Poppy couldn't believe that just that morning they had broken her blood ward. It seemed like a lifetime ago. She should be feeling elated. She had learned more about the forest in one day than she had gathered from all her hours of study, poring over her parents journals; more than she had in her whole life so far. Far from jubilant, she just felt sweaty and anxious. "We need to . . . figure out how to talk to the Holly . . . I guess . . . now that we're here."

Nula lifted her hands. "Okay, but where *is* she? Looks to me like we're just standing around in a hollow tree."

Poppy scowled, but Mack looked affronted. "It's beautiful! Look at the craftsmanship!"

Nula's ear flicked as if a fly buzzed nearby. "Sure. It's a *fancy* hollow tree. The Faery Queen's throne room is fancier though."

Mack frowned. "Fancier doesn't mean better."

"Well, if you say so."

Poppy stepped forward so they didn't have to argue around her. The light had shifted on the smaller tree, and she moved closer to get a better look.

It was strange. There were no windows, but somehow there was light shifting over the smooth bark of the inner tree. It looked like sunshine. How? She moved up the shallow rooted steps. It wasn't just light moving over the surface, it was shadow too, as if something moved just under the surface. She reached out to touch it and fell back with a shout.

Bright hazel eyes looked down at her. The bark shifted with a sound like a sigh, and a narrow face pushed from the surface. Her skin looked soft—not like bark at all, and was golden and brown, like warmed honey. Long dark tendrils hung around her face like tiny branches. A delicate crown of sparkling black thorns and red holly berries rested on her head.

Nula's voice came in a whisper. "Now *she* is fancy."

Poppy glanced at Mack and almost laughed. She could have knocked him down with a breath, he was so enthralled. She nudged him and he straightened, closing his mouth.

The Holly Oak's smooth shoulders appeared next, followed by her arms, which lifted into a graceful stretch. A rustling sound, and the bark below her collarbones shifted into a gown of russet and gold leaves.

The Holly Oak smiled, her hazel eyes sparkling with amusement. She lifted one arm to point directly at Poppy. "You are Pandora Sunshine Bright. I can see your mother and your father in you. Come here." Her voice was deep and rough.

Poppy swallowed and stepped back up on the dais. "Just Poppy," she whispered.

The tree gave her a gentle smile. "Poppy, then. Come closer. I won't bite." The Holly Oak lifted one hand to shield her mouth so the others couldn't see. "I don't have to," she confided.

Poppy's mouth twitched. She did as she was asked.

The Holly Oak reached up and took Poppy's chin in her fingers. Her grip was gentle, but firm—strong. Poppy held very still. She could sense the care the Holly Oak used, as if in other circumstances, she could choose to snap bone with her bare fingers.

The Oak turned Poppy's face first to one side, and then the other. She let go, and Poppy fell back a step. "You have your parents' bravery, I think." She smiled as her hazel eyes narrowed. "But I think . . . not yet their wisdom." She leaned forward from the tree, as though peeling herself away from it. "So, why are you here, Poppy Sunshine? Did your parents send you?"

"Send me? My—my parents? No. They're in the wood too though, hunting something called the Soul Jar. They think it's a malediction that was maybe altered by—"

Poppy sputtered to a halt as the smile melted off the Holly Oak's face. "I'm familiar with that rumor. But *I* think you must be mistaken."

Dark clouds appeared to roll over the Holly Oak's face. Poppy faltered. "You—you mean it's not a malediction? They can't be changed to have an altered purpose?"

"No, your parents are right about that. I don't know who has learned to change a malediction's purpose and bind it with their blood. It must be a creature with great power. Nonetheless, that is certainly what this Soul Jar is." She paused. "What I *meant* was, your parents aren't hunting the Soul Jar. They aren't in the Grimwood at all."

"What?" Poppy shook her head. "No, they have to be. Where else would they be? Jute said they were."

The Holly Oak leaned farther out, until Poppy was forced to step back off the dais to make way for the folds of her gown. "I cannot see them, or sense them. That can mean only one of two things."

Poppy's stomach dropped through the floor.

"It means they are dead, or they have crossed the fog."

A small cry escaped Poppy's lips, but the Holly Oak only straightened. Her eyes never left Poppy's face. "I am sorry to be the bearer of these tidings."

"No. That's wrong."

"It is not."

"They can't be dead."

"Then they are outside the fog."

"Why would they leave?" Mack asked, stepping forward. "I don't think they'd do that. You said . . . you said the Soul Jar was real. What does it do?"

The tree cocked her head at him. "Hello, elf."

Mack flushed and dropped his head. "Mackintosh nee Gala, ma'am. I go by Mack."

"Mack," the Oak acknowledged. "What does the Soul Jar do? Though I have not beheld it, I expect that, as its name implies, it traps souls—or the energy of souls."

"That's what we thought too." Mack agreed.

Nula stepped up on Poppy's other side. "So, could they be in there, then? Could Poppy's parents have gotten caught in the Soul Jar? Would that explain why you can't see them?"

Poppy's heart raced. If her parents were stuck in the Soul Jar . . . then there was a chance she could get them out. Wasn't there? She held her breath.

"Greetings, pooka." Nula blushed dark blue under the Oak's scrutiny. "Trapped *inside* a malediction. That is an interesting theory . . ."

Dog, sensing Poppy's anxiety, leaned into her leg. Poppy dropped one cold hand down against Eta's warm neck.

"It seems unlikely," the tree finished.

"But—" Nula and Poppy said in unison.

Nula whipped the air with her tail. "Maybe you just don't know as much as you think you do," she snapped.

The Holly Oak's hazel eyes focused on Nula. "And maybe, little pooka . . . maybe I know *more* than *you* think I do."

"Stop it," Mack hissed at Nula. "You're not helping."

Nula's ears flattened.

"Can you see my house?" Poppy asked.

"Your home is of the wood, and so within my sight and sense."

"And they're not there?"

The tree shook her head, sending her leafy gown rustling.

"What about the Hollows?" Mack asked. "Can you see there?"

The gold-brown skin of the Holly Oak's face darkened. "I cannot."

Poppy scowled. "My parents aren't welcome in Strange Hollow—not in any of the Hollows, especially now that Governor Gale is in charge."

Mack grimaced. "That leaves the fog."

"The fog does not belong to me," the Holly Oak said. "My magic called it, and maintains it, but it is a free being. I cannot see within, or beyond it."

Poppy felt the blood drain from her face. Mack looked queasy. "The fog . . . is really alive?"

"Its very nature is to obscure. Its task is to hold the Grimwood and the Hollows together, bound by my magic, and bound to it as well."

The tree held up one hand as Poppy opened her mouth to speak. "Peace. I can only tell you what I know to be true. My power extends to all the trees and soil of the forest— only as far as the edge of Strange Hollow. If they are in the wood, this *Soul Jar* is the only place I know of where I might not know of their presence. Perhaps they are not dead."

The wave of relief that washed over Poppy was so strong she thought she might be sick. Her parents weren't dead. They couldn't be. She wouldn't let it be. And they weren't gone forever into the outside world either—or lost in the fog. They would never leave the Grimwood behind. They were *caught*. And that meant they could be freed.

The Holly Oak's dark brows furrowed. "Be careful, Poppy. Hope is food for the soul of every living being—yours included, but it can lead us astray. What you hope for is *possible*. The Soul Jar might have your parents. It is also possible this has not taken place."

Poppy swallowed the bitterness in her throat, grateful to have Mack and Nula at her side. "If they're trapped I'll find them," Poppy insisted. She wouldn't allow even a sliver of doubt to ring in her words. They were alive and they needed her help. She would help them. That had to be the end of it. If she heard even the tiniest bit of doubt in her own voice, she might stop believing she could do it.

The tree considered her and frowned. "The Grimwood is no place for children. My advice to you—go home and wait. This forest is perilous during the day, and even more so at night."

Poppy shook her head. "I'm not going home. I'm going

to find the Soul Jar and get my parents out." Mack's breath caught at the brazenness of her tone, but it was only the truth. To give the Holly Oak less would be wrong.

"Very well . . ." The tree gave an amused snort that was so unexpected, it made Nula snort too. "I will not force you. To do so would cost me more than I can spare. You must make your own choices, and suffer your own consequences."

Poppy gritted her teeth. "Can you explain how the maledictions work or—or who might have altered one? Can you do anything to help? What about the Soul Jar? Do you know anything more about that? Will you?"

For a moment, the Holly Oak looked almost sad. "Will I what?"

"Will you help?"

"I am many things, Poppy Sunshine. I am not without power, but I am rooted here. There is very little I can do to help you." The tree brushed one hand over her lap, sending the leaves rustling as if in a breeze. "What I can do, I will." She paused. "When I first met your parents, I acknowledged their right to hunt maledictions. Permission was not mine to withhold, and it seemed only fair. To show that I understood their reasoning, I even acknowledged their bravery, and sacrifice, as only I am able."

Poppy and Mack shared a look. She had always wondered if the Holly Oak made her house. Now she knew.

"As to your other questions," the Oak continued. "The

answers are: I cannot, I could only guess, I will try, what about it, no, and as I said . . . if I can."

Poppy scowled, trying to remember what she'd asked to match up the answers. Her chest grew tight, but when she looked up into the Holly Oak's face, she was surprised to find the tree's hazel eyes glistening with sap. "I've not had dealings with many of your people, but David and Jasmine have my respect—they are better than most. I would *like* to help you.

"You asked about the nature of the maledictions. I am sorry that I cannot give you more of the answers you're seeking. There are things I cannot say."

Mack reached to grip Poppy's shoulder. "Cannot, or will not?"

The Holly Oak shifted, lifting her sap-stained face to Mack. "Cannot." She grimaced. "What I have told you already was uncomfortable for me."

Mack gave a stiff nod. "I understand."

A smile played over the Holly Oak's mouth, never quite landing. "I've always liked elves. You are wise observers. Almost as wise as trees." She held out her palms. "I am rooted. My senses allow me knowledge, but my magic lies in the trees and soil. I have done what I can."

Poppy clenched her fists. "But you haven't *done* anything!"

The Holly Oak smiled gently at her. "Your parents did not share with me how clever *you* are. Stubborn, disobedient, impulsive . . . all those qualities they told me of, but they left out how clever you are."

Poppy sputtered, unsure whether she was being complimented or insulted.

The tree considered her, tapping her chin with one long finger. The gesture made her look strangely human. She gave Poppy a meaningful look. "I told you it is my magic that holds us all together. You must understand that all magic comes with a cost." She stiffened and gave a small sudden gasp. Her slender fingers clutched at her head.

Poppy reached out. "Are you all right?"

A shiver of leaves, and the tree slowly straightened. Poppy gasped. The Oak's face was streaked in sparkling black.

"I am fine. Thank you." But the Holly Oak's voice was ragged, and Poppy couldn't stop looking at the streaks that now marred her face.

The Holly Oak turned to consider Mack, and then Nula. Her eyes rested for some time on Dog. "Your parents gave you a gift that is fit for a queen," she said, and Poppy caught a fleeting look of sorrow, or perhaps regret, cross her face. It was gone before she could be sure.

"I'm not certain you were wise to bring them," the tree added, and Poppy wondered whether she was referring to Dog, or to Mack and Nula. Regardless, she knew the Holly Oak was right. It had been selfish of her to want them with her.

The Holly Oak pointed one finger at her. "Do *not* get yourself killed, Poppy Sunshine. If your parents are not dead—if they escape and you are not alive to see it, *I* will never hear the end of it."

Poppy flushed. Before she could stop herself, one more question slipped out. "What now?" she asked.

The tree shifted, her form moving in and out of the bark of the tree as if she were speaking from behind a thin veil—a breeze shifting it so that Poppy had to narrow her eyes to track her. She was much taller than Poppy had realized.

"Well," the Holly Oak's voice began to fade as her form sank back from the surface. "Since you will not do what you should, the decision is yours. *You* must decide." She turned away, disappearing behind walls of bark.

CHAPTER NINE

The night was full and dark by the time they left the Holly Oak's chamber, this time by the front doors, which swung open onto a wide, comfortable platform.

"Well, that was weird," Nula said, turning to Mack. "Her face . . . did you get the feeling—"

Mack raised one eyebrow. "I definitely did."

"What do you think it was?" Nula asked.

"Let's get out of here first," Mack insisted, leading the way down the curved stair.

Poppy couldn't follow what they were talking about and she couldn't stop thinking about her parents. By the time they reached the bottom of the stairs, her heart had squeezed into a tiny knot. Mack cast a concerned look at her as she took a shuddering breath.

She had to force the fear out of her head. She couldn't allow herself to doubt. If fear dug its claws into her, she'd crumble right here and not get up again. They were alive. She would find them, and free them. She ran the words through her head like a warning.

Under the pavilions, food had been laid out, and all the creatures still waiting for an audience with the Holly Oak milled around. Some chatted softly with one another, but all fell silent when Poppy and her friends arrived. Eyes of all colors turned to watch them pass. Two of the were-wolves standing on their hind legs let out low snarls, and Dog instantly bristled.

"Easy, Dog," Poppy murmured. She turned slowly. Every face, without exception, seemed angry. Apparently, jumping the line was not to be forgiven. Her gaze fell on the hobbled old woman with the clawed hand. Gnarled and bent, she looked back with sparkling ice-blue eyes that were so full of malignant intent that a cold sweat burst across Poppy's forehead. When the woman smiled, she felt the blood drain from her face. Her teeth were sharp—and there were too many.

Poppy stumbled back. "Maybe we should . . ."

"Go somewhere else?" Mack suggested, tugging at Dog's collar. "Yeah. Nula already went."

Poppy backed up, moving away from the pavilion until, afraid of falling, she turned. Nula's tufted ears were just visible beyond a mass of roots at the edge of the meadow, where the cobbles of the Alcyon rose to meet it. Poppy shivered. She wished she'd remembered to pack a jacket.

"Make any friends?" Nula quipped as they joined her, ducking down behind the roots.

Mack's mouth twitched as he settled to the ground, his back against the biggest section of root. Poppy pulled a face and flopped to sit against the tree.

Mack scooted closer and nudged her. "You okay?"

Nula shifted nearer. "I wonder who has them!"

Mack scrubbed a hand over his face. "And why!"

"Can't be anything good," Nula muttered.

Poppy didn't answer either of them as she fought back a wave of nausea. Instead, she dug the last of the sandwiches out of her pack and passed them around. She gave the last one to Dog. "We just have to find them, that's all. That's what we need to focus on." Her voice hitched. "We . . . we just need to find them."

Mack gave her a sympathetic look and changed the subject, unwrapping his sandwich. "Well, one thing's for sure. The Holly Oak is under a geis. I'm sure of it."

Nula took a vigorous bite of her sandwich. "Defnutluh."

Poppy squinted at her, then turned to Mack. "What's a geis . . . wait, is that . . . is that like a spell or something?" She rooted around in her backpack.

"Sort of," Mack began.

"Wait, I think I remember that. It's in my glossary." She pulled out her notebook and flipped to the back.

"Geis—a vow or curse. Wait." She flipped the page. "That's it?" She closed the book with a sigh. "That's it."

Mack held up a finger as he finished chewing. After a moment he explained, "It means she made a promise."

Nula spoke through another bite of sandwich. "Made of stone."

"Huh?"

The pooka swallowed. "Promises—they're made of stone in the Grimwood. That's what they say."

"Made of . . . stone?"

"It means they're unbreakable. Promises can't be broken."

"What kind of promise did the Holly Oak make?" Poppy wondered.

Mack's eyes cracked open. "Something she knows that she's not allowed to tell."

"I agree." Nula's face grew somber. It made her look older, and stranger.

Poppy fell quiet for a moment, thinking. "What do you think it's about?"

Mack took a deep breath. "Hard to know for sure. What did she say, again? Right before she went weird?"

Nula snorted. "Well, she told Poppy she was clever. Maybe that's what made her go weird."

"Hey!"

Nula smiled. "Sorry. Couldn't help it. She said . . . uh . . . she said her magic holds us together, and that magic has a cost. Blah blah blah . . . Every tree . . . blah blah."

"That's right!" Mack sat up. "She said all magic comes with a cost."

Poppy chewed, considering the Oak's words. She said her power was in the trees and the soil . . . That would mean that her power was in *everything* in the wood.

"What does it matter?" Nula shook off the gloom and took a happy bite of her sandwich. "I don't see how any of that helps. If we went to the faeries . . . but I know you won't do that." She lay back and laced her fingers under her head. "So, what now, oh stubborn one?" she asked.

Poppy rubbed her forehead. "Yeah, okay, fine. Let's try the faeries."

Nula sat up. "Really?"

"That's a terrible idea. No one can trust the faeries," Mack grumbled.

Poppy frowned. "What's so terrible about it?"

Nula snarled. Poppy hadn't noticed she had sharp canines. "They might leave things out sometimes, but the truth is, the faeries have what everyone wants, probably what you want, too."

Mack's expression turned shocked. He stared at Nula. "Oh yeah, and what do I want?"

"The truth is that most creatures envy the Fae," Nula said imperiously. "They have it all. Beauty. Power. Beauty."

"They're *liars*," Mack spat back.

"Just because they don't stick to your smug elven ways—with your whole 'Do right, and you'll be right' thing—"

Color rose in Mack's cheeks. "Our '*thing*'? That is our *code*."

Nula went on as though he hadn't spoken. "The faeries have things you could never hope to—"

"Yeah, they have *tricks*. They are always trying to trap you. Fae believe they're better than everyone—"

Nula's bluish skin had darkened. "The Fae love to have rare things, and they love to know things first. That's all." She leaned to Poppy who was watching the argument unfold, unsure whether to intervene or not. She'd never seen Mack get so worked up. Dog whined, inching closer to the elf.

"They'll fall all over themselves to dine with a human in the woods, never mind one traveling with an elf, and a . . . a three-headed-dog. They're the rarest thing of all!" Nula flushed.

Mack rose and brushed off his hands. "Collecting every rare thing in the wood, just to possess it because they can, does *not* make them better."

"Sure," Nula said in a singsong voice that made Poppy hop up as well, as Mack stomped off. Poppy followed him around the next hump of roots.

She could still hear Nula humming as she walked toward Mack. His back was turned and his hands clenched into fists. "I know you want answers, Poppy," he said through gritted teeth. "And I know we need to free your parents . . . but you promised if I gave you advice, you'd listen. And I'm telling you. Do *not* go to the faeries."

Poppy paused. She had never seen Mack look fierce and frightened at the same time. She put a hand on his shoulder. "It's just what makes the most sense, Mack. Nula says they like her, and—if she's right and the faeries keep track of rare things, they're sure to know something about the Soul Jar! Maybe they'll know more about the Holly Oak's geis too. I mean . . . don't you want answers too?"

The hurt look in his eyes made her blood race to her cheeks. Her chest got tight, but Mack was just being overly cautious, as usual.

His shoulders slumped. "Just whatever you do, don't make any bargains with them." His eyes hardened. "Swear you won't."

Poppy nodded. "I swear."

"They're not to be trusted, Poppy." He paused. "And I'm really not sure about the pooka either."

Before Poppy could reply, Nula's tufted ears appeared behind them over the top edge of some roots. "Peace, Mack! Come look. I made us all a place to sleep."

They followed her back to where Dog lay asleep already. Several large piles of colorful feathers waited for them. Poppy stared at Nula. "How did you do that?"

Nula gave a delighted laugh, her blue cheeks flushing. "I changed into a Misere bird. It's their molting season," she explained when they gave her blank looks.

Poppy shook her head, silently promising herself she'd find out more about those birds when she wasn't so tired. Despite her exhaustion, Poppy lay awake for a long time after Mack and Nula drifted off. In the quiet, she couldn't avoid her fears. She stared up at the branches of the Holly Oak, and at the stars that covered the sky in bright friendly twinkles. The moon was dark, and the stars seemed to stretch out forever.

Her thoughts were like stones rolling through a flood, banging together and scattering under the surge. Her parents were gone. She had always known it would happen eventually, ever since she was a little girl. The nightmares—those came and went, but now that they were real, she didn't even have Jute to comfort her. In the unfolding night, fear poured out of Poppy like smoke from a fire, until it was thick around her and hard to breathe.

She squeezed her eyes shut and took a deep breath through her nose, the way Jute had taught her to do, letting it leave her lips in a single slow exhale. She did it again. Then she counted her "at leasts."

One—*at least Mom and Dad are alive*, she appealed to the sky. She had to believe she would know—feel it somehow—if they weren't. Two—*at least I got into the Grimwood*. Three—*at least my friends are with me*. Four—*we have some food*. Five—*Dog's here*. Six—*we're safe for the night*. Seven—*at least it's not too late*. Slowly, as she thought of more "at leasts," her breath steadied, and some of the weight lifted off her chest. Bits of hope reigned in her heartache, but all the "at leasts" in the world couldn't shut down her fear completely. Not until her parents were home and safe.

Maybe the faeries would be able to help. Poppy rolled onto her side to turn the thought into an "at least," then stilled at the sound of lowered voices on the other side of the roots.

"It sprang up out of nowhere," one low voice snarled, moving closer.

"Nothing comes from nowhere," the other answered.

Poppy very carefully moved so that she was crouched under the edge of the root. Whoever they were, they couldn't have been more than twenty feet away. She peeked over the edge.

She could make out two silhouettes in the darkness. Their long muzzles and sharp ears gave them away as two of the werewolves from the pavilion. She'd read about them in her parents' journals, but—her father's drawings hadn't been right at all. His drawings had shown them hunched forward, almost leaning. These two stood on their hind legs, straight and tall.

"Well, our pack leader said there was no scent left behind. The fuel was something bitter, wrapped in glass."

What were they talking about?

"Did the grassland burn?"

A fire.

"Much of it. A passing witch was able to put it out, but now we're in her debt, and you know how that goes."

"Bad news. In debt to a witch."

"Right, so you can imagine what my wife said when I told her—seeing as we just moved to that part of the forest."

"And you with pups to think of."

"True. True."

"Anyone hurt?"

Did they really hunt in packs? Poppy wondered. Were they really as fast as her father said?

"One of the elder wolves was badly burned—and several shelters burned too."

"So, you're here to tell her about it."

They're here to talk to the Holly Oak about a fire, Poppy realized.

"I got a grievance, so I'm here to make a report. See what the Holly Oak says is to be done."

The voices had started to fade as they moved away. A breeze blew through Poppy's hair, and wafted across the meadow. The second werewolf tipped his face toward the sky, and for a second, Poppy thought he was going to howl. Then he whipped around to face the rock where she was hiding, hunched and leaning forward. She ducked down, her heart pounding.

She tried not to breathe.

"What's the matter, Louis?"

"Smell someone."

"Ahhh. Well, don't get in a tizzy. You can't do anything about that here, and you know it."

"*Might* be that human who cut in front of the line to see the Holly Oak."

The first werewolf let out a low snarl. "That's tempting, I admit, but it's not worth it. Kill anything here, and you're as good as dead yourself. The Oak will have you tied to a picker and send you to the thorn trees."

Poppy stayed pressed to the roots, out of sight. As soon as they were gone, she slipped carefully back into her pile of feathers and fell right to sleep.

She was the first to wake in the morning, and before she even rubbed the sleep out of her eyes, she reached for her pack, rummaging her hand all the way to the bottom. She caught the end of the gold chain where her necklace lay curled at the bottom, and gently pulled.

She stared at it, the gold locket gleaming softly in the palm of her hand. She didn't understand why, but she was afraid to open it. It was as if looking at her parents in the locket would bring things full circle—make their danger final in some way. Her head knew it wasn't true, but her pulse still fluttered in her throat. After a moment or two, she pried open the little heart.

On one side was a tiny painting of her father, his red-gold hair shining. She'd gotten the small gap in her front teeth from him. The other side of the locket held a painting of her mother, with her black hair loose. Her bright eyes looked right into Poppy's. *Do whatever you must,* they seemed to say. *We need you now.*

She snapped it shut and put it around her neck with shaking hands.

When she felt better, she got up and shook Mack and Nula awake. Mack rolled to his feet with a groan, stretching his arms up so high that his T-shirt rose halfway up his chest. Nula refused to do anything but grunt. After the third time Poppy poked her, she rolled over and turned herself into a mouse.

"How far is it to the faeries?" she asked, picking Nula up and holding her on an open palm.

Nula yawned, and hopped off Poppy's hand to turn back into herself. "A day's walk . . . from the dock where we left."

Poppy looked at Mack. "Back the way we came," she said with a sigh.

Mack shrugged. "Good. Maybe we'll see Jute. Maybe he'll have a better idea than going to the faeries." He forced a laugh. "Maybe you'll listen to him, since you won't listen to me."

Instead of answering, Poppy headed for the dock. Mack knew Jute didn't leave the house unless he had to, and she didn't want to fight. She shoved her hand into her pocket to get the gold for the Boatman . . . then her stomach fell.

She stopped walking.

After a moment, Mack and Nula both turned. "What's wrong?" the pooka asked. "You look like you're going to be sick."

Poppy took a breath. "I don't have enough gold left for the Boatman. "I must have lost one along the way . . ." Her shoulders slumped. "I only have two pieces—not three."

Nula grimaced and Mack's body tensed. "I just hope it's enough," he said, moving toward the dock.

Nula slowed to walk with Poppy. "He can waste energy hoping it's enough," she hissed. "I'll hope the Boatman doesn't eat us for breakfast."

CHAPTER TEN

When they got to the end of the dock, Mack rang for the Boatman. The ripple of sound seemed dimmer here—farther away, as if it rose from under the salt sea. They stood watching the water—Poppy shifting her weight back and forth, rattling her two coins in her pocket, Mack shaking his arms, and Nula twisting the end of her tail. Even Dog gave a little whine.

And then the Boatman rose—without a sound, as if he had been just waiting there, under the water. It was just as creepy, and just as silent as the first time, and it made Poppy's skin go cold. She remembered their first journey with the Boatman. His laughter had sent her body into uncontrollable shivers, as if she had been a mouse hearing the cry of a hawk. She hoped he wouldn't laugh again, or worse, be angry that they had called him and didn't have enough coins to pay.

She tried to fill her voice with steely confidence. "This is all the gold I have," she said, dropping the two coins into his palm. "I hope it will do."

She lifted her chin and met the Boatman's eyes. They were cold, but burned all the same. It felt like a long time before he acquiesced, his thick fingers curling around the coins.

They clambered onto the boat. Again, he watched Dog.

"The elf might make a good meal," Nula offered under her breath. "If you're feeling peckish."

Poppy elbowed her, then settled herself in the bottom of the boat. "Back to where we started, please," she whispered when the Boatman looked at her expectantly. She thought she knew what to expect, but when the boat pulled away and he began to laugh, she startled, every hair on her body rising, as if lightning had struck the ground next to her.

This time she kept her face raised as the boat sped across the Alcyon sea. The Boatman's oar, she noticed, wasn't actually an oar. Instead, he stood in the prow with a long pole, raising and dropping it into the water as if he were measuring the depth of the water instead of traveling it. He raised it up, and dropped it down . . . raised it up, and dropped it down. Poppy watched the water race by as they picked up speed. She could have sworn slender shadows slipped through the water alongside them as they passed.

It was only minutes—though Poppy was certain it was a long way across—until he drove them up the estuary of the Veena river, whose tributaries ran all over the Grimwood. The boat sped along, turning the canopy of trees to a blur, as though time and space were only inklings of their imagination.

They jerked to the right as the river took a different path, or perhaps it was a different river altogether. It curved, veering violently, first to one side and then the other. Poppy and Nula clung together. Nula's tail was wrapped so tight around Poppy's ribs that she gasped for air. Mack threw himself on top of Dog to hold them in, gripping the side of the boat.

At one point, Poppy thought she heard a feral scream, and wondered if there were things other than rocks and fallen branches in the water, bucking at their little craft to try to dislodge them.

All the while, the Boatman laughed, the sound growing sharper in her ears—a hundred tiny knives, cutting away her hopes and bravery with each passing moment.

When the boat stopped at last, back at the dock where they had first begun, all of them—even Dog—toppled onto the dock like it was the sweetest of homecomings. Nula and Poppy stumbled to their feet. Dog wobbled after them.

"He took us on the cheapskate's route." Nula gulped. "We're lucky to be alive." She rose to point a finger at Poppy. "Never again."

Poppy crossed her heart.

The still air in the wood was already thick with the heat of the day. Huge stands of pale birch scattered through the woods and made it look brighter, their white bark and shivering leaves both beautiful and eerie. Through the trees, Poppy could see that the sun was nearly halfway up the sky.

"Which way to the faeries?" Poppy asked. Mack's face grew stormy.

Nula pointed. "That way. West."

Mack had turned away to look across the river into the woods toward Strange Hollow. "When we do go back, we should stay on this side of the river. It will take longer, but at least we won't have to run from the banshee."

"You know," Nula said, swatting a mosquito with her tail. "I've been thinking about that banshee."

Mack raised an eyebrow and led the way, setting a fast pace westward, as if he was eager to get it over with. "What about her?"

Poppy and Dog fell in on one side of Mack, not quite at a run to keep up.

Nula caught up on the other side of Mack. "I'm thinking it might not have been a gravestone."

Poppy grimaced and slapped a mosquito. "What else could it have been?"

"A passage stone."

"What's a passage stone?" Poppy asked.

"That's not a real thing," Mack scoffed at the same time.

"It is too."

"It is not. Maybe they were a real thing a long time ago, but if they were, I don't think they do what the stories say anymore," Mack said, pulling a face. "Now they're just markers. That's all."

"Why have I never heard of this?" Poppy nudged Mack and almost tripped over a fallen branch. They were moving so fast, she had to keep her eyes on the ground.

"Nothing to tell."

Nula's ear twitched. "My people used to use them all the time—they say. Just because you've never—"

"Well, has it happened to you?"

"No, but—"

Mack had never sounded so smug. "Do you know *anyone* it's happened to?"

Nula scowled.

"Well, there you go. Not every old story is true. The stones are just really old markers. They have symbols on them. The end."

Nula turned to Poppy. "You know those standing stones at the edge of the Grimwood?"

"The big ones with the symbols carved in them?"

"Yeah. Those are passage stones. There are stories that say they can take you somewhere else."

Mack nose-sighed.

Nula ignored him. "Every time you walk past one there's a chance you'll wind up in some other part of the Grimwood."

"Kind of like when someone goes into the fog?" Poppy

asked, wondering why she hadn't read about this in any of her parents' journals.

Nula shrugged. "I don't know anything about the fog," she admitted.

Poppy stopped walking, closing her eyes for a few seconds to try to picture where she had seen the tall stones before. "Hey, wait up," she called, hurrying to catch up to Mack. "So, that big stone at the edge of the trees just down the valley. Is that one?"

Mack lifted a shoulder. "Yeah."

"What about all the stones where the kids play?" she added. "Those can't be . . . what did you call them?"

Nula had fallen behind. "Passage stones," she called.

"I don't know," Mack admitted, slapping at a mosquito. "Maybe. But there's nothing magical about them. They're just stones."

"Huh." Poppy had to admit, it did seem pretty unlikely. There had to be at least seven of them right in the valley. Kids played around them all the time, and she'd never heard of anyone falling through one into the Grimwood.

Nula was still talking behind them. "Some of them are really old—especially the ones in the wood. That's what made me wonder. Sometimes they're pretty mossy and crumbly, like that one with the banshee."

"So, are you saying that might be why the banshee's not in my parents' journals? That's why they've never seen her?"

Mack slowed down to let Nula catch up. She cocked

her head at Poppy. "Is that what I'm saying? I just thought maybe that's why she was so aggressive—she was there by accident. That maybe it wasn't her gravestone at all."

Mack interrupted. "What, like she fell through from somewhere else?"

"Yeah. Maybe." A wicked grin spread over Nula's face. She shot a look at Mack. "We could walk by there and find out."

"No way," Poppy said.

"Umm, no," Mack said at the same time.

Nula laughed. "Anyway, there are stones all along the edge of the wood if you know where to look," she interjected. "But there are some really old ones in the deep . . . and I guess in other parts of the wood too."

The sun was above them, beating down through the trees, and Poppy stopped to catch her breath. She watched a purple and neon-blue tentacular as it bent long arms to its mouth one at a time, wiping them clean of the pollen that dusted the air.

Poppy's throat felt raw and sweat dripped into her eyes. They had come around a second bend in the river. If they left the Grimwood here, just beyond the edge of the forest, she thought they'd come to Golden Hollow. It was as good a time as any to rest a minute.

A bead of sweat ran down her back. "So . . . they're landmarks to keep you from getting lost? It would be cool if there was a map of them. If someone can figure out how the magic works, they could use them to get around." She leaned against a birch and lifted her canteen, guzzling the cool water, then handed it to Nula. Mack had his own, and she knew he was happy to share with Dog.

Nula blew a raspberry. "They might keep you from getting *yourself* lost, but that doesn't mean they keep the Grimwood from getting you lost." She lifted the canteen and took a sip. "And who knows if you'd get back in one piece." She paused, then shot Poppy a grin. "Might be fun."

Suddenly, Mack froze, his posture so sharp that the rest of them froze too. The elf was listening so hard Poppy could feel it—danger, acute and tangible. A bolt of adrenaline ran down her back.

"I hear footsteps," Mack mouthed, pointing down to where his toes dug into the soil. "And I think I hear voices."

Nula shifted. "I don't hear anything except—"

And then the tree behind her exploded in flame.

Dog started barking, all three heads wild with fury and fear, but before anyone else could react, a whistling sound raced through the trees. Another tree burst into fire.

"Let's go!" Poppy called, and ran toward the river. Mack was by her side in an instant. "Where's Nula?" she asked.

"Bird," Mack said, careening into her as a tree to his

right blew up. They toppled to the ground, Dog barking and lunging to tug at their sleeves.

Poppy stumbled to her feet and helped Mack up. They ran again. The air was full of whistles now, each followed by a tree exploding.

Heat filled the air, and something sharp hit Poppy's cheek. She cried out.

Crackling sounds surrounded them as another impact knocked them down. The soil began to sizzle, turning dark behind them, the color seeping over the ground toward them, withering the plants. A sparkling black thorn tree pushed out of the earth, twisting into itself. The fire around it went out.

"Look out!" Poppy cried and scuttled back, tugging Mack with her.

Poppy's cheek stung. She lifted her hand and it came away red.

Nula appeared a few feet away, deeper in the wood. "This way!" she called, waving them on. "Hurry!"

They stumbled to their feet and raced for Nula.

They had only gone a few steps when Poppy heard a whooshing sound, followed by more sizzling. She skidded to a stop, turning back to look.

Her mouth fell open. "Mack!" she called forward. "Mack, look!"

He spun around in time to see thorn trees rising next to each of the burning trees.

Everywhere the black soil touched, the ground sizzled

and crackled, plumes of dark smoke shot into the air—
and the fire went out.

The normal trees blackened and crumbled like char-
coal. A grove of thorn trees had emerged, fully grown and
darkly sparkling. The fire was gone, but the burnt trees
were withering—turning brown and falling to ash.

Poppy's throat tightened as the giant maple tree Mack
had leaned on blackened and died.

Mack stood behind her, with one hand on her shoulder. "The thorn trees protect the Grimwood. They always
have."

Nula, who had become the small blue bird again,
perched on his shoulder.

"Thorns!" Poppy swore. "What was that? Where did
those fires come from? They . . . they shot through the
air." She looked at Mack. "Have you seen that before? Was
it lightning?"

"No. I don't know," Mack said in a low voice.

"Was that . . . it seemed like an attack. Did someone
just *attack* us?"

Mack pressed his lips together. "I don't know. I heard
those footsteps, but . . . I don't think so . . . maybe." He
dug his toes into the dirt. "Something doesn't feel right
though. Let's get out of here," he added.

"Agreed."

They moved west as fast as they could. No one spoke
a word. It was as if any sound might shatter everything
that remained.

CHAPTER ELEVEN

The sun was starting to set. As the light turned golden, Poppy thought of her house, a picture of it flashing in her mind, gleaming in the morning sunshine, the roots turned warm as honey. The image made her heart skip a beat.

For the first time, she missed it. It was true, she had been lonely there, but the thought of Jute, there by himself with no one to look after, made her heart ache. He must be worried sick. Her parents' faces flashed in her mind. She could see her mother bent over a book, with her hair wild from her pushing her hands into it. She remembered an image of her father, stirring a pot of some potion in the lab, his thousand-yard stare making it clear his mind was elsewhere. They weren't around much, but they were hers, and she wanted them back—all of them, together.

Poppy knelt down and cuddled Dog's three heads. "Maybe I should have left you at home with Jute," she said, pressing her face into Eta's, then Two's, and finally

Brutus's. Predictably, he slobbered her cheek. Mack laughed as she stood to scrub at it with her sleeve.

Mogwen birds sang choruses from the treetops, and though the scent of smoke clung to her clothes and hair, she could still smell pine sap and wild honeysuckle in the air.

The trees were thick, forcing them to walk single file. Nula led the way.

They'd been walking for an hour without saying much when the trees opened up a little, and Mack had the space to walk next to Poppy and Nula again. "I was always told the *noble* Fae didn't think much of pooka. I mean, they call you the *lesser* Fae," he said. "How did you meet them anyway?"

Nula's tail whipped back and forth. "I'm just lucky. I met them by chance and . . . they think I'm different— special. They might believe most of us are *lesser*, but they'll talk to me. For sure."

He exchanged a look with Poppy. "Special how?" he asked.

Nula blushed such a dark blue that her cheeks looked bruised. "They didn't go into details. They like me. That's all."

Mack gave a terse "huh."

"Is it much farther?" Poppy asked.

Nula sniffed, and stroked Brutus's ears as she walked. "We should reach the Rowan Gate before too long—that's the entrance to the queen's realm." She peered up at the treetops. "They might even be watching us already."

Mack peered into the trees. "Be careful when we get there, Poppy. Watch what you say."

"That's true." Nula confirmed. "Every word matters with the faeries." She lifted her chin. "That's their integrity."

"Integrity is one way to put it." Mack scowled. "Nasty piece of work is another. Just be careful what you agree to, okay? Every word counts, so think before you talk, and don't get creative."

Poppy almost snapped that she always thought before she spoke, but one look at Mack's face held her back. He was worried for real. She could tell from the way his eyebrows crumpled together at the bridge of his nose. "Okay," she agreed.

He shoved his hands into his pockets as if he couldn't think what else to do with them. "What are you going to trade? You'll have to give them something for information about your parents—or for anything they know about the Soul Jar."

Nula startled.

Poppy gave him a blank look.

"You do know they're not going to just . . . offer it to you for free, right? These are Fae we're talking about."

Poppy's cheeks warmed. There was only one thing of value that she had with her now. Her thoughts turned to the little gold locket hanging around her neck. She reached up to touch it, rubbing its surface gently.

Mack's eyes widened slightly at the sight of it. "Are you sure?"

There was a pang behind her ribs, but that was all. She wished she'd been able to keep it with her longer—that she had worn it more—but she knew what had to be done. She reached her hands around and moved her ponytail, unclasping the necklace her parents had given her.

"This should do it, don't you think?"

Mack looked to Nula. "Will it?"

It was Nula's turn to blush. "Oh, sure. Gold works fine. It's all a matter of . . . it's all a matter of what they want. I—sorry, I probably should have mentioned they'd be wanting payment."

Poppy traded looks with Mack again. Nula was acting strangely. Probably just nervous, despite her proclaimed confidence. Poppy figured there was a good chance Nula didn't really know what she was doing any more than she and Mack did. She quickly pried the little pictures out of her locket and zipped them safely into her pocket.

Poppy turned to ask Nula if something was bothering her, but before she could, she caught sight of something in the distance. "Is that—"

Nula gave her a glorious smile. "That's the gate into the Fae realm," she confirmed.

It was much bigger than Poppy expected. Two enormous trees soared up into an archway draped in clusters of red berries. Beams of sunlight shot to the ground all around the gate in a golden circle, which cast the rest of the woods into shadow.

She scanned the trees around them. There was nothing there to see except the occasional Mogwen, but the sense that they were being watched grew, prickling at her skin. As they approached, she saw that two guards stood to either side of the arch, legs stiff and faces stern. Their black armor was shot through with silver designs that shone coldly in the sun. As they got closer, Poppy spotted more guards in the trees nearby.

Their skin was shadow blue—darker than Nula's, and their fine, sharp features, together with the dark circles under their eyes made them look about as friendly as a punch in the nose. They all had jet-black braids that matched the shadows stretching under their eyes and down their cheeks like tears. Each had a tall silver pike at their side. Poppy's mouth went dry as they got closer, but the guards didn't even twitch, and for a moment she wondered if they were real. Nula pushed past Mack and Poppy to approach them. The guard on the left frowned as the pooka raised up on her toes to whisper in his ear.

Nula pointed toward Poppy, then turned back to the guard, who didn't acknowledge she had said anything at all.

Nula frowned and leaned in again, this time pointing at Poppy and Dog. The guard's dark eyes grew hard and bright—the only sign that he had heard her.

Nula harrumphed and stomped to the other guard.

"She'll want to see me," Poppy heard her say as she stuck one fist on her hip. "I'm telling you."

The second guard's eyes shifted to Mack. Mack drew himself up to look his biggest. "You're not Fae," the guard to the right of the gateway said in a voice that was warmer than expected, considering the coldness of her expression.

Nula's other fist rose to her hip. "I—I am! I'm lesser Fae. But believe me, the queen is going to want what we have to offer."

"No."

Nula stepped back, a look of shock settling on her face. "No? But—"

The male guard smirked. "We have strict orders not to—"

"Let in nobodies," the female guard finished.

Nula closed her mouth, the skin along her cheekbones turning a deep blue.

Brutus snarled. Mack nudged Poppy with his elbow.

Poppy cleared her throat. "I, um, have gold to trade," she offered. "For information."

"Just tell her Nula's here." Nula's hands came off her hips and twisted in front of her. "Tell her. She'll want to see me."

"Why would she want to see *you*?"

"I—she just will. She—" Nula whispered something else in the male guard's ear. Poppy could practically hear Mack scowl.

"I don't believe you," the guard said.

"You better listen to her," Poppy called. "They like her, you know. You're going to get in big trouble for talking to her like that."

The guard rolled his eyes at her, and Poppy sent him a look that would peel paint. Then, while Nula continued to argue with both guards, Poppy studied the gate. It didn't really seem like much of a barrier—more symbolic. Maybe they could just sneak around it while the guards were distracted. She nudged Mack and stepped toward the rowan trees.

Mack shook his head, reaching out with his hand low to try to pull her back. Poppy sidestepped and took another step toward the gate. There was a whistling sound and two arrows plunked into the ground just in front of Poppy's feet.

Poppy swallowed and stepped back to stand by Mack.

Nula, meanwhile, was showing signs of having a fit. "I'll find a way to tell her I was here! And when she gets word of what you called me, she's going to—she's going to turn you both into newts."

"We have our orders," the male guard snarled. "Do your worst, pooka."

Nula stood completely still for the time it took Poppy to blink, then—*zimpf*—a little white weasel disappeared through the gate.

"I'll skin you for that," he shouted after her, then exchanged a look with the other guard.

"Think the queen will come?" the female asked in a low voice.

"Doubt it. That pooka was lying."

"All I know is you better hope she doesn't bring the queen with her. If she was lying, you just let the pooka get past you into the realm. If she wasn't lying, you should have taken them in under guard. Either way, the queen will be none too pleased with you."

"And what were *you* doing, might I ask, while I was—"

"I'm just saying."

Poppy leaned toward Mack. "Did she go to get the queen?"

Mack stared in the direction Nula had disappeared. "I just hope she's right about them liking her."

Poppy tightened her ponytail and thought. The Fae guards stood unmoving, but she could feel others, watching from the trees.

It seemed like ages, but couldn't have been more than a few excruciating minutes until a whoosh of feathers caught Poppy's eye.

Nula was back, looking like she'd flown through a thorn bush. Her expression was orbidding. Whatever had happened, the pooka hadn't come out on top.

Poppy opened her mouth to ask what had happened, but another look at Nula's stormy face changed her mind. The pooka would tell them when she was ready. An image of her mother flashed through Poppy's thoughts. She was sketching a faery at her desk while Poppy watched. She could even hear her mother's voice, clear and bright. *There are three things faeries can't resist . . . a rarity, a gamble, and a riddle. They will try to deny it, of course. They always obscure the truth, but in the end, they'll give in. They are dangerous—very—but they always keep their word.* Poppy cleared her throat. "The faeries . . . they think they're pretty smart, right?"

Mack's eyes narrowed as if he knew she was up to something. "They think they're the smartest—the best of the best in every way."

Nula kicked a tree.

"So they're proud," Poppy went on, her eyes pinned on Nula. "And . . . they like to take risks?"

Mack nodded. "What are you getting at?"

Poppy didn't answer. Instead she strode toward the guards. They straightened. "So," Poppy began. "I've heard faeries know everything there is to know, but I don't think I believe it. You don't seem so smart. So, I think . . ." She paused. "I think I can outsmart you."

"Poppy," Mack hissed.

She swished her hand at him. "Here's my challenge. Answer my riddle correctly and we'll go away . . . but if you can't answer it correctly, then you have to let us through."

The female guard scoffed. "As if any human question could trouble us."

"Why should we?" the other guard said at the same time.

Mack appeared at her side, glowering.

"No reason," Poppy admitted. "But if you don't . . . I'll know you can't."

"What do we gain should we win?"

Poppy hesitated, then bent to dig in her pack. A smirk danced across her face as she held up . . . "We're almost out of apples. But I'll spare this one, if you answer correctly."

The guards looked at each other.

Poppy turned the fruit so that the sunlight gleamed against its pink-red skin. "Beth has the juiciest . . . the most luscious apples." She raised an eyebrow at them. "You don't get too many of these in the deep . . . do you?"

The female snorted. "Fine," she said. "Ask your riddle. It will be amusing to see you try."

"And if you can't answer, you'll let us in. Right?"

The male guard relaxed, a tight sneer working its way across his face. "As you say."

Mack stepped back. Poppy could feel the disapproval radiating off him, but what else could she do? Nula had struck out. She had to at least try. Her parents were counting on her.

"Good," she said to the guards, raising her hands to her hips. "Here's my riddle. Only one color, but rarely one size. Stuck at the bottom, but easily flies. Present in sun, but never in rain. It does no harm, and feels no pain."

The male guard frowned and cast an uncertain look

at the other, who had gone quite pale. Then his mouth twitched. He began to laugh—a rough, grating sound.

Poppy smirked.

"You have no idea, do you," he said as the female guard grew even paler. "The queen is going to have your hide!"

"She won't," Poppy insisted. "She'll tell you that you did the right thing."

The guard seemed to take a breath.

Poppy turned to the male guard. "Want to know the answer?"

"Don't tell him," the guard grumbled, crossing her arms.

Poppy met the guard's eyes and smiled. "Do you?"

He rolled his eyes. "Fine. Your victory. It's only a silly riddle—a child's game. What's the answer?"

Poppy tried not to look smug. "A shadow."

"Good one," he admitted when he had thought it through.

"Well," the female guard sneered. "You better hope she's right about the queen as well, or we're both mulch."

Poppy dropped the apple back into her pack as Nula appeared at her side. Both she and Mack watched the guards as they passed.

"They're with me," Poppy reminded.

The male guard threw up his hands. "Go on, then. Our fate's in the queen's hands." He gave Dog an admiring glance. "But feel free to leave your cerberus in our care.

They're the first I've seen." His black eyes shone at her from the shadows of his face. "Or perhaps I could win them from you. Another riddle?"

"They stay with me," Poppy said firmly. Dog was the best thing her parents had ever done. She wasn't letting them out of her sight.

"I can't believe your riddle trick worked!" Mack blurted as the three of them passed under the archway of rowan trees.

"It's the Grimwood," Nula said irritably. "Of course it worked! Riddles are like gold coins around here— everyone takes them."

Poppy grinned. "Guess faeries aren't so smart after all."

Mack tried to frown at her, but laughed despite himself. "Okay then, now what, oh wise one?"

"Now, we go see what the queen knows about the Soul Jar." Poppy grimaced.

CHAPTER TWELVE

The Faery Queen was easy to find. There were no rooms or alcoves in her "throne room"— just places where the trees had been cleared and replaced with sharp, manicured hedges and lawns, trimmed in geometric shapes, and arched trellises. They were marked by tall vases used as if they were exclamation points. Everything was tidy and tightly controlled. Even the vines were trained to do as they were told, spreading gracefully across the spaces between the trees in pleasing symmetrical designs, like screens—or walls—on the outside edges of the garden. They grew denser as Poppy and her friends moved forward. Crystal raindrops hung in the trees and in the trellises, catching the light and shooting rainbows over the ground.

Poppy shuddered. It all reminded her of a series of tunnel webs, leading them along. The delicate green beauty should have been pleasing, but it made Poppy's skin crawl. It was so perfect it turned her stomach, like overripe fruit, too colorful and too sweet.

The dulcet tones of a harp floated on the air, growing louder as they moved deeper into the wood. They saw no houses anywhere—no signs of a village or of life generally, just the open gardens through the trees, and the dense screens of vines, narrowing as they walked.

Poppy gave Mack a questioning look.

He pointed one finger upward. "They live in the canopy," he explained.

The harp music grew louder, and they passed between two hedges in bloom, the sweet scent of their tiny white blossoms thick and cloying. They'd been trimmed to look like Fae, with blossoms for eyes, and a spill of flowers for hair. The blooms poured out of their open palms and open mouths.

A long path covered in white snowdrops opened, stretching to a point ahead of them. The flowers beneath their feet let off a bruised scent as they walked over them. Dog sneezed.

The scent stuck to the back of Poppy's throat, and for some reason, this, more than anything else, made Poppy wonder if going to the faeries might be a mistake. She hadn't realized how much light and fresh air there was in the green iron tang of the wood. She hadn't noticed it, she supposed, because it was everywhere. Everywhere but here. Here, the Grimwood smelled as though it had been sitting too long in the sun.

She looked up and her breath caught in her throat.

At the very tip of the white path, the Faery Queen sat on a throne of gnarled black wood, polished to gleaming and shot through with silver—but that wasn't what made her gasp. It was the enormous spiders, nearly as large as horses, stretching along the path to the throne. There were at least ten of them, each accompanied by a faery handmaiden standing nearby to help spin out their silk into skeins. Large baskets sat on the ground, filled with the completed skeins.

The Faery Queen cleared her throat, and Poppy's eyes snapped back to her. She was tall. Taller than any of the others, and needle thin. Her gown was made of spider lace, covered in tiny diamonds—or at least Poppy thought they might be diamonds. Then again, they might be crystals . . . or dew drops. All she knew was she didn't want to get close enough to find out.

The queen's face was gaunt, and deep blue—with a bruised, shadowed look below her dark eyes and across her cheekbones. She watched them approach almost eagerly, her thin lip curling as her gaze fell on Nula.

Nula flushed and dropped into a deep curtsy. "Great Queen," she began as Mack and Poppy scrambled to sketch bows of their own. "You who are wise beyond measure, lovelier than stars, strong as the—"

"I see my hedge did not deter you, pooka. But never mind. You've brought strangers." The queen's voice was airy and high, like breath through a bell, and Poppy thought that if she heard that voice in a moonlit glade, she would never in a million years picture the queen as she really looked.

Poppy drew up, and beside her, Mack shifted his weight. "We're seeking information, Your Majesty," she interjected. "Nula says your people know everything there is to know in the Grimwood."

The force of the queen's consideration fell on Poppy, and it was like being pinned by a curious collector. Sweat broke out across her forehead.

"That is true," said the queen.

"I hope what I brought pleases you," Nula interrupted.

The queen stilled. "We shall see, Fionnula of the pooka-kind. They interest me adequately."

Nula bowed her head. "Thank you, Your Grace."

The queen's eyes fell on Dog. "Let's have a look at that cerberus!" Her long fingers, black at the nails, gripped the smooth arms of her throne as she rose. Each side was carved to look like an arm itself, ending in hands carved into fists. "How did a *human* come to have such a treasure?" the Faery Queen purred.

Poppy's heart sped as she gripped Dog's collar. She wished—truly wished—for the first time that she'd left them at home. Something about the queen made her want to tuck all her friends into the shadows. "They were a gift from my parents," she said. "That's why I'm here—my parents, I mean."

The Faery Queen's grip relaxed, but her attention seemed to sharpen. "Go on."

"I—my parents . . . David and Jasmine Bright. They hunt maledictions."

The Faery Queen gave a derisive sniff. "Are you here to accuse me of something, girl?"

"What? I'm not—I just hoped . . ." Poppy steeled her spine and continued. "I want to know what you know about a certain malediction. It's called the Soul Jar. I want to know if you know where it is, or how to . . . how to get someone out of it. I think my parents might be stuck inside."

The queen studied Nula. "What makes you think I have those answers?" She paused. "And if I did, why would I give them to you? Your people are nothing to me."

"I have some gold. I'll give it to you—I just . . . I just need to know if you know anything about the Soul Jar—or my parents."

The queen exhaled, weaving her long fingers across her chest as she moved to recline again in her throne. "That is interesting."

Mack stilled. "What can you tell us?"

Her head snapped to him, almost as if she hadn't seen him until he spoke. "An elf! Fascinating." She turned to Poppy again. "You do travel in interesting company, girl. I have decided, however, on the cost of your answers." She examined her pointed nails. "I would like your cerberus."

"What? No!"

Nula shifted uneasily next to her. "You won't have a choice, Poppy," she mumbled. "You can't say no to the Faery Queen."

"No!"

Next to her, Mack had let out a low snarl.

"I will not," Poppy told the queen.

The queen's face hardened. "You are not worthy of this creature."

"Dog is my family, and you can't have them."

The queen's fingers wrapped tightly around the fists of her throne. "I see. You offer me gold coins?"

"Not coins—it's . . . it's a gold locket. But yes, I offer a trade. Gold, in exchange for information."

"Gold I have already, in uncountable amounts."

Poppy said nothing.

Another sniff. "Join my court."

"Yes!" Nula cried.

The queen frowned. "I'm not talking to you—pooka." Her voice could have cut glass. "There is no gift that could prevail upon me to let the lesser folk into my midst."

Nula's ears flattened, and Poppy felt a pang of pity for her friend. Then she realized what the queen had just said. "You're asking . . . *me* to join your court?" Poppy sputtered.

The queen held out her arms as if putting her realm on display. "You interest me. I see you are braver than others of your kind. And you seem to attract the attention of the Grimwood folk—that interests me too." She flicked her fingers at Mack and Nula. "What do they see in you, I wonder."

Poppy's mouth had gone dry. She should feel honored, probably, but instead she was slightly nauseous.

"What is your name?" the queen asked, her voice like a barb.

"Poppy . . . um, Pandora Sunshine, Your Majesty."

The queen studied her, taking in her all-black clothing and serious expression. "Your parents have a sense of humor, then."

"What?" Poppy said blankly.

"And what is your answer, Pandora?"

Mack gripped her arm. "Don't do it, Poppy. If you agree, they'll keep you here forever. You'll just be another servant to her."

"Shush, elf." The queen flicked her finger and a glob of spider's web threw itself over Mack's mouth. "You speak too freely."

"Mack!" Poppy cried, helpless as she watched him peel the sticky web away from his face and struggle to get it off his hands.

The queen looked smug, but when Poppy turned to ask Nula what to do, she saw that her friend's blue skin had gone so pale she was almost white. Poppy startled at the inexplicable hurt in Nula's gold eyes.

"Well?" the queen asked. "Will you be honored among all other humans?" She clapped her hands, and all the spiders' handmaidens moved toward the throne.

"Umm. I—you honor me, great Queen."

"I do! Wonderful—"

"But unfortunately, I'm not at liberty to accept. I apologize, Your Majesty, but I came here to trade gold for information, and gold is all I have to offer."

A pause, and the air seemed to grow heavy around her. The queen's expression forced Poppy back a step. The thought flew through her head that maybe they should just leave. "If you don't know about my parents"—she hurried to get the words out—"then . . . maybe you can just point me in the direction of the Soul Jar . . . ?"

A longer pause. Mack drew back a step, pulling Poppy with him.

The queen's voice was cold—dripping with venom. "Very well, Poppy Sunshine." She nodded at the nearest handmaiden, who stepped forward and held out her hand. Poppy hurriedly fished out her locket and poured it into the faery's cold palm. Despite the pang in her chest as the queen's fingers closed around it, relief washed over her. She couldn't wait to get out of here.

The handmaiden returned to the queen's side.

"Your parents I know nothing of—and care nothing for," the queen began. "But I *can* indeed put you on the path of the Soul Jar."

Poppy took an involuntary step forward. "You can? Thank you! I—"

The queen held up the locket. "A little gold piece of your heart, however, is not enough."

Poppy froze.

"You will not part with your cerberus. You will not join my court." Her long fingers drummed on the arm of her throne. "It seems to me you have altogether too much will for someone so weak." Her fingers stopped. "So! You must pay with the sweat of your brow. I will give you a challenge. Complete it, and I will acknowledge you worthy of the information that you seek. Fail, and I take what I want from you in exchange. That is a bargain worth making."

"Poppy . . . ," Mack warned.

"Done!" Poppy snapped as Mack bristled at her side.

The slow smile that grew on the queen's face forced Poppy back another step. Should she have taken more time to consider? She forced herself to stand straighter. "What's the challenge?"

The queen nodded toward another handmaiden. The slight faery, eyes downcast, brought her a small blue bottle.

"Your challenge is a song."

"A song?"

The queen smiled. Her teeth were small and pale. "Take this bottle."

Poppy stepped forward and took it, hurrying back to Mack's side.

"I warn you, however. Do not open it. It was made specifically to hold the Valkyries' battle song."

The bottle was smooth and cold in her hand, despite the heat of the day. "But I don't—"

The queen waved her hand. "You have twenty-four hours. If you're late, or return without the song, my bargain is won."

"Twenty-four hours? You never said—"

The queen's dark brows rose. "All Fae agreements are either for the duration of a single day, or for the duration of a year and a day . . . or, occasionally, one hundred years and a day. Everyone knows this. It is our way. Besides which, I was under the impression, girl, that you were in a hurry."

There was no way she was leaving her parents trapped inside a malediction for a year! "Fine. A day. Twenty-four hours."

The queen gave a nod, her smile wide. "As you wish. Our bargain is struck. As a show of good faith, I will suggest you begin at the bluff meadow."

Nula's voice was barely a whisper. "Your Grace . . . Your Grace, if I could just ask . . ."

"I don't like your face, pooka."

Poppy gave an audible gasp, her eyes shooting to Nula. The pooka looked stricken.

Poppy hadn't liked the Faery Queen before—but now a curl of anger heated her belly.

"Your kind are weak and cowardly," the queen continued. "You have nothing to offer me that I desire except your absence."

Mack hissed like he'd been burned, and Nula seemed to shrink back as though each word was a punch.

"Go now, before I get rid of you permanently. *That* is my thanks."

Nula spun around. The look she shot at Poppy felt like a blow.

Poppy opened her mouth to apologize—she wasn't sure what for—but before she could utter a word, Nula tucked her head and fled. She didn't even bother to change forms.

"Nula!" Poppy called, but the pooka was gone.

Poppy turned to Mack, but he wouldn't look at her. Without saying a word, they hurried after Nula. They only stopped to rest when they were far enough away that they could no longer hear the music of the harp on the breeze.

It was as if the forest came back to life around them. Even the air was warmer. Poppy let out a breath she hadn't realized she was holding and lifted up the little bottle to the light.

It was small, about the size of her palm. The pale blue glass shimmered a little when she turned it. They had twenty-four hours to find the Valkyries and catch their song. Then she'd get all the information she needed about the Soul Jar and track it down. A surge of anxiety raced through her.

Behind her Mack was strangely quiet. She turned, thinking she'd show him the bottle, but stumbled back in surprise. He was standing with his arms crossed, glaring at her with his copper eyes flashing as if they could set fire to the trees.

He didn't wait for her to ask what was wrong.

"How could you?"

"What?"

"You *swore*. You promised me you wouldn't bargain with the faeries."

Heat rushed to Poppy's cheeks. "Mack—they're my parents! I—"

He stabbed a hand into his hair. "I know! I know they're your parents, Pop. I get it. But you can't find them if you get killed on the way!"

"*Get killed?* Mack! You're overreacting."

"No—stop saying that! Stop calling me a worrier— that's just your excuse not to listen to me and you know it!"

"An excuse? Are you kidding me?" Poppy felt something snap inside her and stomped forward to yell in his face. "MY PARENTS ARE TRAPPED! I have the best *excuse* in the world."

Mack's face contorted, the hurt in his eyes knocking Poppy back better than a shove. "If you cared about me . . .

you would have kept your promise. You would trust me and let me help. But you don't," he snarled. "Not when it counts."

Poppy couldn't believe this was happening. Her voice rose to a wail against her will. "I *do* trust—"

"You made a deal with the Faery Queen, Poppy! Do you even know what a Valkyrie is . . . or how to find the bluff meadow?"

"I—"

He met her eyes. "How far is it? Is it dangerous? How do we catch their song?"

"I don't know, but it doesn't matter. I have to do it! And it doesn't help to have you second-guessing every choice I make! I have to find them. How can you even think I would say no—if there's a chance?"

"What chance? The chance that this magical forest will just let you do what you want with no consequences? IN TWENTY-FOUR HOURS?" he roared.

Mack was *yelling* at her. A sick feeling began to build in Poppy's stomach. His anger had caught him off guard too. He slumped against a tree and turned to face her.

When he spoke again, his voice was soft and sad. "You think you know better than everyone around you, but I know these woods better than you, Poppy. That's a fact." He wiped a tear off his cheek. "I don't know everything . . . but you—you just throw yourself into things all the time. You don't think. You don't care what your choices cost the people who care about you."

There was a bitter taste at the back of Poppy's throat and heat burned her cheeks. "What should I have done, Mack? If we'd done things your way, we would still be waiting at the Holly Oak! You know, it's easy for you to say that we should play by the rules. It's not *your* parents that are missing! It's not you that spent your whole life trapped at the edge of Strange Hollow, between your own people and the Grimwood."

They glared at each other across the distance, until Poppy began to feel sick again.

Mack's voice was almost a whisper. "Fine. Learn the hard way. It's obvious that nothing I say can stop you . . . but I choose the elven way—Do right, and you'll be right. I promised Jute I would stay, and I will. I keep my promises. But our friendship—I don't know if I can do it anymore, Poppy." And with that, Mack turned and strode into the forest.

CHAPTER THIRTEEN

Poppy's feet made no sound on the carpet of soft pine needles as she walked away. She needed a minute to compose herself. There was no way she was going to let Mack see her cry.

Sitting next to Poppy, Eta and Brutus were of two minds, with Eta leaning into Poppy, and Brutus staring toward where Mack had stopped, back turned, a distance away. Two let out a plaintive cry.

Mack's words hurt, but at least it gave her something to focus on besides the guilt and dread that washed over her when he said she didn't care—that she could learn the hard way. He was being unfair, and if she could be angry at him for it, then she didn't have to think about what he said. She didn't have to wonder if he was right. She didn't have to consider whether it was even possible to find her parents . . . if they were even alive. She pushed every doubt to the side and focused on feeling the low, steady burn in her chest.

A small sniff from behind a tree told Poppy that Nula

was back. Mack must have realized it too, because he straightened.

"Nula?" Poppy called.

"Yes?"

"Why are you hiding behind a tree?"

"Because you shouldn't have to look at me. She said I'm—I'm nobody . . . *nothing*—no one wants me."

"Come out. That's not true," Poppy said at the same time that Mack turned and said, "You're someone."

"*We* want you," Poppy added gently, glancing at Mack. The pooka sniffed. "You do?"

"The faeries have always thought they're better than everyone else." Mack rolled his eyes. "They can't stand to think they're just like the rest of us."

"But they're not," Nula protested. "They're so much . . . more."

"Are not," Poppy insisted.

"They're not," Mack agreed, and the kindness in his voice forced a lump into Poppy's throat.

Nula's tail swished like a pendulum from behind the tree. "But they're so beautiful."

"I don't think so," Poppy managed to say. "I think they're creepy . . . with their streaky eyes, and those giant spiders spinning silk for them, are you kidding?"

Nula stepped out and cocked her head at Poppy and gave a small, watery laugh.

Mack gave Nula a gentle smile. "Beauty is what we do

and who we are. Physical beauty is nothing compared to loyalty, and wit, and kindness."

"I'm witty." Nula sniffed again.

Mack laughed, and Poppy dropped her gaze to her boots, fighting tears. She'd never fought with Mack before—not like this. It was like bleeding—painful, and irritating, and messy all at once. *You did promise*, a voice in her head implored. Poppy felt the hurt in Mack's gaze, but she kept her eyes on the ground.

"Agreed," Poppy answered Nula at last, her throat tight. She gritted her teeth. It wasn't fair for Mack to be angry at her. He wasn't the one whose parents were trapped in some kind of soul catcher. What if she couldn't get them back? He was supposed to be on her side.

Nula leaned against the tree. "Do you really believe that stuff . . . that stuff about beauty though?" Her cheeks were tearstained, bright tracks over her blue skin.

Mack moved to put one hand on Nula's shoulder, and the anger rushed out of Poppy in an instant, leaving her hollow and tired. "When you get to know Mack better," she said, "you'll realize that he's *usually* right."

Nula must have heard the bite in her voice, because she shot a look at Mack, and then back to Poppy again.

"Are you two okay?" she asked.

Mack didn't answer. Instead he looked up through the

canopy. "The sun is setting. We need to make sure we're safe for the night."

Poppy shook her head. "We can't stop for the night. We only have twenty-four hours to find the Valkyries and capture their song."

"Right." Mack's shoulders tightened. "But walking through the Grimwood at night isn't an option for us . . . which," he added, "I'm sure the Faery Queen knew when she made that deal with you."

Poppy swallowed.

"We'll just have to make the best of it. And maybe we'll get farther, faster if we get some rest. I'm going to get us some food. If I were you, I'd get out the salt and iron shavings, and make a circle big enough for all of us to sleep in."

Poppy muttered about Mack being a know-it-all as she pulled the bag of shavings from her pack. Nula dragged over a big flat stone for a cook fire. After seeing the thorn trees spring up out of nowhere to douse the fires they'd escaped, it seemed wise to keep flames off the soil. Poppy sprinkled the coarse grains of salt, dappled with thin curls of iron in a huge circle around them. She enclosed a large ash tree to lean against, and made sure the circle was big enough for all of them to sit around the fire, and to take turns lying down.

Once the circle was finished, Poppy gathered windfall wood to get them through the night. Nula helped. The forest was peaceful. Spike frogs thrummed in the trees and along the riverbed, and even the crickets were starting to carouse at the edge of the stream, as the wind creaked through the trees. They settled in to wait for Mack, and Dog curled up next to her, Eta resting her chin on Poppy's lap.

She hoped her parents were okay. They were tough— she knew that much from reading their journals. They would fight back if they could. She hated the quiet for allowing all her thoughts to rush in. Were they in pain? If it had been her that had gotten caught, how long would it have been before they even noticed she was gone? She shook the thoughts away, but others came rushing in to take their place.

She hoped Jute was okay. He would have noticed she was missing right away. And Mack.

Mack. A lump rose again in her throat and she swallowed hard. After a while Poppy's eyes grew heavy, despite the ache in her chest. The leaves danced above her, shimmering in the early evening light. Her parents were in danger. She knew that. But even knowing it, and even considering what had happened with the faeries just a short time before, it was hard, in that moment, to imagine anyone fearing the Grimwood. It's like a bear, she thought, as her mind began to drift. Harmless when it's resting, but dangerous when disturbed.

Poppy must have dozed, because when she opened

her eyes, the forest was the deep blue of past dusk. A sweet salty smoke drifted over their camp and she sat up. Mack's eyes were closed, but he sat with his back against the big tree and his arms crossed, as though daring anyone to disturb him.

Mack had banked the fire and set their single pan across some coals. Poppy moved closer to see what was in it. Tentaculars, cut into strips and sizzling in water with cress and fresh green onion. Her mouth watered.

Nula was wide awake too. She crouched near the edge of the circle with a book open on the ground next to her. Her blue skin almost made her disappear in the evening light. She wasn't reading the book though—she was poking it with a stick. Poppy watched her for a moment, her brain trying to make sense of what she was seeing. When her thoughts caught up with her mouth, she asked the pooka what she was doing.

Nula cocked her head. "I'm poking this book."

"Okay, yes. I see that you're poking it. *Why* are you poking it . . . and where did it come from?"

"I'm poking it to try and get it to show me what it's hiding. And I got it from the Holly Oak."

"The Holly Oak gave you a book? Can I see?"

"Sure. And no. She didn't give it to me. I nicked it."

Poppy moved too fast. The rush of dizziness made her head throb. "You . . . you stole it from the Holly Oak?"

Nula stopped poking. "I guess. Technically. But it was

practically begging me to take it. You should have seen it, glittering away on that shelf in the closet. She must have known I'd take it."

Poppy shook her head. The book was just plain brown leather. "What are you talking about? What shelf?" Behind her Mack let out a gentle snore, and Poppy lowered her voice to a hiss. "What were you *thinking*? You can't take things from the Holly Oak. What if she finds out?"

"If she cared, she would have stopped me. She could, you know. Anyway, I told you. It wanted me to take it. Come see." Nula picked it up and held it out.

Against her better judgment, Poppy shifted to her knees so she could crawl over to the pooka. If Mack found out they were in possession of a book the pooka had stolen from the oldest, and most revered creature in the Grimwood, he would never speak to her again. She almost didn't want to know about it herself.

Almost.

The book was small and thin—unassuming. The brown leather cover was embossed with the image of a tree inside a circle of clasped hands. The page edges were silver. Poppy's breath tightened in her chest as she reached out to take it.

It was heavy—much heavier than it should have been with so few pages, as though the secrets it held had a weight of their own. She opened it.

The pages were blank.

Except—in the middle of the book, there were several pages that looked as though someone had tried to write something and failed. A huge splotch of ink spread over the inside, like someone's pen had vomited on the book's inner seam. She turned the page. Blank again, but with a splotch on the left-hand page. The next was on the right.

Altogether there were seven pages with ink splotches.

"Seven pages," Nula said. Her voice was as somber as Poppy had ever heard it. "Look out for sevens in the wood," she said in a low voice. "And threes. Sometimes nines."

"Nine is just three threes," Poppy said absently as she let the pages ruffle through her fingers. "What is it, do you think? A journal or something?"

Nula shook her head. "Nothing ordinary like that. Feel how heavy it is? It's magic. I'd bet anything."

Nula poked it with the stick, despite the fact that Poppy was still holding it. "But it's useless if it won't give up its secrets."

"Stop that." Poppy pushed away the stick and rubbed at the first ink splotch. She wasn't really sure why, but she believed Nula—that the book had something magic in it. It occurred to her—too late now—that it could have been a malediction. She shouldn't have touched it at all.

She narrowed her eyes at the pooka, but Nula hadn't gone into any kind of trance. She hadn't left the circle to wander into the wood in search of a thorn grove either. Poppy's heart returned to its normal rhythm and she turned her attention back to the book. "I wonder what it is."

"Inklings," Mack said just behind her in a soft voice that made Nula yelp and jump a mile.

"Sorry," Mack laughed. "I didn't realize you weren't paying attention to the elf sneaking up behind you."

"Very funny."

"Where did that come from?" he asked.

Poppy and Nula locked eyes. There was a heartbeat of silence that Poppy was sure would tip Mack off. Without taking her eyes off Poppy, Nula said, "Just a book. I've been trying to figure out how to unlock it, but the whole thing just lies there."

Mack held out his hand and Poppy set the book in his palm. She scooted closer. Was he still angry?

He didn't look at her, but took the book, frowning at the weight. "The ink just lies there because it isn't ink."

Poppy grimaced. "Well then, what is it? Moldy cheese?"

"Like I said, inklings," he answered coldly. "Give me your knife."

Poppy's heart flipped, but she pulled the small blade from her boot and handed it over. Mack took the tip of the knife and made a cut on the pad of his pointer finger. Poppy sucked in her breath.

"It's like most everything in the Grimwood," he explained.

"Ohhhh—out for blood," Nula finished, leaning forward. "Inklings, you say? I've never seen them before."

"What are they?" Poppy asked as Mack's blood began to drip onto the pages. She drew back as the ink blot rolled over the book toward the blood and seemed to absorb it through the page.

"Nine drops," Mack said, squeezing his fingertip. "That's seven." He grimaced. "They're creatures—wood folk, like us. But they live off the magic trapped in books. Plenty of magical books in the Grimwood." He aimed a stiff smile at the ground. "Everybody's got one."

"Not glittery ones," Nula muttered.

Mack shot her a strange look. "Annnnyway, the inklings sort of hibernate in there, until you feed them, and then they remember their places again. There," he sighed, popping his finger in his mouth as the last drop fell to the page. A moment later, the ink on the page began to roll.

CHAPTER FOURTEEN

The inklings shifted and rolled like black sand, first over one page and then the other, until at last small curls peeled away to form themselves into words.

> Stay away from the Grimwood, child.
> Stay away from the fog.
> Stay away from the thorn trees, child.
> Stay away from the bog.
> Tooth for tooth.
> Blood or bone.
> Promises are made of stone.
> Know your place, and
> Watch the weather.
> Wood and home must rise together.

A shiver passed over Poppy. "That's like the rhyme they say in Strange Hollow."

"The first bit, anyway," Mack acknowledged.

"How's that one go, then?" Nula asked.

Poppy swallowed, her mouth suddenly dry. "Stay away from the Grimwood, child. Stay away from the fog. Stay away from the thorn trees, child. Stay away from the bog. Keep the promise. Rue the day. The Grimwood is no place to play. Close the shutters. Lock the doors. They come for you on twos and fours. They come for you on twos and fours."

"What do you say that for? That's scary."

Poppy gave a small nod. "It's a children's rhyme. A warning. And, I think it's supposed to amplify the warding . . . to keep away the monsters. But it doesn't work."

"Humans are weird," Mack acknowledged.

"Well, it sounds like a bargain if you ask me," Nula said.

He cocked his head. "How do you figure?"

Poppy blanched at the word "bargain." "Well, they do both mention promises—that's a bit like a bargain, isn't it?

"Only if they get something in return," Mack grumbled, digging his toes into the forest floor.

What do you think it means?"

"And why did the Holly Oak have it?" Nula added.

Mack froze. "What?"

"I mean . . . why . . . did . . . the Holly Oak *also* have it?"

Mack frowned but said nothing.

"Give me the knife," Poppy said. "I'll do the other pages."

"No," Mack said, stabbing another finger.

"Fine," Poppy muttered under her breath.

The other pages were different. There were six of them—three on either side of the rhyme. Each one was a drawing, and the inklings sketched them in like wood-cuts. The first one showed monsters in a village—fires and screaming people. Arms and legs. It was gross.

Mack flipped the page, while both Poppy and Nula peered over his shoulders. The second drawing was of a young woman with a kerchief over her hair. She stood in front of the remaining villagers with her hands up like she was trying to get them to listen. In the third picture the same woman led all the people into the forest. A huge tree stood in front of them. "Is that the Holly Oak?" Poppy asked, but Mack had already turned the page. The fourth page—right in the middle—was the rhyme.

Nula reached for the knife and Mack gave it to her. Her blood was blue, with a pearly sheen. It beaded on the page until the inklings swirled around it like ravenous parasites. The next image was of the woman and the tree facing each other. Behind the woman stood all the people, and behind the tree—a horde of beasts and mon-sters. Poppy recognized the giant spiders of the faery court.

The sixth page was different again from the others. It was a circle of hands, and a tree in the middle. "Like the cover," Poppy whispered. The pairs of hands shivered, as if they shook one another.

The last picture was of a grove of thorn trees. The inklings ran over the pages, making the thorny whips thrash.

"What does it mean?" Poppy asked.

"Nothing good, I bet," Nula muttered.

Poppy shuddered and slapped the book closed, in Mack's lap. He startled and looked at her but turned away when she caught his eye.

"Now that's a weird book." Nula grimaced, slipping the book out of Mack's hands and back into the pocket of her tunic.

I'm sorry about our fight, Mack. Poppy thought the words but couldn't bring herself to say them. Instead she turned her back on him as he pulled a tentacular from the pan, blowing on it and tossing it from hand to hand before popping it into his mouth. He hadn't said a word.

Nula stared at Poppy, then back at Mack, her expression speculative.

"We should rest for a few hours," Mack said. "We're going to need it."

Nula's face darkened, but she let it be. They ate the tentaculars without talking, and each of them found a patch of dirt and got comfortable.

They slept in shifts. Poppy woke once to see Mack sitting cross-legged at the edge of the circle. Dog sat next to him. Across the narrow band of salt and iron, a tall black dog with long fur and red eyes sat watching them. More red eyes gleamed from the darkness. None of them moved.

"Mack?" Poppy breathed the words. "Are you okay?"

He nodded. "They won't cross the circle. You can go back to sleep."

A few hours before dawn, when it was her turn to watch, Nula woke her, yawning. Poppy crept over and sat next to her to watch the last embers of their fire.

Nula pointed vaguely toward the east. "There's a couple of trolls over there. They already came by once, but they couldn't cross the circle."

"Nula?"

"Hm?"

"How come the salt and iron don't bother you and Mack?"

"Hm? Oh . . . ill intent."

"Huh—"

"We don't have ill intent. That's what the salt and the iron keep out. We aren't looking to cause harm to anyone inside the circle, so it doesn't react to us. Can't hurt that you invited us in, as well." She laughed.

"Is that why you can go into the Hollows too, because you don't want to hurt anyone?"

Nula considered. "Maybe. I don't know what keeps other things out of the Hollows, but nothing's ever stopped me—definitely not those useless carved statues."

Poppy grinned. "Mack's always wanted to go see it for himself."

Nula studied her. "What's up with you two, anyway?"

"I don't know. He's angry." Poppy rested her chin on her knees.

"Yeah, I got that."

Poppy pressed her lips tight, as though holding the words back would keep them from being true. "I promised him I wouldn't bargain with the faeries."

Nula blanched. "Ah. But then you did it anyway. Yeah, that sucks."

Poppy pulled her hair back into a ponytail. "I had to. How else was I—"

"Yeah, I get it. You had to. But you didn't even . . . you broke your promise to him, and it took you about one second. You didn't talk to him about it first or anything."

Poppy moved her forehead to her knees.

"I can see why he's angry at you. You . . . you weren't being a good friend. And you made him small."

Poppy lifted her face. "Huh?"

"You made him small. You know . . . small in your life, like he doesn't matter."

Poppy turned her head away. "Nula?"

"Hm?"

"What do you think that book is about?"

"Change the subject much?" Nula shook her head.

"Yeah, okay. The book. I don't know, but it's powerful."
She paused. "Honestly, I sort of want to put it back."

Poppy turned back to give her a sympathetic smile.

"Welp," Nula said, brushing the dirt off her hands.
"I'm going to get a little sleep before the sun comes up . . .
but if you want my advice." She nudged Poppy with
her elbow. "And I *know* you do. You should tell Mack
you're sorry. You messed up, so you should own that."

Poppy's cheeks heated, but she didn't have the heart to
snap at Nula. A moment later, she didn't want to anyway.
She wanted to cry.

The pooka lay down under the tree and was asleep the
moment she closed her eyes.

Poppy didn't cry. She sat watching the wood, spinning
the pooka's words in her head. She could hear the trolls
crashing through the underbrush—farther away, then
nearer, then off in the distance again.

She wondered what they were doing. She wondered
what they looked like. She briefly considered leaving the
circle to go find out, but if anything happened, time might
not be the worst thing she'd lose. She considered waking
Mack up to tell him she was making the right choice and
not being reckless, but instead, she turned her thoughts to
Nula's strange stolen book, and its even stranger rhyme.

Why was it so similar—but also so different, from the
rhyme in Strange Hollow? Which one was the original? It
was the center of the whole book—so it must be important.

As she was pondering how to sneak the book away from Nula while she slept, the trolls crashed out of the undergrowth. Poppy scrambled to her feet.

They were wrestling each other. The trees creaked and swayed around them as they gripped each other's forearms, locked together by their enormous racks of antlers, drawing back, then coming together again with such force it shook the ground.

The trolls took no notice of her. They were enormous, and pale white, and except for the fact that their arms and legs bulged with muscles, they looked nothing like Poppy had imagined.

They were shaped like people, but way bigger—the tops of their antlers reaching well into the tree branches. Their faces were strange too—long and lumpy—with pointed white teeth that gleamed and snapped as they twisted their antlers first one way and then the other, shoving to try to gain an advantage.

They broke apart.

The one with the long blond braid grunted. "Gives it up, Myrtle."

The other one chuckled and shook dark curls. "Nah. Don't thinks I will. How 'bout you gives it up, Gregor?"

"Can't. I likes winning too much."

They drove at each other again, their antlers crashing together with a sound like snapping limbs. "You knows it doesn't matter," Myrtle ground out. "The elders won't declares a new general until they finds out who mades the fire near the nesting grounds."

Gregor chuckled. "S'pose you're right. But still, I won't chance losin'."

"Well, yer givin' me a headaches . . . and I don't likes to waste my times."

"Sun's coming up soon. Truce, then?"

"Yeah. For nows. Truce."

They drew back, untangling their antlers to stand still, both of them panting.

"Anyways," Myrtle said. "Since the sun's risin', as you says, we shoulds be goin'."

"Don't wants to get turned to stones."

Poppy heard herself speak before she'd even realized she was considering it. "That's true? You really turn to stone in the sun?"

The two trolls looked over, their yellow eyes gleaming, and suddenly Poppy wished she hadn't called attention to herself.

"Well, well."

"It speaks."

"That's a different ones."

"Is it, then? I can't tells them apart."

"Can you nots, then? The one from earliers is blue. And there—see that's another ones sitting there againsts the tree."

"That one's an elf."

"Is he deads?"

Poppy shook her head. "Of course not! He's just sleeping."

"Oh. Good." A mournful look crossed Myrtle's face. "But we can't gets him."

"Not with the salts."

"Not with the salts and the irons."

Goose bumps rose on Poppy's arms. She cleared her throat. "So the sun really turns you to stone?"

The troll with the braid nodded. "Let's goes, Myrtle. She's makin' me hungrys."

"Me toos, Gregor. I wishes we could eat 'er. She's biggish, so we'd haves to breaks her and . . ."

"No, couldn't breaks her. We got no pot. Can't cooks 'er. No fires in the woods. We'd haves to brings her back and shares her."

"True. True." The dark-haired one gave a huff of laughter. "Now that'd puts us in a fix."

"Thorn trees likety splikity. Let's goes, Myrtle. I've had enoughs."

"Wait!" Poppy called. "Did you say something about a fire . . . in your nesting ground?"

They had started to turn away, but paused now, and moved nearer instead—a lumbering, shambling gait that made Poppy back farther away from the edge of the circle.

"We did indeeds. What do you knows about it?"

"Nothing really. I know there was a fire near some werewolves' homes, and . . . and we got caught in one too.

The thorn trees put it out. Are . . . are either of those near where you nest?"

"Why are you askin' 'bouts our nesting ground?"

"Takes it easys, Gregor. She's just sayin'. Other fires, you says? Fire grows the thorn trees every time. Who's doin' the makin'? Says if you knows."

Poppy shook her head. "I don't knows . . . know. But there seem to be a lot of them springing up."

"And thorn trees," the blond troll lamented. "The Oak's gots to defend the wood." He shook his enormous head. "Can't just lets it go burnin'."

"The Oak?" Poppy asked, nearly stepping out of the circle in her excitement. "Did you say the Oak has to defend the wood . . . with the thorn trees?"

"Oh sures. Thems hers too. It's all hers." They stood staring at her for a moment, their eyes gleaming. One started to drool, and Poppy stepped back. Her back hit the trunk of the tree. She let out a yelp as a hand wrapped around her ankle. She looked down to see Mack staring back.

Staring at the trolls, he rose slowly to his feet next to her.

As one, the trolls turned and shambled away, still muttering. "I thinks it's the faeries doin' the burnings. They always likes to be on tops."

"Nah. I thinks it's that bog biddy—she's a nasty one."

"Nah. Not hers, Myrtle. She's stucks in the bog. What does such as hers wants with fire?"

"Wells, who else?"

"Wells, the thorn trees don't burn when they puts it out. Maybe it's thems."

"You needs your head examined for worms, I thinks, Gregor. They's nasty, but they's just doin' their jobs. Besides, why woulds they puts them out if they starts them?"

Their voices faded as they moved away into the wood. Poppy stared after them, her heartbeat fast. She had hoped to find adventure in the Grimwood, but more than that, she'd hoped to find answers. No . . . she had *expected* to find answers. Here was one she had waited for. It wasn't just the regular trees the Holly Oak controlled. The thorn trees were hers too. Did that make the maledictions hers as well?

She fisted her hands. More questions! She knew what a thorn tree looked like—and a troll—and she was beginning to understand why it was a bad idea to deal with faeries. But when it came to understanding the Grimwood—freeing her parents and being a part of something bigger together, all she'd found were more secrets and more questions. The forest wasn't like she thought it would be.

She turned to Mack and opened her mouth to tell him about what she'd learned, but he just gave her a sad look and settled back down against the tree, closing his eyes.

She blinked rapidly. And then there was Mack. She might have lost his friendship for good.

Dog came over to stand next to her. The night was beginning to slip toward dawn. Brutus bumped her leg with his cinder-block head, and she let one hand uncurl and rest on their side. "We have to figure this out and free Mom and Dad, guys . . . and I've got to find a way to make it up to Mack."

Nula came and stood next to her on the other side, rubbing her eyes.

"How much time do you think is left, Nula?" Poppy's voice caught.

Nula considered. "The forest folk don't really think much about time, you know. They don't really need to, unless—"

"Unless they happen to have made a bargain with the Fae."

Nula flushed. "Right . . . but, the sun sets late, and rises early, so I'd say . . . I'd say it's been about six hours."

"Six hours." Poppy blanched. "Then we only have eighteen hours left."

"Plenty of time." Nula gave a stiff chuckle that wasn't at all reassuring before she lay back down and closed her eyes.

Poppy stretched out next to Nula and Dog, but instead of closing her eyes, she watched the sky begin to turn green as it slipped toward morning. Dawn couldn't come fast enough.

CHAPTER
FIFTEEN

An hour or so later, when the sun had finally stretched golden tendrils over the tops of the trees, Poppy woke Nula. Mack's eyes popped open as if he'd been awake all along. Maybe he had. The light was still dim through the trees, but they didn't have a moment to spare. The queen had told them to start at bluff meadow.

"Do you think the queen was lying when she told us where to begin?" Poppy asked aloud.

"Faeries don't lie!" Nula called back from where she walked ahead.

Mack considered, his copper hair knotted where his head had rested against the tree. "No, but they don't tell the *full* truth either. Certainly not to help us out. She gave us that information for a reason."

"But why? Doesn't she want to win?"

He sketched a frown, but just looked tired. "That's the thing about the faeries," he said. "They always win."

Poppy grimaced.

"Listen, Poppy. If you don't get the Valkyrie song before this evening, she wins, and gets to take whatever she wants from you—including you, by the way. You remember she wanted you to join her court, right?"

Poppy swallowed.

"And if you do happen to succeed, she gets the Valkyrie song without risking anything herself. She wins no matter what." Mack dropped his hand to her shoulder, then snatched it back again. "We do have one small advantage."

"What?" Poppy heard the tremor in her voice.

He brushed dirt off the backs of his legs. "I thought about it last night, and I think I know where the bluff meadow is."

They moved quickly, passing lone thorn trees—the first Poppy had seen since the ones that had sprung up to put out the fire.

For the whole first hour they walked, Poppy talked. If she kept the words flowing, she didn't have to think about her parents, or about her argument with Mack. If she kept talking, she didn't even have to think about what might happen if the Faery Queen won.

She told Mack and Nula about the thorn trees being part of the Holly Oak. When Mack walked ahead, she talked to Nula about the weather and the trolls until at last, Nula fell silent, and then Poppy talked *at* her.

Nula caught up with Mack and, after a long look over her shoulder at Poppy, gave him a glare that held at least two lectures about something. Mack shook his head, and continued to keep his distance.

Though she'd never been a nervous talker, Poppy grew chattier than she'd ever been in her life. She made observations about the forest as they walked. She wondered out loud about different species of tentaculars. She wondered out loud about the migration patterns of Mogwen. She wondered out loud whether it would rain, and how the thorn trees knew about the fire, and how they had put it out.

She wondered out loud about anything and everything that might distract her from the fact that her parents' souls were stuck somewhere and maybe injured, and maybe worse. She didn't want to think about how Mack was angry with her, and how that was her fault for always pushing her way through. She tried to push away the passage of time, and the possibility of failure. She wanted to hide it all under a thick pile of questions the way a squirrel buries a nut for the winter.

The wall between her and Mack wouldn't budge, and she didn't know how to fix it. He was only here because of his promise to Jute. They were running out of time . . . and they hadn't even reached the bluff meadow. Her stomach churned, and her problems wouldn't stay down. Instead they grew, like the heat of the day, becoming more real with every mile. Sweat dripped down Poppy's back.

When two hours had passed, and they were still

surrounded by trees, she began to panic. There was no chance she could win against the Faery Queen. She walked faster and faster until Nula got exasperated with trying to keep up and turned herself into a deer, sprinting ahead into the wood. Mack walked behind her and said nothing.

After the third hour, Poppy had to slow down again, her breath ragged. The panic that had been fueling her began fading into despair. She had a stitch in her side, and her throat was raw from breathing fast. Mack was right. Dealing with faeries was a really bad idea. Foolish.

Like her.

If she lost, they would have to run—hide somehow, or at least she would. She wouldn't drag her friends into her mess. And then what about her parents? And she still didn't have any of the answers she needed.

They had been walking for almost four hours when they came to a full-fledged grove of thorn trees, stretching into the distance. Even Dog seemed to tiptoe as they skirted the edges. In the stillness, Poppy's renewed effort at distracting herself with chatter clattered to a halt.

The smell was rank—thick and rotten. The black trees sparkled beautifully in the glimmers of late morning sunlight as it sifted down through the canopy, but the whole place felt somber and sad, and almost smothering. It was as though someone had dropped a heavy blanket over the whole grove.

Bones littered the ground, some old and crumbling.

Poppy could make out . . . other things, wrapped in the whips—things that were long past help.

There were several holes in the loose rich soil under the trees, as though something had pushed up through the ground to escape.

Maledictions, Poppy thought, her pulse hammering.

Fifteen minutes later, Mack broke into a run. Poppy exchanged looks with Nula, who had become herself again sometime in the previous hour, and ran after him, her heart lifting as the forest opened up onto a huge meadow. Tall grasses stretched out to the edge of a cliff. A huge bird circled in the distance.

Eta and Brutus barked happily, their tail wagging. Two woke up, tongue lolling as his head jostled between his two siblings like they were playing monkey in the middle. They all disappeared into the tall grass.

Poppy couldn't help the laugh that bubbled up. She took a deep breath. The air was sweet and smelled of dust and sunlight. She hadn't realized how closed in the Grimwood had become—how stifling.

She laughed again. "Now what?"

"We should go west," Nula said. "Wood folk always like the west."

Mack shook his head. "Valkyries are immortal battle maidens, not wood folk . . . and this is the perfect place for a battle," he argued. "This is the meadows. We should wait for them here."

Nula scowled. "You think they're just going to show up?"

"Okay, well, it's a better idea than just walking west."

Poppy followed the trail of bent grasses that Dog had left in their wake, moving away from Mack and Nula's bickering. She closed her eyes and inhaled. The air cleared her mind, settling her doubts.

She was still in the Grimwood, and her wager with the Faery Queen wasn't just a threat. It was an opportunity. If she succeeded, she would be on the track of the Soul Jar in no time. She *would* rescue her parents.

She could do this. She'd been preparing all of her life. She dropped her backpack to the ground and pulled out her notebook, scanning all the notes she'd made from her parents' journals—looking for any mention of the bluff meadow or of Valkyrie.

Behind her, Mack and Nula had finished bickering, and like her had paused to take in the meadow. Dog was barking, so Mack threw a stick for them. A smile played over his face as he looked out across toward the bluff.

Poppy closed her eyes and took another deep breath. When she opened them, she made out water sparkling in the distance, far below the cliffs. She wondered if it was the Alcyon. Farther still she could see more bluffs, and flashed to the vision she had seen while she was standing on the stairs of the Holly Oak, looking out. It had to be the Alcyon! She was on those bluffs—the ones she had seen—high above the fathomless salt sea, surrounded by forest. Her heart skipped a beat.

Battle maidens, Mack had called the Valkyrie. The phrase rang a bell in her mind . . . reminded her of something she had heard. Across the distance a bird let out a piercing cry, jogging her memory. Her parents had talked about a bird they wanted to see one day . . . a bird that was beloved by battle maidens. She flipped to her glossary.

There it was, in the B section! Battle maidens, also called Valkyrie, are warrior women (immortal) who get to choose who lives or dies at any battle they attend. In the northern homeland of the Valkyrie, warriors consider it an honor to be chosen to go with them to the afterlife. Their battle cry is a fierce weapon, honed from the souls of the fallen. They are said to ride a bird called a Kohko. It is made of iron and fire and will answer only to the same.

A shriek echoed across the meadow, and a shadow darkened the sky above them, rippling out across the grasses like a wave. She looked up and knew what she had to do.

"Dog!" she called, rooting through her pack. "Dog! Come!"

They appeared at her side, covered in grass seed, all three of them sparkly-eyed and panting. She smirked. "Good Dog! Now, stay close to me."

She yanked out her little iron bell and set it on the ground, fishing down into her pack. Across the meadow,

Mack and Nula had seen the shadow too. They ran toward her, their eyes wide. Mack was shouting.

They were in for a surprise. She just hoped it was a good one.

She exhaled with relief as she found what she was looking for and hurried to pull the last of Dog's bone from her pack, waving it back and forth over her head, so the bird would be sure to see. Brutus gave an offended woof, but Poppy kept a firm grip on their collar.

Mack and Nula arrived, short of breath, at her side.

"What are you doing?" Mack asked.

On her other side, Nula watched her with stark amazement, as if she might spring another head.

"I'm calling us a ride." Poppy tipped her chin at the silhouette of the enormous bird, growing larger against the sun. It had veered toward them.

Mack's mouth opened and shut, and opened again. "Not on that?"

Poppy grinned.

Mack grabbed her arm with one hand, and Dog's collar with the other, yanking them both back, as if he would spin them back into the forest to hide.

"Mack! This is right. I'm sure of it."

His face didn't change expression, but he let go, and stood beside her, his body still and tense.

Poppy had told him she was certain . . . but as the bird grew closer, Poppy's doubt grew. Its wings spanned almost the whole meadow. The sun shone against it as it got closer, disappearing into thick silver-black feathers the color of iron. It opened its hooked beak to scream, red eyes glittering like fire.

"Ummmmmm," said Nula, grabbing hold of Poppy's pocket and disappearing inside. Poppy patted the mouse idly, her heart in her throat.

Mack pulled the net gun from Poppy's pack. "If you get us killed, my mother's going to kill us both. You haven't met her yet, Poppy, but believe me, if I'm dead, you won't want to."

The bird's shadow fell over them and Poppy gave him a small smirk. They both knew the bird wouldn't even notice the net. Poppy left her knife in her boot.

Tensed to run, Poppy stepped forward, waving the bone in the air. The bird answered, letting out a shriek that split the air. It pulled up, lowering its black-taloned feet to the ground. Its muscled legs, each as big as Poppy, were covered in thick feathers.

She tossed the bone upward, and let out her breath as the bird snapped it out of the air and dropped the bone down its gullet. Eta whined. Poppy caught a glimpse of a long black harness, covered in bells. A huge black saddle, with a rectangular basket at the back boosted her confidence.

She took a step forward.

The bird spun, beak wide—and stabbed forward.

Poppy let out a yelp and jumped back, knocking Mack to the ground. Dog began to bark.

The bird turned toward them.

"No!" Poppy screamed.

Dog stood their ground, legs wide, all three heads snarling.

The bird let out another cry and stabbed again.

Dog shot to the left of it, finding their stance again and moving forward, their snarls intensifying.

"We have to help them," Mack cried, running to Dog's side. In her pocket, Nula was spinning in circles. The pooka appeared at her side again, tearing Poppy's pocket. "It's magic!" she hissed, diving into Poppy's other pocket.

Poppy stared at the bird. Think! Think! She couldn't think. The tinkling of bells was incessant and distracting.

Bells! Bells! That's it!

The bird dived again and Mack cried out, shooting a net that landed covering half the bird's head. It shook the net off without a thought and stabbed its beak at the ground again and again.

Dog lunged, barking to try to drive the bird off.

Poppy's blood was rushing so fast she thought she might pass out. She grabbed for the iron bell where it had fallen, her fingertips reaching out to touch the smooth, cool metal. She yanked it up and held it high in the air. The long wooden handle was so delicate compared to the handle of her knife, but she rang it hard, filling the air with its cold, clear song.

The bird stilled and turned toward her.

Poppy bent forward, still ringing the bell for all she was worth. She took a deep, shuddering breath, and kept her arm swinging, but after a moment stood straight.

Mack was staring at her.

"Get Dog . . . please," she said quietly. "Pick them up and get on."

To his credit, Mack didn't ask questions. He grabbed Dog, who had also stilled and had eyes only for Poppy, and approached the bird. Poppy stepped nearer, holding the bell high in the air in front of the bird.

As if in a trance, the bird lowered one wing, and Mack, after a quick glance back at her, climbed up into the saddle. He put Dog in the basket and closed the lid, fastening the small hooks.

Poppy went next. Her arm had gone numb, but she waved the bell as though her life depended on it. She was pretty sure it did.

She climbed up in front of Mack, still ringing. The saddle had black leather loops on the sides—handholds. Mack had already grabbed his. She met his eyes over her shoulder, and he nodded.

Poppy took a deep breath and shoved the handle of the bell between her teeth, grabbing hold of the loops.

The air continued ringing for a moment after the

clapper fell silent, but as soon as the sound stopped resonating, the bird squawked and shook its head as though shaking off a biting insect. It shuffled its powerful legs, stamping as it spun toward the cliffs. The whoosh of its giant wings flattened the grasses.

Poppy screamed through gritted teeth as it ran toward the edge of the cliff, launching them off the edge.

CHAPTER SIXTEEN

Wind whipped through Poppy's hair and ruffled the bird's feathers as they picked up speed. It circled, gaining height as their shadow passed over the meadow where they had been standing moments before. The bird arced downward, angling toward the glittering sea far below them. A moment later it evened out, moving farther out over the open water.

There the bird paused, hanging high in the air, hovering with neither weight nor care. A joyful rush of air filled Poppy's lungs.

And then the bird dived—straight down.

The wind ripped away Poppy's scream. The bell fell, toppling from her teeth. Behind her Mack screamed too, and inside the basket, Dog let out a keening whine.

The bird let out a cry as they plummeted toward the bell, spiraling toward the sea.

Poppy glimpsed the Holly Oak island and saw the bell disappear into the Alcyon as the bird let out another sharp cry—lifting them up—back into the sunlit sky.

She looked back at Mack, who had turned a sickly shade of green. Her whole body shook, and she squeezed her eyes shut. They were *so* high up. "Are you all right?" she called back, trying not to think about it.

Mack coughed out a yes, and she blew out a breath.

The bird rose and rose, and each time it beat its enormous wings Poppy wondered how far they had gone. After a few beats of its wings, she forced herself to open her eyes, and though her heart was in her throat, she couldn't help smiling. Ahead of them rose a chalk-white bluff and in the distance, Poppy could see people standing on the rocky landscape—watching their approach.

She nudged Mack and felt him draw in a breath behind her.

They were close enough now for Poppy to see that the watchers were women. The sunlight gleamed and sparked off their armor, so bright they were hard to see. Poppy counted seven of them, all wearing helmets, with long spears in their hands and swords at their waists. They stood in formation, like the tip of an arrow, pointing right at Poppy. The woman at the tip stepped forward to greet them as the bird set down on the cliffside.

Poppy slid from the saddle. Mack let Dog out and jumped down with them in his arms to stand behind her.

The woman's red braids hung from her helmet like soft chains of copper. The sun behind her was so bright that her head and shoulders were edged with light, as if she was on fire. The woman shifted her weight, casting her own face into shadow. Poppy caught a glimpse of ice-blue eyes and sharp, pale features before the woman shifted again and Poppy had to look away. The armor of all three women sparkled, so bright in the sun that it made her eyes water painfully.

Mack's voice dropped low. "Poppy . . . be careful."

She scowled, and opened her mouth to protest, then changed her mind and leaned closer to listen instead.

Mack went on. "The Faery Queen sent us straight to them. She didn't want to do this herself."

Poppy let his words sink in. He was right, of course. It was Mack's special, and most annoying, talent. She sighed. It was time she gave him the same respect he always showed her, and listened.

"You're right," she whispered back. "We should be on our guard for tricks . . ."

His eyes had widened. "Yeah—okay. It's clear the Valkyries are a danger she didn't want to face herself. Just . . . go slow, okay?"

She let Mack see that she had heard him—had understood, then turned to the women.

Nula *poofed* out of her pocket, appearing at her side, and Poppy wished she could see the women's faces properly, to know if they were startled. They kept the angle of the sunlight just right to hide their faces, and their emotions, if they had any.

At her side, Dog let out a long, low growl, and though none of the women had spoken a word, Poppy sensed a shift in the air. She had the strange thought that there was more to them than just their bodies . . . that while their forms stood waiting, their spirits pushed at some invisible boundary, testing whether it could hold them back.

Still the women didn't speak. Poppy could see the corded muscles of their necks, tight with strain.

Poppy's pulse fluttered in answer, but she knew—her instinct focused on the predators watching her—that showing fear now would be a fatal error. These women were just as dangerous as any other monster of the wood.

"Are you the Valkyries?" Poppy asked, lifting her chin.

Nula leaned to whisper in her ear. "They're supposed to be very proud—flatter them, if you can."

The woman at the front stepped forward and looked straight down at Poppy, and seemed to grow taller. Mack tried to tug her back, but Poppy resisted and lifted her eyes to meet the woman's face.

"I am Brynne, general of these great battle maidens. We wait for war. Why have you sought us out? You are no warrior."

Poppy almost argued with her, but bit the inside of her cheek instead. Flatter them, Nula had said. "Great General!" she began, trying to sound as formal as Brynne had. "I have longed all my life to learn the ways of the Valkyrie battle maidens."

This wasn't precisely true. Still, Poppy wanted to know everything about the Grimwood, and they *were* in it.

Brynne gave a derisive snort. "Only the greatest of gods can make a battle maiden. You are foolish to pursue it."

"Is it true that you choose who lives and dies in battle?"

Brynne threw back her shoulders. "It *is* true. When we attend a battle, we choose those who have the greatest fire within them—the ones who are fiercest as they face death. Only they are worthy to dine with us in the great halls of the dead."

"Wow—that's really cool. You must be . . . you must be really strong, and brave . . . and . . . and wise."

"Yes."

Mack nudged her.

Too much? Not enough? Poppy wasn't sure. "I bet you're fast as lightning," she added.

The compliment was like a match.

Suddenly all seven of the Valkyries burst into action—breaking into pairs and swinging their swords at each other, so they sparked and clanged.

"Yes," said Brynne, striking a pose with her sword. "We are beauty and dread." She struck another pose. "We are terror and deliverance." She lunged into a third pose, her sword arm cast like a scorpion's sting, over her head. "We are redemption and glory and—"

"And you're singers?"

The Valkyries froze. Brynne stood, stepping closer,

and this time Mack did drag Poppy back. Dog moved to block the Valkyrie general, baring their teeth.

A cold wind whipped through Poppy and she shivered. "I—I mean, I've heard you sing?"

"What do you know of the song of the Valkyries?"

Poppy swallowed. "Only that it's the most glorious . . . most mind-numbing."

"Stunning," Mack chimed in.

"The finest of all songs," Nula squeaked.

"Hmph," Brynne huffed, turning her attention to Dog. Poppy held out her hand—as if she could have stopped a Valkyrie—as Brynne crouched to look each of Dog's heads in the face. Dog stilled, and Poppy tasted bile. If the Valkyrie did something to Dog, Poppy wasn't sure what she would do . . . but it would take more than Mack to stop her.

"This is a fine beast. From whence do they hail?"

Poppy drew back. "Uhh . . . They hail from here. From the Grimwood."

Brynne rested one hand on Brutus's head. Eta let out a whine.

"They do not. Their heritage is in another place—as it is for all in this place you call the Grimwood. Do you know their heritage or do you not?"

"Dog was born in the Grimwood."

Brynne rose. "It matters not. You will be honored to gift them to us."

Poppy crossed her arms. "No. I will not be honored. I will *never* part with them."

Brynne drew herself to her full height, glowering down at Poppy.

"I *will* be honored to hear your song."

Brynne's eyes flashed. "You wish to hear our battle song?"

The Valkyries behind her seemed almost to rustle, like reeds on a riverbank.

"I do."

"The song we sing to call out the souls of our chosen. The song we sing as we head into battle, to declare to all those about to spill blood that their lives are ours to cull— and ours to judge? That is the song you wish to hear?"

Poppy's mouth had gone dry.

From inside her pocket, Nula pushed up the small blue bottle, and Poppy took it, twisting the cork in her fingers. With her other hand, she reached out and pushed Mack backward two steps, to bring them closer to the bird. Maybe they could jump on and—

Brynne lifted her hand and with a cry, the bird lifted off without them, shooting straight up into the blue sky, rising higher and higher.

There was a sucking sound—as if someone had taken a huge inhale and pulled all the air from around them. Brynne and the other Valkyries opened their mouths, and there was a bright, loud ringing sound.

Poppy didn't wait to figure out what was happening. She yanked open the bottle and pointed it at the Valkyrie general.

There was a pop and a whoosh. The air was back again. Poppy replaced the cork and shoved the bottle deep into the front pocket of her jeans. She had done it—she had captured the Valkyries' song.

Everything was still for a moment. She could see Brynne's face fully now—and all the others' as well, like she hadn't been able to before. It was as though the sun had disappeared behind a cloud, though there wasn't a single one in the sky.

Brynne shook her head as if shaking off sleep and glanced over either shoulder at her battle sisters.

Then she turned back to Poppy.

Then she pulled her sword.

Poppy gasped and spun around, but there was nowhere to run. The bird was gone, and the Valkyries' formation kept them blocked from the wide grassland behind them.

She caught sight of Mack's alarmed expression as the Valkyries stalked toward them with slow, purposeful steps, their eyes suddenly dark and gleaming against their pale skin. Brynne's were fixed on Poppy.

Behind them, the cliff fell away fifty feet or more to the fathomless waters. Poppy swallowed. It wasn't so far . . . there was a good chance they would live. Probably.

"We have to jump off the cliff," Poppy muttered, try-ing to keep the Valkyries from seeing her lips move. Her knees shook as she backed up.

Mack shook his head. "Hitting the water will be more like hitting stone at this height."

Poppy met his eyes. "I don't think we have a choice."

Nula appeared at her side. She cast them a sympa-thetic look and changed into a swallow, zipping out into the open air. Mack stared out for a moment as if willing another solution to make itself known. Then without a word, he reached down to sling Dog over his shoulder, and turned to meet Poppy's eyes. "Now?"

"Now!" Poppy shouted as she grabbed his hand, and jumped.

CHAPTER
SEVENTEEN

This time they didn't scream. The air rushing past was like a scream itself—sharp and cold. The wind was so strong Poppy couldn't open her eyes at all. It whistled painfully in her ears and flapped at the fabric of her hoodie, whipping her long black hair against her face. She sensed that Mack and Dog, and even Nula, were still with her, but she couldn't see them. Fear stiffened all her muscles and made breathing impossible.

Her feet pierced the water with a shock of pain, rushing downward through the still, salt sea. For a moment Poppy's eyes flew open, but she only saw the dark shapes of Mack and Dog hanging in the water, before her eyes were burning with salt. She tried to move in their direction as she rose to the surface, arms outstretched to grab them if she could.

Mack broke the surface, sputtering, as Poppy took her first gasp of air. Nula—at least she assumed it was Nula, had become a dolphin, and held Dog to the surface, swimming in graceful circles around them.

Poppy's feet stung, and her legs ached from hitting the water. She took deep, choking breaths as she turned, looking for any hint of shoreline. In the distance, she could see the Holly Oak island. Behind them, and all around, were cliffs. No shoreline in sight. The river and shallows were on the other side of the Alcyon.

"We've got to get to the island."

Mack grimaced, and Poppy moved toward him. "Are you okay?"

"I—my shoulder." He was holding it as he bobbed awkwardly.

She couldn't see much through his hand, but the strange angle told her he'd knocked it out of the socket. "Can you put it back?"

Mack blanched, but gave a stiff nod. "I think so. Put a hand against my back and when I hit it, push." He took a breath and hit himself hard, knocking the shoulder back with a grunt. He closed his eyes, floating on his back for a moment. When he opened them, his eyes narrowed. "Look," he said.

Poppy followed his gaze up the cliffside. At the top, the Valkyries peered down over the edge, their armor sparking in the afternoon sun.

"I hope they don't stay angry," Poppy sputtered.

"But you caught their song." Mack smiled at her.

"Yes." Poppy grinned back. "I did."

They swam for the island, Mack moving slow to favor

his shoulder. The quiet between them grew heavy. Poppy knew she needed to talk to him—say something about what she'd done, and she didn't think she could wait any longer to do it.

"Mack?" Poppy kept her eyes pinned to the Holly Oak island.

"What?" he puffed.

"I'm really sorry."

A long pause.

Poppy risked a quick look. His expression was hard—his copper eyes fixed on her. She looked away again, her cheeks heating. She took a deep breath. "I'm sorry for what I did. Breaking my promise . . . it was reckless."

"Yeah, it was."

Poppy swallowed her pride. "You're my best friend," her voice hitched. "I should have trusted your advice and been more careful—more thoughtful. Also, I made you a promise, and that meant something, and I didn't keep it. And I should have . . . I should have at least talked to you about it."

He was quiet, swimming next to her, but she risked another look. His expression had softened. "I'm sorry too," he said. "Finding your parents is the most important thing right now. You needed me, and . . . I was really harsh. I'm sorry."

"You were just trying to keep me safe." Poppy forced herself to stop swimming and look Mack fully in the face.

His eyes widened, and he stopped swimming, treading water as she wiped her eyes. "It's just splashes," she said. "I'm not crying."

He looked away.

"Mack?"

He looked back.

"Thank you for caring. I'll do better, okay? I'll really try. Please don't give up on being my friend."

Their eyes locked for a heartbeat . . . then two. Mack gave her his best smile. "I won't, Poppy. I promise." Then he lifted his good arm and sent a splash of water right at her face. Poppy ducked, laughing, and swam toward shore again.

The sun was scorching, drying the salt on their skin until it stung. Poppy's eyes burned. While she and Mack struggled along, Dog seemed to be enjoying Nula's bursts of assistance. They'd made a game of it, with Dog paddling along, then falling behind, waiting until the dolphin came up beneath them to shove them forward with a few flips of her tail. Two's tongue lolled, and Eta and Brutus looked like they were smiling. After the third time, they even wagged their tail, slapping the water as Nula approached.

Poppy almost laughed, but she needed all her breath. Her whole body hurt, and next to her, Mack's face had grown grim. He was hurting too.

"Hey, Mackintosh."

He turned his head, his copper eyes dark.

"I forbid you to drown."

His eyebrows rose and he choked on a laugh.

"If we're going to die in the Grimwood, it's going to be much more exciting than sinking—I can promise you that."

He snorted. "Only you, Poppy Sunshine, would forbid us to die boring."

Poppy tried to laugh, but had to pinch her mouth shut to keep the water out. "Someone has to do it," she retorted, and focused on the island. It was getting closer, and there was someone on the shore. "Who is that?"

Mack had spotted them too. "Is that—"

"It's Jute!"

At that moment, Nula's tail slapped the water, splashing their faces. "Hey!" Poppy cried. But Nula's only response was to shoot around and give her back a painful shove. Poppy spun to yell at her, then froze.

Far off in the dark water behind them, a long black muzzle lifted silently. It was followed by black eyes and a floating black mane that she could almost sense more than see. There was a flash of red where the horse's nostrils flared.

Poppy's heart flew into her throat. "M—Mack?"

She heard his intake of breath.

Another head rose next to the first, this one the deep green of thick water. Only the smallest ripples showed in the water as others rose to join them.

Nula was already rushing Dog forward through the water when one word left Mack's lips. "Swim," he said.

"What are those?"

"Kelpies," he said, and the tremor in his voice scared her more than anything. "Swim, Poppy. Swim as fast and as quiet as you can. Maybe they haven't seen us."

But Poppy knew as well as Mack did that the kelpies knew they were there.

Poppy had read about kelpies in her parents' journals, but their notes hadn't said anything about them being in the Alcyon—only in ponds and lakes.

She supposed her parents had never fallen into the Grimwood's fathomless sea. Maybe no one else had either.

Or maybe they just hadn't lived to tell about it.

Water horses, the kelpies were sometimes called. They gained legs for the land only on the summer and winter solstices . . . long enough to lure something to them. Their beauty was so magnetic that sometimes their victims would even climb up on their backs.

But once you were in its power, a kelpie would race into the water and drown you. Then eat you. Not necessarily in that order.

For once in her life, Poppy didn't want to know any more than that.

They swam.

There didn't seem to be enough air.

I didn't mean it, she thought. *I didn't mean it, about*

dying an exciting death. I want to die a boring death—a quiet, boring death . . . a long time from now.

She wondered if it was the last time she would ever see Jute. The tall hob paced the shore, his long arms laced over his head. He could see the kelpies too.

Tears swam in her eyes, mingling with the salt sea.

Then Jute did something she'd never seen before. He stretched out his arms toward her, as if he could catch her hands and pull her to him, even from so far away. At first it only made her heart ache, but as she watched, his arms began to grow. They twisted and stretched, moving toward them.

Nula reached the shore ahead of Poppy and Mack, and transformed back into herself, with Dog on her heels.

"Swim, Mack! Swim!" Poppy screamed.

"My shoulder—" Mack grunted. He was slowing down . . . falling behind.

Still Jute's arms stretched.

The ripples in the water grew closer.

"Go," Mack choked, but Poppy grabbed his hand, tugging him forward. "No way. I won't leave you!"

They were barely moving.

Something brushed against her leg.

Impossible though it seemed, Jute's arms had reached them. One vine-like arm wrapped around her wrist as the other hooked itself around Mack. The hob tugged hard, and Mack cried out as they shot forward, skimming the water like flying fish.

Behind them she felt the water pulling at her feet, like a wake building, and she heard splashes.

She looked back.

The kelpies churned the water, utterly silent, their heads and necks high. Their sharp teeth gnashed, eyes rolling with fury or hunger, the herd rolling toward them like a wave.

Poppy screamed.

Jute yanked.

She landed on the pebbled shore next to Mack, her face pressed into Jute's long toes.

The rushing sound continued. A few yards from the shore, the water horses pawed the water with their forelegs, their strange undulating bodies moving them forward and back again, so that they seemed to hover there.

"The Holly Oak is sacred ground," Mack spoke into the stones pressed to his cheek. Nula paced the beach behind them, muttering to herself as Dog trotted at her heels.

Jute studied the pooka but said nothing as he pulled Poppy to her feet. She turned her face into his scratchy wool sweater, and he wrapped his arms around her. His arms had returned to normal, but his knuckles and fingertips were still twiggy.

"I didn't know you could do that," Poppy said, stilling at the sound of his two hearts beating their syncopated rhythm.

"Neither did I," he said, pulling her closer. "I guess we've discovered another of my special hob powers."

"Nice of them to show up when you need them." Poppy gave a hysterical laugh as Jute kissed the top of her head.

"Poppy Sunshine. Little bug. You're safe," Jute murmered. "I have you."

She squeezed harder. "I'm sorry for tricking you, Jute."

"Shh, shh, shh. Never mind."

"I didn't think it would be so hard," she confided.

"I know."

"It's not like I expected—not at all."

Jute held her tight, the rumble of his voice tickling her ear. "Expectations are often just a trick we play on ourselves," he said, patting her back. "The truth is always something more than we expect—and always something less as well. Contentment comes when we learn to be grateful for the good things in front of us."

Poppy turned her face farther into him, breathing in the smell of wool, and warmth, and the sharp green scent that was her uncle. "What if I can't be content?" she asked with a quaver in her voice.

He chuckled and wrapped the long fingers of one hand around her chin, lifting her face until she was looking into his speckled eyes. "Contentment isn't something we *are*," Jute explained. "It's only a place we visit for a while. But it grows familiar over time, like a crooked little house on a map of strange lands—where there's always a light in the window." He sighed, letting go of her face. "When I first felt contentment, it came from a sense of belonging—from feeling kinship with myself and those I love." He paused. "It came slowly, as I discovered who I was, and what made my heart sing. And after a time, it got easier to find my way back."

Poppy wrapped her arms around Jute's middle and squeezed until he woofed. "You're young," he insisted. "Still seeking . . . but one day contentment will be as familiar as an old friend."

Jute let go of Poppy and reached over to ruffle Mack's hair. He seemed to size up Nula for the first time. "A new friend, Poppy?"

"That's Nula. Nula, this is my uncle Jute."

Jute dipped his head. "A pooka, if I'm not mistaken?"

To her credit, Nula didn't question the family relation. Instead, she blushed blue and gave him a quiet smile. "Fionnula, really. Nula is just a nickname."

Jute smiled gently. "You're a good swimmer—and I see you've taken a shine to Dog."

Nula dipped her head. "Everyone likes Dog. And it's nice to meet you."

A twig snapped behind her, and Poppy spun to look behind her. Something moved behind an outcrop of rocks. She hesitated, then left Jute and the others talking, and moved closer.

She'd only taken a few steps when an old woman

leaned out from behind a boulder. A bright kerchief held down wisps of white hair, and her eyes glittered. She beckoned for Poppy to come closer.

Poppy glanced back at Jute. He was explaining something to Mack and Nula—probably something wise . . . and heavy. She turned back.

"Come," the old woman mouthed eagerly. "Come."

Poppy went.

CHAPTER EIGHTEEN

The old woman's stomach growled.

Poppy moved to the other side of the rocks where Jute and the others couldn't see. She fumbled in her bag, and found one last apple. When she held it out, the woman patted her arm with her wrinkled hand and gave Poppy a sad look. "Such nice manners. Slice it up for me, dear?"

Poppy pulled her little knife from her boot. She cut the apple into slices and held one out. "Are you . . . are you a witch?"

The woman hesitated, then snatched a piece of apple. "Hasn't anyone told you not to talk to strangers in the wood, child—especially not old women?"

Poppy pulled back. "We have talked about that, actually. But this is the Holly Oak island. It's sacred ground . . . right?"

The woman gave her a wide smile. She was missing teeth, but the ones she had were sharp and yellow. She winked. "Good thing for you."

"So you are a witch! A bad one!" Poppy couldn't help the tiny thrill that ran down her back.

The old woman bit the slice of apple, chewing slowly. "Well, I'm no faery godmother," she laughed, bits of spit and apple flying. Her face grew serious. "But never mind about me. Let's talk about you. *You're* the human girl . . . the one wandering around the wood like it's a playground."

Poppy's jaw dropped. "I'm not wandering around—I'm trying to find my parents, and before that—"

"Listen. You're here . . . and a good thing too. The Grimwood folk need you." Her fingers wrapped around Poppy's wrist like iron bands. "That's the marrow of it, girl. That's the marrow."

"Need my help how?" Poppy tried to pull free, but the woman's grip only tightened.

"I'm not here to eat you, child. We need you to remember the promise."

"What promise?"

Her eyes flashed. "The promise of Prudence Barebone," she snarled.

Poppy startled. "Who?"

The woman frowned. "Prudence. Barebone."

"Who's that?"

"Who? Who? So sad. Like a little owl." Her wrinkles deepened. "You should know her name. Some say she is the mother of all this." She waved her free hand to take in the trees and the shore and the fathomless sea.

"Why do they call her that? Who—I mean, what did she do?"

"When I was a girl, *every* child knew this story." She huffed a breath. "Prudence Barebone made the promise—the very first, between the people and the Grimwood."

"Tell me," Poppy breathed.

The woman took another bite of apple and chuckled. "The Holly Oak was just a sapling looking for a place to root for good, or so I was told. The people kept burning back the wood. They didn't want her, or her dark forest of monsters and magic. Too dangerous. Too strange." She chuckled again. "They soon learned the Oak doesn't take kindly to fire."

Poppy felt her eyes widen. "The thorn groves . . . the old ones in the deep! That's when they grew!"

The woman snorted, but Poppy hurried on. "What about Prudence—did *she* want the Grimwood?"

"Well, she's dirt dead and long gone. Can't ask her." The woman let go of Poppy's arm. Poppy rubbed at the bruises forming from the witch's grip.

"But since I'm an old woman," she continued, "I can say what I think, and I'm not afraid to give you my opinion of young Prudence. She was pragmatic—a young lady not too much older than you, I'd guess. She was greedy too. That seems clear enough. There was only Strange Hollow then—none of the other Hollows, mind you. The people tried to burn the wood, and the Oak fought back—sent all its creatures into the Hollow. It wasn't pretty. There was a great battle . . . and it went badly for everyone.

"It wasn't what the Oak wanted, of course. She was just trying to root herself—trying to build a home for all. I doubt Prudence had any true understanding, but she saw the way things were going, nonetheless. She convinced the people of Strange Hollow that the Holly Oak would continue to fight for the wood and its creatures . . . for its place in the larger world. It didn't take much to convince them that it was a fight that humans couldn't hope to win."

Poppy thought suddenly of the strange little book Nula had taken, and the rhyme the inklings had remembered for them. "Tooth for tooth," she recalled. "Blood or bone."

The woman squinted. "You've heard it, then."

In a flash, Poppy remembered one of the images in the book. The tree and the woman, with all the people of the Hollows and the creatures of the wood stretched out behind them. "The promise of Prudence Barebone," she breathed, covering her surprise by poking her head out from behind the rocks to look at Nula. She and Mack were still talking with Jute, but Mack narrowed his eyes at her, like he was sure she was up to something.

She ducked back behind the rock.

What *was* the little book Nula had taken from the Holly Oak? "So . . . what did Prudence do?" she asked the witch.

"Well, she did what anyone does in this cursed wood when they're in trouble. She bound herself in a different way—a way she could choose, and she took something for herself in the bargain."

Bells went off in Poppy's head. "She made a promise."

The old woman's eyes lit. "Prudence made a promise."

Poppy wasn't sure whether it was the light in the woman's eyes, or the ringing of her words, but for a moment it made Poppy's hair stand on end. "What promise?"

The woman cackled. "A promise for the ages. A promise for all time. For all of us."

"With the Holly Oak?"

"With the Holly Oak." The woman gazed meaningfully at the apple slices in Poppy's hand and Poppy handed her some more.

The old woman went on, chewing. "Prudence was afraid, you see. She didn't want to grow old and die." She breathed a long sigh. "So, she bargained extra years—for everyone. She wasn't selfish, only greedy. She asked for reasonable safety—a ban on any creature entering the Hollows who meant humans harm. The Oak couldn't grant immortality, so Prudence asked for long and healthy lives, more than double a human lifespan. Bountiful harvests. No snow."

A sour taste crawled up the back of Poppy's throat. "But can the Holly Oak give us all that? I mean, how? What . . . what did Prudence promise in return?"

The woman shot her a sharp look. "Clever girl. All magic has a price, and what Prudence asked for was costly. She promised peace, I suppose you could say. She promised the humans wouldn't harm the wood, and that they would stay, bound to the magic of the wood and the fog, protectors should the fog ever fail." She bit off another piece of apple. "Then they all signed it. Every last one."

Poppy shivered. The witch hadn't actually named the price Prudence had paid, but before she could push her for more answers, the old woman leaned in. Her breath smelled like something had crawled in her mouth and died. "Then Prudence made a mistake."

Poppy tried not to gag. This was important. She could feel it.

The woman began to back away. "She swore the Oak to secrecy. Now, only the rhyme remains . . . and these days you all have even forgotten that."

The last time they were here, the Holly Oak had been trying to tell them something . . . something she wasn't able to say. A geis, Mack had called it.

Poppy looked up. The woman was fading from view, her form shifting into mist. "Wait!" Poppy cried.

The woman's glittering eyes were the last to go. A whisper echoed in Poppy's ear. "Don't forget," it said.

"What's all the shouting about?" Mack's voice called.

Poppy spun around. The rocks that had blocked her

and the old woman from view were gone. The shore was flat and clear. Everyone was staring at her.

Her scalp prickled. "Jute? Did any of you see where that old woman went? Or . . . or the rocks?"

Mack pulled a face. "What woman? What rocks?"

Jute shook his head. "No one's here but us, my dear."

"I was just talking to her! She was old, and she had—"

"No, you weren't," Nula scoffed. "You've been over there muttering to yourself for the last fifteen minutes." She rolled her eyes. "I just thought you were *in a mood.*"

"No. I'm not in *a mood.* I was talking to someone. Right here! Behind some rocks! An old woman."

Mack and Jute both looked concerned, but Nula came closer and pulled at Poppy's arms, looking her up and down, then spun her around and did the same on the other side.

"What are you doing?"

"She didn't bite you, did she?"

"No, she didn't bite me!"

Nula narrowed her eyes at Poppy as though she didn't quite believe her. "But you *did say* it was an old woman?"

Poppy nodded.

"Well, I guess you're lucky, then."

"Whyyyy?"

Nula rubbed her shoulder. "Even good witches can bite."

Poppy gaped. "How did you know?"

Nula swatted Poppy with her tail. "I told you. You have to watch out for old women in the wood. They're never just grannies. What did she want?"

Poppy looked at Mack and Jute. "She wanted to tell me a story."

Mack and Jute exchanged a look. Jute shook his head. "There's no time for stories, Poppy." He pulled her into a hug. "Mack told me what's happened. You have to get that magic bottle back to the Faery Queen." He held Poppy away, then dug one hand into his pocket. "Hold out your hand."

He dropped a handful of gold coins into her palm.

Nula groaned.

Jute closed Poppy's fingers around the coins. "There's no time to waste. The Holly Oak sent for me. I'll go to her, and you can explain everything later—once you've fulfilled your bargain."

"But—"

"Just hurry," he said, brushing his fingers over her cheek. "I love you too." His hand dropped to his side and he met each of their eyes, before turning away. "Now," he said. "Run."

They raced along the shore as Poppy's thoughts flew to the Boatman, and then to the kelpies. Just the thought of the Boatman made sweat break out across her skin, but there was nothing—not even a bargain with the Faery

Queen—that would make her get back in the Alcyon sea and swim.

She led the way, moving as fast as she could. She had no idea how much time was left, but she knew it wasn't much. She tried to tally the time it had taken to reach the Valkyrie—to fly across the sea to the far cliffs. How long had they been in the water? How many hours had passed since dawn?

How many more would it take to reach the Faery Queen again?

Limbs heavy with exhaustion, they ran for the dilapidated dock, stumbling over cobbles and roots around the uneven shoreline. Mack was on her heels, with Nula and Dog pushing them forward. When the dock came into view, she put on a burst of speed, reaching into her pocket to close her fist around the small blue bottle.

Would the Faery Queen have the information she needed? Would it be enough? And how did the promise of Prudence Barebone weave into this mess? It did—she was sure of it. That promise had something to do, not just with the Soul Jar, but with all the maledictions. Which meant it involved her parents.

If she could just figure it out, maybe she could help all of them—in the wood and out. One thing was for sure. As soon as she got out of this mess with the faeries, she would sit down with Mack and Nula, tell them what the witch had told her, and take another good look at that book.

Nula was clanging the bell at the end of the dock like

her life depended on it. Poppy had never seen the pooka so agitated. *Maybe because she always turns into something else and runs away when she's upset.* One day, Nula would have to choose her alternate form, as all pookas did—the form she would spend at least half her adult life in. Poppy wondered what her friend would choose. She hoped she would be around to see it.

The Boatman rose, silent and threatening as ever. Almost gleeful, he held out his hand. Perhaps he thought she wouldn't have the coins to pay.

She wasn't sorry to disappoint him.

They suffered through the ride, though this time he took the easy, paid-full-price part of the river. As easy as it ever got anyway, and as soon as they stumbled out, they ran again, racing through the wood—walking only long enough to catch their breath, before they ran again. Poppy searched the wood for the Rowan Gate that marked the entry to the Faery Queen's territory. She could almost feel the passage of time now. It ticked through her entire body, kicking her pulse off its normal rhythm like a downbeat drum.

How much longer? An hour . . . less? A few minutes?

Please let us get there in time, Poppy begged the Grimwood. Please let her be forgiving if we're late. Let her be so impressed with the Valkyries' song that she tells us everything she knows. Let my parents be safe. The Faery Queen will know where the Soul Jar is . . . and once we have it, we'll free my parents. *She'll tell us where it is. We'll get there in time. She'll tell us where it is. We'll get there in time.*

Poppy's thoughts flew ahead of her with wings that were soft and full of promises.

The queen was waiting at the gate—the very picture of a peaceful welcoming, with white flowers in her straight black hair. She was flanked on either side by her guards, still as stone in the shadows of the great Rowan arch.

The queen peered into the wood, and in her palm sat a huge hourglass filled with sand. Poppy could see, even from a distance, that only the tiniest bit of sand remained.

As they ran, time seemed to slow. Poppy couldn't look away from the Faery Queen's dark eyes. Poppy's heart rose into her throat as they closed in, sinking again as she saw the last few grains of sand fall. A bell tolled, shaking the trees.

"No!" Poppy shouted.

The queen's expression grew smug and satisfied, and she clapped her hands like a child as they skidded to a stop at her feet. "You're late," she said, her smile widening. "You're too late."

CHAPTER NINETEEN

The Faery Queen grinned at them—a flower, over-ripe and oversweet. "You see," she explained. "I knew you couldn't do it. I *knew* that I would get my wish."

"But we did do it," Poppy exclaimed at the same time that Mack cried, "A few seconds! That's all—just seconds."

"As if that matters to me," the queen said, turning to Mack. "You're like all the rest of your kind, aren't you? So concerned with *doing right*," her voice turned mocking. "Well! See where it gets you? Nowhere!"

Mack crossed his arms. "It keeps our hearts clean. Unlike yours."

"Pish. What do I want with a clean heart? A heart is there to be used—like any other thing in the world. Useful, until it's used up." She stepped forward from the line of her guards.

Poppy's hands had grown cold. She let one fall to Eta's head, drawing Dog close for comfort. She had lost. What would the queen take? Would she make Poppy become a servant in the faery court? Poppy gritted her teeth. If she did, Mack would help get word to the Holly Oak—she was sure of it. Dog leaned into her, muscles quivering.

There were more faery guards now. And where were those giant spiders with their creepy handmaidens spinning out their spider silk?

The queen strolled around Mack, one pointed finger trailing over his back as she passed. He shivered. "Let me tell you something for free, young man. Keeping your heart clean will not help you. Following the rules will not help you. If you want to win, you need to—"

Mack shook his head. "Cheat? Steal? Turn away from what's right?"

"Milksop! No. If you want to win, you must learn to *leverage*."

Poppy scoffed. "What does that even mean?"

The queen's expression darkened, the shadows under her eyes deepening as she shifted her attention to Poppy. Her voice grew deeper. "It means using what you know to gain an advantage."

"It means cheating." At his sides, Mack's hands fisted, every muscle in his body tight.

"Does it?"

Mack looked nothing like himself as he fought to contain his anger. *And where was Nula?* Poppy looked behind them and spotted her. The pooka had backed up, and was standing a few feet away. It was this, more than anything, that made Poppy's heart begin to race. Nula was shaking so hard, Poppy could see it from a distance, but the pooka didn't change forms, and she didn't run. Her expression was fierce and . . . defiant? Did Nula know something?

She knew something.

Poppy tried to catch her eyes, but the pooka wouldn't look away from the faeries.

The queen had made her way back around to face Mack. "The Fae never cheat," she said tightly, raising her dark eyes to meet Mack's steady copper gaze. "The Fae watch a thing until we understand it, and then we find the cracks and the loops and the holes, and we slip through and cut your throat before you know we're there."

Poppy looked up. The trees were filled with Fae in dark glittering armor. As she watched, the giant spiders emerged, moving forward out of the trees to stand behind the queen. The spiders' handmaidens, their dark hair pulled tight, rode their backs—and they were armed with blowguns.

She reached for Mack's arm and gave it a shake, but he wouldn't look at her.

"Now." The queen whipped around to Poppy. "About that bargain." She held out her hand and an enormous meaty bone appeared, hanging in the air over her palm. Dog moved away from Poppy's side, the bone taking Brutus's full attention.

Her stomach dropped. "Dog," she hissed. "Come!"

But Dog's full attention was on the bone. Two whined.

"I believe we stipulated that if I didn't get my song in time, I could take something else." Her eyes narrowed. "Something of my choosing."

Poppy felt the blood drain from her face. The queen's tight smile grew in response.

"No!" Mack said. "You can't!"

Her smile widened. "Can't I?" She turned to look at Dog, and shifted the bone in the air, watching as Brutus's eyes followed it.

Eta looked back at Poppy and whimpered.

Poppy couldn't speak. She almost couldn't see. She turned to Mack, but his expression reflected hers.

"No," he said softly and reached down to try to hold Dog back.

"None of that," the queen growled and flicked her hand at him. Mack froze.

"Mack!" Poppy cried as the queen stretched the bone up above her head. "Good Dog," she purred, and flung the bone through the Rowan Gate into the wood behind her. It vanished into the distance, and with a bark of joy, Brutus followed, taking Eta and Two with him.

"NO!" Poppy wailed, running forward to chase them, as whatever held Mack back gave way and he toppled forward into the dirt.

"Eta! Two! Brutus!" Poppy sobbed, unable to hold back her tears.

The queen knocked Poppy's feet out from under her and she landed flat on her back, all the air knocked from her lungs. "Now," the queen said, looking down at her. "Where is my song?"

Nula appeared at Poppy's side and helped her up. "That wasn't the bargain," she snapped, leaning close. "The words were clear. The song or something else. The song OR something else." She let go of Poppy's arm and moved back behind Mack.

A wave of gratitude washed over Poppy. It wasn't enough to dull the pain of Dog's loss—not even close, but she had never been more grateful to have Nula's friendship.

Her spine hardened as she turned to the queen. "No." She lifted her tearstained face. "We agreed. I would bring you the song in exchange for the information I need, and if I failed, you would take something else *instead*. You took something else. You don't get anything more." She widened her stance, and Mack moved to her side.

"You've been paid." Poppy crossed her arms as though they could hold back her heartache. Each moment her heart beat on without Dog at her side was like being stabbed. She wanted to drop to the ground and sob. "Now, keep your promise."

"Damnation," the queen spat, spinning to glare at Nula. Her smile was back in an instant. "Very well. Why not. You were promised information. Now you will have it."

All the strength vanished from Nula's face. "No," she begged.

"About the Soul Jar," Poppy insisted. "And about my parents."

"Yes, yes. Very well." The queen waved her hand in the air. "As you wish, my dear. And let this be a lesson to you."

"What lesson?" Mack ground out.

"To be careful what you ask for, of course," said the queen. She began to pace, circling the three of them like a bird of prey that's spotted its next meal and is only waiting for the right moment to drop out of the sky.

"The Grimwood belongs to the Holly Oak. Everyone is here by-her-leave. Every tree of the wood is connected to her, including the thorn trees. And that means everything belonging to the thorn trees is connected to her. That includes the Soul Jar and—"

Poppy's jaw dropped. "The Holly Oak makes the maledictions?"

"As for your parents, I can tell you only one thing for certain—they are *not* in the Soul Jar."

Poppy rocked back. "They have to be. If they're not in the Soul Jar . . . then . . ." Poppy's teeth caught the inside of her cheek. She tasted blood.

The queen's expression turned sly. "If I were a *betting* person, Poppy Sunshine," she hissed. "If *I* were *you*, I would look to your own people. They're the *real* monsters, you know."

Poppy's thoughts faltered as she tried to make sense

of the Faery Queen's words. "You . . . you think my parents were taken . . . by people?"

The Faery Queen moved on, her predatory smile the only answer. "You also asked if I knew how to find the Soul Jar. And. I. Do.

"I do indeed. I know a great deal more than that, in fact."

She turned back to Poppy, the full force of her attention falling on Poppy's fist where it closed around the small blue bottle. "Not only can I tell you where the Soul Jar is. I can tell you who made it . . . and what it holds . . . and I can tell you *who* used it."

Poppy couldn't breathe. She raised her fist and uncurled her fingers. The little blue bottle lay in her palm, cool against the thin scab that had formed when Nula broke her blood ward. A fine mist swirled inside the bottle. "This . . . this is the Soul Jar?" Her voice was a whisper.

"It is." The queen's voice was smug.

Poppy stared at the queen. Her voice was strained. "It was you. You made the Soul Jar. You changed the malediction."

The queen snapped her fingers in the air. "As easy as any blood ward. I can't believe no one ever thought of it before." She laughed. "Well, I can."

"Blood makes the rules in the wood." Poppy swallowed, her gaze fixing on the bottle with slow horror. "And we—*I* used it to catch the Valkyries' song? But . . .

it's called the Soul Jar." Poppy hated the pleading tone in her own voice, but she couldn't control it. "It's the Soul Jar . . . and this is a *song* . . . not a soul."

"What is a song, if not the expression of a soul?" The queen's smile grew sickly sweet at the look on Poppy's face. She patted Poppy's cheek with an icy cold hand. "Never mind, dear. You couldn't have known. What use do the Valkyries have for souls of their own? None at all! They're immortal, after all.

"But the Valkyries' song is another matter. All songs have some power, but their song? *Their song* is one of the greatest weapons ever made. They say it is forged from little pieces of the souls they collect in the heat of battle." She tipped her chin at the bottle, clasping her hands at her back. "So . . . I'm afraid what you took from them was not really a *song* at all."

"Their song is made of souls?" Mack gulped. "*We* took people's souls?"

The queen's eyes flashed. "Indeed, you did. And you did very well too!" Her voice held pride—and not in them.

"Don't give it to her," Nula called from behind Poppy. "You don't have to! You already paid her."

Her friend's words were like a switch. All Poppy's pain—her anguish over Dog, the shock of being tricked into taking the Valkyries' song of souls—all of it ignited. But before she could use it to set fire to the world, the Faery Queen leaped forward and slapped Nula. The crack of her palm against Nula's cheek ricocheted through the trees.

Nula cried out, and fell back as Mack let out a snarl, and moved to step between them. Poppy gave a horrified gasp.

The queen stalked around them. "You should think carefully before you risk yourself to protect this creature." Her voice came from deep in her chest and sounded old . . . and angry.

"Leave her alone," Mack said, pushing Nula behind him.

They had to get out of here. Poppy gritted her teeth and turned to Mack and Nula, her fingers rubbing at the half-healed wound on her palm. Mack gave her a puzzled look, his gaze dropping to her hands. Understanding flooded his eyes.

Poppy waited. She wouldn't make the choice recklessly. She wanted Mack with her every step of the way.

"Do it!" Nula cried, catching on, and Mack nodded.

Without a word Poppy tore open the wound, letting her blood cover the Soul Jar. At the same time, she cried, "You will harm none! You will harm none! You will harm none!"

The Faery Queen's face registered shock as Poppy pulled out the stopper and released the Valkyries' song.

CHAPTER TWENTY

A whistling sound filled the glade. Everyone froze, preparing for a blow. For several long moments nothing happened. The queen's expression lengthened. Deep lines of withheld fury distorted her expression, but she held her troops steady with a raised hand—watching.

It wasn't anything like being up on the cliff with the Valkyries. There was no pressure in the air—no sense of something gathering. *Was the song useless, then, without the Valkyries there to wield it?* The forces of the Fae army, all gathered in neat rows behind the queen, shuffled and shifted.

The wood remained quiet, and Mack began to tug Poppy back. The shadows of the Faery Queen's face grew longer still, and she drew a slender blade out of thin air. Four more spiders with handmaidens on their backs moved forward to stand behind the queen. Poppy counted seven of them in the glade now, the dim evening light reflecting in each of their eight black eyes.

She looked down at the little bottle, still clutched in her bloody palm. She'd undone the malediction . . . but maybe the song wasn't loose yet. Poppy searched the wood for anything that could help. A large stone leaned against the white birch next to Mack, and without another thought, Poppy lifted the bottle and smashed it against the stone.

It shattered with the chime of breaking glass, and then came a sucking sound, like the breaking of a seal, and the Valkyries appeared, hovering above the trees, answering the call of their own magic in an instant. They dropped out of the sky, landing in crouches, their armor too bright to see.

She, Mack, and Nula were somehow behind the Valkyries. They could have turned and run . . . or hidden, but Poppy couldn't retreat without clearing the air.

"I'm sorry, Brynne," she called, and the Valkyrie commander, still crouched, motionless, turned her head—the only sign that she heard.

Poppy hurried to say what had to be said. "The Faery Queen told me the bottle would only catch some of your song. She tricked me. I meant no harm. Please accept my apology." Her throat tightened as she added, "She took Dog—my cerberus."

The sharp line of the Valkyrie's jaw clenched and she rose to her feet, turning her face back to the Fae. There was no telling what the commander of the Valkyries might have said in response, because at that moment, the queen let out a yowl like the cry of a cat, and attacked.

Poppy jumped, stumbling, but Mack hauled her up again. Nula was a panther at her side.

"Run!" Poppy said, and they ran, the clash of metal ringing through the woods behind them, and a rising wail in the wind.

She didn't look back, but to either side of them Poppy could see spiders through the trees, keeping pace with them, as the handmaidens in their black saddles watched.

"They're waiting for us to get tired," Mack shouted.

"What are we going to do?" Poppy gasped.

Nula let out a fierce roar.

"She's right," Mack said, panting for breath. "We'll have to fight. How's your aim?"

Her lungs burned already, but Poppy stammered, "Th—the net gun? What good will that do?"

They veered left as Mack led the way. "Lots, if you hit the spiders' legs," he called back. "The handmaidens won't leave them, even if the spiders fall." He launched over a fallen log, turning to make sure Poppy cleared it too. "My mother says they're connected somehow."

Poppy shivered—whether it was from the breeze against her sweat-covered skin, or the thought of being bonded to a gigantic spider, it was hard to say.

The spiders weren't getting closer—weren't

attacking—but they were staying near, the handmaidens' black eyes never moving from their quarry.

Poppy reached back as they ran, tugging the net gun free. Aiming was almost impossible. There was no break in the trees, and Poppy lost two nets trying to aim between them. "This isn't working! We need a clearing!"

Nula snarled and pulled in front, leading them away to the east.

"There." Mack pointed ahead of them. "The trees thin out over there."

"Are you sure?"

"Nope! But Nula seems to know what she's doing." The panther's paws kicked up dirt, and the spiders stayed with them to either side.

The trees *did* thin out, and Poppy quickly took aim, firing a net at one of the three spiders to her right. It wrapped around two of the spider's legs, toppling it so that it rolled, end over end, throwing its handmaiden from the saddle. "One down!" Poppy whooped.

But she was out of breath. It was getting harder.

"Keep going," Mack wheezed. There was a hiss from her left and one of the handmaidens lifted something, pointing it at Poppy. She dodged, just as a blob of black goo flew past her and hit a tree.

"What is that stuff?"

"Web, I think," Mack panted. "Hit another one, Poppy. Hurry. We can't keep this up much longer, and there are a lot more of them."

Poppy aimed at the one that had shot at them, and missed. One quick look at the cartridge told her she only had three nets left.

She aimed again—and this time hit one of the spiders to her left—though still not the one that had shot at them. "There are five still chasing us," she yelled, tripping over a stick, and catching herself just in time.

Silently, two of the spiders broke away, peeling out of the trees to run behind Mack and Poppy.

Poppy's throat was raw. Something hit her in the back, hardening instantly. She stumbled forward with a grunt. It was harder to breathe now. She caught sight of thorn trees in the distance. Another glob of web flew past—this time from the right, and this time, it hit Mack.

It had a cord.

Without pausing to think, Poppy pulled her knife and sliced the cord. All she could think of was the thorn trees, with their whips that reeled you in. She wasn't going to let these handmaidens get their hands on Mack.

Another thwack as a glob hit the back of her knee. "Mack!" she cried out as it hardened, making it impossible to bend. She fell forward.

With a grunt he threw her over his shoulder, and put on a burst of speed.

"Head to the thorn grove," Poppy called as his shoulder dug into her guts. There was a pause, and then she felt him nod.

"Nula! Follow us," she cried, and forced the top of her

body to lift so she could aim the net gun. Without having to focus on running, she hit one of the spiders directly behind them, and then the other.

"Three left," she called to Mack as the last of the spiders and handmaidens moved behind them, chasing them down.

The trees cleared. Black soil and old scattered bones crunched under Mack's feet. Thorn trees glittered all around them, stretching as far as they could see.

Mack had slowed.

Nula raced past.

"Keep going!" Poppy shouted. "Don't stop for anything!" She pushed her hands into Mack's lower back, straining to see behind them. Her net gun—empty now—was still clasped in her hand. She held her breath, then let it out again as the last three spiders followed them in.

As if the pounding of all those feet had woken the thorn grove up, whips smashed the ground behind and in front of them. Mack half ran and half danced to avoid them.

The spiders were huge targets with nowhere to hide. Their handmaidens didn't last long. The whips plucked them off the spiders' backs, wrapping them in coils as they flew through the air.

The handmaidens didn't make a sound.

The spiders kept pushing forward, but didn't last

much longer. The first one got wrapped in the whips of two different trees that wrestled for their prize.

Poppy looked away, squeezing her eyes shut.

Mack was breathing hard. "Hold on, Poppy," he said. "We're almost through."

A few more seconds, and they would be safe on the other side.

CHAPTER
TWENTY-ONE

They fell out of the thorn grove and onto the forest floor, panting and sweaty. Mack closed his eyes, his face contorted with pain. Poppy's head pounded from bouncing as Mack ran, but she blew out a breath and turned to examine Mack's face. "Thanks," she whispered.

His copper eyes cracked open, and he gave her a twitch of a smile. His cheeks were flushed. "Thanks yourself," he said.

She grinned at him.

Nula lay on her back, clutching her tail to her chest and staring up through the canopy. Dusk had fallen, and shadows played over her face like thoughts.

They all grew quiet.

The wood was thick with the scent of pine, and high in the trees, the spike frogs thrummed their drone-like song. Poppy picked at the thick black glob behind her knee.

Now that they had survived the battle—the events

of the last few hours were catching up to her. The glob peeled away, leaving her skin raw and angry. A tear ran down her cheek and she wiped it away angrily. They kept coming, and she let out a broken sob.

"Poppy?" Mack sat up.

"Are you hurt?" Nula put a hand on her back.

"She took Dog! Dog's gone!" Nula snatched her hand back as Poppy buried her forehead into her knees and wept. "We could have died! I could have gotten all of us killed. Oh, Dog!"

Mack's hand settled on her shoulder. "I'm so sorry, Pop. I'm so sorry. I should have tried harder. I should have grabbed them sooner. I—I could almost break that web. If I had—"

"No, Mack." Poppy sniffed, wiping her face on her sleeve. "There's nothing you could have done. If I had just listened to you in the first place—" She choked back another wave of tears.

"Listen, Poppy." Mack's voice was strained. "I know it's not much . . . but they'll take really good care of Dog. They'll be safe—until we can figure out how to get them back."

Poppy blew out a deep breath and stood up. "You're right. And we have to find Mom and Dad. Do you think the Faery Queen might be right about them being in the Hollows?"

"Yes," Nula said.

"Maybe," Mack drew out at the same time.

"Why would someone take them? Why would they do that?" *I would be so scared if it was me.* Poppy tried to imagine her parents scared, then shook the thought away. It made her nauseous.

She flashed on the image of Governor Gale's sneering expression as he loomed over her in town. Her memory shifted back years, and she heard his voice from where she had stood listening behind the kitchen door. "One day, you won't be so smug," he'd said. "One day someone will teach you a lesson."

She wiped her face again and met Mack's gaze. "The governor really doesn't like us," she admitted. "But he's still a human being. And he's still the governor. I don't think he'd let people get away with violence. And even if he doesn't want to help my parents . . . or me, he won't allow people to break the law in Strange Hollow, right?"

"The part I don't understand," Mack said, ignoring her question, "is, why would humans take your parents in the first place. What's the point?"

"'Cause it's their fault," Nula said.

Both Mack and Poppy stared at her. Poppy pressed her lips tight. "What do you mean—"

"I mean, that's not what *I* think," the pooka assured her. "But I'd bet my own blood that it's what they think in the Hollows. Humans are always looking for someone to blame, and people in Strange Hollow think your parents are in league with the Grimwood, right? That they're spies, or that they have something to do with the maledictions taking people? Well, maybe they decided to do something about it."

Mack's face fell. "Sounds plausible to me, Poppy."

Poppy frowned. "Well, there *have* been a lot of maledictions lately."

"More than usual?" Nula asked.

"Yes—I think so. And they did put up all those new wards," Poppy admitted. "But the governor is brand-new!" She threw her hands up. "And he keeps telling people he's going to 'make the woods fair.' Blaming the people trying to help is *not* fair!"

Mack leaned against a tree. "My mom says that *fair* is like *beauty*. Just depends who's judging."

Nula's face was sad. "They're just afraid. Fear turns all the other feelings into hate."

Poppy began to pace. "So . . . maybe we just need to try and prove to them that my parents are on their side."

Mack grimaced. "I mean, your parents have been telling them that for years. Why would they believe us?"

They fell silent again. After a minute Poppy asked, "Well then, what about that other stuff the Faery Queen said, the stuff about the maledictions being connected to the Holly Oak? If that's true, we could—"

Nula sniffed. "Like I said, faeries don't lie."

Mack snorted. "Yeah, but you can bet there's more to the story."

The story! The promise of Prudence Barebone! Poppy gasped. "I know what to do."

Despite all of them being jumpy and Mack threatening to set a circle for the night after every few steps, they all followed the sound of the river. It didn't take very long, but even so, it was all-the-way dark by the time they found another dock. Poppy wondered if there was a limit to how many times you could ride with the Boatman before he shoved you off the boat. She grimaced, glad that at least Jute had given her plenty of coins. It hadn't gotten any less scary, but cutting through the water under the storm of the Boatman's laughter had taken on a dreamlike, déjà-vu quality. She thought he might finally speak when he noticed that Dog was gone . . . but his eyes only flashed, and his laughter carried a cruel edge that she hadn't noticed before.

Poppy needed to go to the Holly Oak one last time— and this time she was going to get some real answers. She just hoped the Oak could be trusted. She wanted the Holly Oak to give a merry laugh and tell them that the Faery Queen could lie just like anyone else . . . and that of course she wasn't behind the maledictions. If it turned out to be true, her parents wouldn't be the only ones in trouble. Regardless, Poppy knew in her gut that somehow Prudence's promise and the disappearance of her parents were connected. She just couldn't see how yet.

The moon had risen by the time they were safely on the island. Its thin crescent had a gleam sharp as any knife's. The three of them stared at the stairs curling all the way up the Holly Oak. Nula nudged her, which Poppy took to mean that the pooka was ready for another dash up the stairs, if such was deemed necessary. She wasn't sure how it had happened, or when exactly, but the pooka had become someone Poppy could count on . . . someone she *did* count on—a friend. Poppy smiled at her. For just a second, with Mack standing nearby too, she had the sense that with the three of them together they might be able to fix things.

The sense of comfort was fleeting—gone as soon as they passed by the pavilions, which were quiet and empty. Poppy wondered if the creatures of the wood sensed something ominous in the air the way she did—a heavy foreboding that shifted like fog. Maybe the folk were all just busy with other things, but maybe they were hunkered down in their dens and nests and villages, waiting for the feeling to pass. She wondered where Jute was, and if he was okay.

Even without running, Poppy was out of breath by the time they reached the double doors to the Holly Oak's chamber. She knocked, and as they waited for the doors to open, Poppy took a moment to really look around. Huge lanterns hung to either side of the doors and cast a warm glow over the wide platform, which wrapped around most of the tree. Twisted limbs grew up into a thick banister along the edge. From there, Poppy could see out over the dark shapes of the whole forest. It stretched for miles in every direction—a sea of dark treetops. Pools of shadow marked the thorn groves.

She could just make out the line of the Grimwood to the north where it broke against the edge of Strange Hollow like a wave, and to the east where it met Dark Hollow, and west to Golden Hollow. To the south, where Trader's Hollow marked the only passage through the fog, she could only see the dark rustling of the trees. Here and there, moonlight danced like sparks on the Veena river as it wound its way through the wood. There was no telling where it started, but it ended at the Alcyon. Beyond it all— past the edges of the Grimwood and past the Hollows, the fog rose, glowing softly, blocking her view of everything beyond except the sky.

A shiver ran down her back as she recalled what the Holly Oak had said about the fog—that it was a being with a will of its own. It protected the magic of the Grimwood from the outside world, holding the wood and the Hollows together, for better or for worse.

The double doors were closed this time—and interesting. She hadn't noticed—the images carved into the warm wood of each of the panels. One panel was carved with the likeness of the Holly Oak leaning from her trunk. In front of her on the second panel, stood a small, thin woman. They reached out to each other as if they were about to shake hands, but the woman had a knife in her other hand. All manner of creatures stood around the Holly Oak, and behind the woman, a gathering of people.

"Ready?" Mack asked.

Poppy gave a stiff nod, but continued to stand still in front of the doors. The image looked familiar.

"Poppy?"

With a jolt she realized it was the same picture in the book Nula had taken. It was a picture of the promise of Prudence Barebone. A shiver ran down her back as she raised a fist to knock again, but this time, before her hand could connect, the doors swung open on their own.

The Holly Oak was waiting—and she didn't look happy. She leaned from the tree at the end of the long chamber, her brown fingers gripping the bark as though she would pull herself out of the trunk altogether.

Poppy was glad Mack and Nula were at her back. They made her brave.

The Holly Oak made a rustling sound. "Where is my book?"

Poppy's heart shot into her throat.

"Book?" Nula squeaked.

"My book—the one I gave you. I know you opened it. I know you read it."

Nula laughed a triumphant "Ha!" She turned to Poppy. "See! I told you! I *told* you the book glittered at me! The Holly Oak wanted me to take it!"

"What?" Mack said, looking from Poppy to Nula and back again. "You—she took that? You *took* that . . . from the *Holly Oak*?!"

Nula looked smug. "No. She *gave* it to me."

Despite herself, Poppy couldn't help asking the first question that popped into her head. "How did you know we read it?"

"I know . . . because I can speak of it."

"The geis is lifted," Mack muttered under his breath. "She couldn't tell us about it, but now that we figured it out ourselves . . ."

"She can," Poppy finished. "So, she really did want Nula to take that book. Oh, that's clever."

"Promises," intoned the tree in words that rang against the soft walls of the chamber. "Promises are made of stone."

Poppy nudged Mack. "I didn't get a chance to tell either of you—what with Dog, and the spiders and everything—I, uh . . . Remember that conversation I had with the witch?"

Nula shook her head. "You mean the old lady you imagined after we almost got eaten by kelpies? That witch?"

Poppy narrowed her eyes at Nula, but nodded. "I didn't imagine it . . . but yeah, her."

"The Grimwood has way too many witches if you ask me." Mack grimaced. "They're unpredictable—slippery as eels in butter."

Poppy hurried on. "Well . . . she told me a story."

Mack had stiffened at her side. "What story?"

Poppy's eyes returned to the Oak. She was swaying a little, almost like she was dancing . . . or in pain.

"Let me see that book, Nula."

The Oak rustled, but her stern expression didn't change as Nula fished the strange little book out of her pocket, and handed it over.

The inklings were beginning to dissipate back into their blobs, but they still had enough form for Poppy to see some of it without cutting her finger again. She turned to the page with the image of the Oak surrounded by clasped hands. She ran her fingers over the page. "The witch said the thorn trees were the Holly Oak's too. I just . . . I didn't make the connection." She turned to Mack.

The Holly Oak pressed her lips together. "All the trees are mine. I told you this."

"What connection?" Mack asked.

"To the maledictions. Like the Faery Queen said." Poppy narrowed her eyes at the Oak. "You left that out. You didn't tell us the maledictions are yours too!"

The Holly Oak didn't speak, but a streak of black rolled over her face. Poppy took that for confirmation.

Mack took Poppy's arm, lowering his voice. "If the

maledictions are truly hers, then she . . . she kills people, Poppy!"

Nula glued herself to Poppy's other side.

"Wait. Listen," Poppy said. She turned away from the Oak so the three of them faced one another in a huddle. "I admit, if it's not just the thorn trees that belong to her and it's the maledictions too, it . . . doesn't look good. But Nula, she gave you the book—or drew your attention to it. That means she wanted us to know about Prudence Barebone. And we know she's been under a geis—unable to tell us everything. Mack, you're the one that said there had to be more to this story, right? The Faery Queen told us the truth, but only part of it."

She spun to the tree. "I want the whole truth—all of it."

The Holly Oak gave Poppy a tight smile. Her dark eyes sparkled—with excitement or anger, Poppy couldn't be sure.

"I cannot tell you what you don't already know, Pandora Sunshine. Not about this."

"Okay, then . . . we'll figure it out. All you have to do is nod when we get it right. Okay?"

The tree studied Poppy as another streak of black furrowed her brow. It cleared and she smiled. "I was right to trust in you, girl. You are as clever as your parents said."

Poppy's cheeks grew hot. She cleared her throat. "You and Prudence Barebone struck a bargain—made a promise."

The tree looked away.

"Prudence wanted to keep the peace, but she wanted more than that . . . didn't she?"

The Holly Oak's expression turned thoughtful. "Yes," she said softly. "Much more."

Nula clutched the tuft of her tail in her hands. "So, keeping the peace . . . that means any creature with ill intent stays out of the Hollows, and the people don't try to cut down the forest. No one gets hurt? That sort of thing?"

Poppy nodded, but Mack shook his head. "But maledictions do hurt people." He lowered his voice. "So . . . is the Oak breaking her promise?"

"Depends how it was worded, I guess." Nula chewed the tip of her tail thoughtfully. "Maybe they said no one could *attack* the Hollows or the wood. Maledictions don't attack."

Poppy considered. "I mean, I don't know if maledictions are . . . alive exactly? But whether they are or not, we know that their magic puts people in a trance. It doesn't *hurt* them. Then the pickers lead them into the wood— they don't hurt anyone themselves either. Each piece by itself is harmless." She turned to the tree. "So, you're not breaking the promise . . . it's more like a trick . . . a series of loopholes."

The Holly Oak's honey gold cheeks grew pink, but she said nothing to defend herself. Her dress of leaves rustled as she shifted uncomfortably.

"Harmless until they get to the thorn trees," Mack amended.

"Right," Poppy acknowledged. "The thorn trees kill people."

"More than just people," Nula objected. "They kill anything they can get their . . . uh, hands on."

Poppy spun to the tree again, who was just waiting . . . her expression shifting between frustration and what Poppy thought might be pride. "But why would you allow that?" she asked.

They fell silent.

"Every creature must be true to its nature." The Holly Oak held out her palms.

Nula shook her head. "But that's not a reason to go to all that trouble. Sure, thorn trees gotta eat. I can see that. But that's different from seeding maledictions that lure people from Poppy's Hollow . . . or some other Hollow."

Poppy met the Holly Oak's bright eyes. "She's right, isn't she?"

The Holly Oak nodded.

"But you can't tell us why."

She shook her head.

"But it is you, isn't it—the maledictions? They're part of your magic."

The Holly Oak looked down to where her fingers twisted against her leafy gown and gave a stiff nod. "It is."

Beside her, Nula breathed in sharply. The pooka had paled to a light blue.

"What's wrong?" Poppy asked.

Nula's voice was so quiet, Poppy had to lean toward her to hear.

"Maybe . . . she had to," Nula choked. "Maybe there was something that she wanted so much—"

"Who? The Oak?" Mack scoffed.

"Or Prudence!" Poppy gasped. "The witch *said* she was greedy. Clever and greedy, but that she wasn't selfish about it. Everyone benefited . . . something like that."

"That's not what I meant," Nula protested.

"Benefited how?" Mack asked.

"What do people in the Hollows have that other people don't?"

"The fog? The wood?"

Poppy shook her head. "I guess, but what else?"

"You don't get sick?"

"That's right . . . " Poppy's heartbeat quickened. "We don't get sick. Plus, we have really long lives." Everything stilled. "Long life," Poppy said, suddenly certain. "The witch said Prudence asked for long life. People in the Hollows . . . live."

Poppy spun to the Holly Oak. "Prudence was afraid of dying!"

"What did I tell you." Nula gave a grim nod. "Fear turns everything rotten. And she *had* to bargain for a long life for everyone. She didn't want to be alone without her family . . . and friends." Nula's voice hitched.

"And magic has a cost." Mack met Poppy's eyes, his face stricken.

Poppy felt the blood drain from her face. "The peace was free, because it was equal. But when Prudence bargained for long life, the maledictions were the cost." Bile rose in her throat. She'd never been so certain of anything. "Maledictions are the price of our extra years. Did they know? Did the people know? Did they *agree* to that?"

The black streaks had stopped writhing over the Holly Oak's warm brown skin. She looked . . . worn. Still beautiful, but older, as though the truth exhausted her. "They—"

Nula groaned. "They probably didn't discuss the specifics. They just saw those extra years . . . and all the beautiful outfits, and all the food. How could they say no?"

Poppy cocked her head at Nula, then turned back to the tree. "What were you going to say?" she asked.

"Wait," Nula said. "I can't stand it anymore! I need to . . ." Nula swallowed. "I have to tell you guys something. Right now. I need . . . I need you to understand."

"Okay, but—"

Mack shook his head at Poppy. "Wait," he said, his brows all bunched up in their worried way, as he turned to Nula.

She was still talking. "You should see how happy everyone is at the dances. It's not like it looked with all the spiders and . . . and the grouchiness."

Grouchiness? Mack and Poppy exchanged confused looks.

Nula swallowed again and looked away. "No one ever dances alone, you know. You always have someone by your side in the faery court. You never have to . . . be alone." She closed her eyes and a blue tear rolled down her cheek. "Oh, the dances," she sighed.

Mack reached out and wrapped his fingers around Poppy's wrist as if he needed a tether. "I don't think we're talking about Prudence Barebone anymore, Poppy."

"Don't you see?" Nula asked, turning her face to meet Poppy's perplexed expression. "If the faeries accepted me . . . really accepted me, that meant I could finally be someone worthy . . . someone who deserved friends."

The pooka's face had flushed a deep blue. She stared down at her lap. "I—I'm so sorry, Poppy. I'm really, really sorry."

Poppy reached out to take her friend's hand, but Nula took a step back. "Nula! What's going on? Sorry for what?"

Mack released Poppy's wrist.

"I . . . I didn't realize," Nula went on. "I didn't think about the *true* cost and . . . now I've ruined everything and I—I can't even fix it! But I'm not under a geis, like the Holly Oak was . . . I have to at least *try* and explain."

"Nula." Mack stepped closer. "What are you trying to tell us?"

"Please, don't come any closer, Mack. If you two try

and make me feel better, I might change my mind and I can't change my mind, because *you're* my friends— not them. Not! Them!" Tears were pouring down Nula's face, but she lifted her chin and met Poppy's startled eyes.

"They promised," she hiccupped. "They promised I could be one of them—part of the faery court for real. They had heard about your cerberus and—" She stopped and held out her palms, pleading.

All at once Poppy's entire body went cold, as if she had fallen through ice. "You . . . you *brought* us to the faeries . . . because they wanted Dog?" She couldn't breathe. "You *traded* Dog to join the Fae?"

"But I don't want that anymore, Poppy! They're terrible! Mack! Please! I didn't know what it would be like!" She was backing up now.

"What *what* would be like?" Mack's voice had turned gentle, and Poppy stared at him and then at Nula, as the cold running through her slowly began to burn. Dog was gone because Nula had betrayed them. The pooka had pretended to be their friend, but it was a lie.

Nula dropped her face into her hands and wept. "Having friends," she wailed. "I didn't know what it would be like—having real friends."

There was the space of a single breath, before the fire in Poppy ignited. "GET OUT OF HERE!" she screamed, charging toward the pooka with her fingers like claws.

Mack grabbed Poppy, holding her back. "Go, Nula," he said.

"I'm sorry," Nula sobbed, and *poofed* into a moth—disappearing up into the ceiling.

Stillness followed Nula's departure. Poppy could hear the blood pounding in her ears.

The Holly Oak broke the silence. "I too am sorry, Poppy Sunshine," she rumbled behind her. "I warned Prudence there would be a cost. The magic it takes to lengthen your lives is great—but even I did not realize how deep, and how dark, that cost would grow."

"Thank you for the truth," Mack managed to say, stumbling as he tried to steer Poppy toward the door.

Poppy couldn't answer. Her chest was hollow. She couldn't see through the thick tears that watered her feet. Mack moved her toward the exit, while Poppy wept as if she could patch up the holes in her heart by filling them with tears.

Everything hurt.

Dog was gone. Nula wasn't her friend at all. She was her enemy. Her parents were trapped somewhere, and she didn't know if she would ever find them. Maybe they weren't alive at all. She had been so sure before. Now, she wasn't sure of anything.

CHAPTER TWENTY-TWO

There was only the cold glow of moonlight to illuminate their way as Mack led Poppy past the pavilions—where only a few creatures milled around—and down to the shore to set up camp for the night. They moved as if they shared a single mind, not speaking a word. Poppy gathered windfall wood, while Mack found a hearthstone and started a small fire. The Alcyon lapped at the shore. The air was crisp and smelled of salt water and ripe blackberries.

Once they were settled, Mack walked back up to the pavilions and got them some dinner. It was roasted meat—hard to say what—in a blackberry sauce, which explained the smell in the air. There were potatoes too, and bitter greens. Poppy picked at her food and tried not to think about her parents, or Nula, or Dog.

She tried not to think about anything. A sharp pain lanced through her chest, and she forced her thoughts to Prudence Barebone and the rhymes of the Grimwood. Everything she had learned tied itself in knots as she tried to make sense of it.

She gave up.

She felt hollowed out. She didn't want to miss Nula, but she did, and it was infuriating. She hoped her parents were okay. She hoped they were planning an escape. She hoped they knew she would try to find them, no matter how long it took.

The sea washed against the cobbled shore throughout the night, but despite its soft song, Poppy still couldn't sleep. She lay awake, staring into the Holly Oak's branches, thinking of everything she'd lost.

When she dozed off at last, her sleep was full of dreams. Images of Dog filled her head. Memories of their soft fur—and the way they would bowl her over each time she came home. She dreamed of Two's eyes, and Brutus's bravery, and Eta . . . sweet Eta, with all her wise looks.

She dreamed that her mother was calling for her. She dreamed of her father apologizing—asking for forgiveness, but she wasn't sure for what, because his words were jumbled and foggy. Even Nula made an appearance. Poppy dreamed that she woke up to find the pooka staring down at her from the tree branches above them. She was crying, and her blue tears dripped down on Poppy's head.

When she opened her eyes for real, there were streaks of pale blue through the branches above her, but there was no one there. Just the breeze rattling the Holly Oak's leaves, and beyond them, the fading stars.

Mack sat with his back against a boulder. She got up

and moved to sit next to him. When the sun finally rose, he had dozed off again, even though he was still sitting up. They had a long way to go to get home. And they still needed to come up with a plan to get her parents back.

The sharp ache raced back in and she shoved all her thoughts deep, far into the shadows of her mind where she wouldn't have to look at them. Instead, she allowed the only thought that mattered to simmer where she could feel the heat of it, and remember. She would get them back. Somehow, she would get her parents back. And then she'd find a way to save Dog.

At the end of the dock, she rang the bell—felt its tolling roll over her body, but she didn't even look up as she dropped the coins in the Boatman's hand. She stepped in and sat in the floor of the boat with her eyes closed, and didn't once bother to wonder which route he had chosen for them this time.

Stumbling back onto the broken-down dock where they had started made Poppy want to cry again—but she had no tears left. The last time she had been here, they had all been together. Mack pointed out some berry bushes that were safe, and they gorged until their stomachs ached. Poppy took out the last of the bread and cheese from the market, too.

"Mack?"

"Hm?"

"Are you sure you want to do this?"

He made a face. "Do what?"

"Help me. Are you sure you don't want to go home—see your family?"

Mack frowned. "I'm sure."

"But—"

"No, Poppy. I'm sure." He paused. "Unless you don't want my help?"

"No! It's not that."

He started walking. "It's not your fault, you know."

"What?"

"It's not your fault—about Dog. And I didn't know about Nula either."

"Maybe you didn't know, but you had a feeling. You said you weren't sure we should trust her."

He grunted. "I did—say that. But that was before we really knew Nula. And . . . and maybe I said it because I was being selfish, wanting to keep your friendship all to myself."

Poppy's eyes jerked to his, and he laughed. "But I was wrong, okay?"

"Well, we both know if I had listened to you, Dog would still be here."

"No. I was wrong about that too . . . about always being so cautious." He stopped walking and turned to face her. "Rules are important—caution too. We need them." He looked down at his feet and Poppy watched with amusement as he dug his toes down into the soil.

"But just being careful all the time doesn't always keep us safe," Mack admitted wryly. "Sometimes you have to take chances."

Poppy swallowed and reached out to squeeze his hand. They stood that way a moment, then the quiet got strange and she let go.

"Anyway." Mack muttered as they started walking again. "You heard Nula. The Faery Queen already knew about Dog. She had her eye on them from the start—before you ever set foot in the forest. She would have found a way to get them."

"You really think so?"

"I really do."

Her throat tightened. "If we can believe anything Nula said at all! Why did she lie to us? All that time! Why didn't she just tell us? I hope I never—"

But before Poppy had finished her sentence, Nula herself stepped out from behind a tree.

She didn't look at Poppy, but her eyes flicked briefly to Mack. Her voice was quiet. "Hi," she said.

"Are you *following* us?" Poppy cried.

The wood seemed to grow still around them, listening.

Mack shifted his feet. "Hi, Nula," he said.

Poppy glared. "What do you want?"

Nula's hands twisted in front of her. "I—I want to make it up."

278

"Make it up?" Poppy's voice was high and tight. "Make it up? Make up that the Faery Queen took my Dog?"

A blue flush had risen in Nula's cheeks. Her tufted ears lay flat, hidden in her thick brown hair. "I'm sorry," she pleaded. "I thought . . . I thought I belonged with them . . . the faeries, I mean. I thought—" She looked up, and her huge gold eyes met Poppy's. "I didn't think *enough* about what it would cost. But I was wrong, Poppy. I don't belong with the Fae. I don't . . . I don't even want to be anywhere near them." Her brows knit together making her face fierce. "They're terrible."

For a moment Poppy couldn't speak. Then she remembered the moment Brutus leaped for the bone— the moment Eta gave her plaintive cry, and rage washed over her. "She TOOK Dog, Nula! She—" Poppy's throat closed. She swallowed, her voice dropping to a threatening whisper. "You lied to us—you were never our friend. You tricked us."

Poppy fought the urge to physically attack Nula—to hurt her the way she was hurting. Instead, she let out a roar that made Nula and Mack both jump, then stormed past them, her hands fisted at her sides. "I never want to see you again! Don't ever come back!"

She was a fair distance ahead when she realized Mack wasn't with her. She spun around with his name on her lips, and froze. He was standing across the path from Nula, saying something. Nula was nodding.

"Mack!" she shouted. He scowled at her, patted Nula's arm, then turned slowly and walked away from her.

When he caught up, Poppy folded her arms. "Good! I'm glad she's gone. Why are you even talking to her? Dog's gone because of her."

Mack arched one eyebrow. "No. Not really."

"What do you mean, *not really*. If it wasn't for her . . ."

"I told you, Pop. The Faery Queen would have found a way. She just used Nula—because she was lonely and because she knew they had something Nula wanted."

"Right." She scoffed. "They had something she wanted . . . like what? Fancy parties and pretty outfits?"

Mack raised an eyebrow. "That's not what she wanted, Poppy. She wanted to be a part of something—and she thought it would, I don't know, make her better?"

"Well, too bad! She's not better! And now she's alone again!"

"She's a lot like you, Pop."

"What? How can you even say that right now?"

Mack didn't answer but considered her for a moment. "Anger is like acid."

"What? What's that supposed to mean?"

Mack leaned against a tree. "That's what Ma tells me when I get angry. She says, anger is like acid. It takes all the shine off things, and eats at what's underneath. She says we should treat it like sour milk."

Poppy turned around, her curiosity getting the better of her. "Sour . . . milk?"

"Yeah."

Poppy waited for him to explain.

He didn't.

"Okay, fine. How do you treat anger like sour milk?"

He grinned at her. "I knew you couldn't stand not knowing." He pushed himself away from the tree. "You treat anger like sour milk by pouring it out. Getting rid of it."

"I'd like to pour sour milk *on* her."

He pulled a face. "I think you just did."

"Seriously, Mack. Don't I have a right to be angry?"

"Of course! I'm angry too. Just . . . not at Nula. Nula didn't take Dog. She knows that lying to us was wrong . . . you can see that she feels it."

Poppy crossed her arms. "I think your mom's wrong, Mack. Anger's not like sour milk. Anger is a reminder."

"A reminder of what?" he asked, catching up with her.

"A reminder of who to let close, and who to stay away from. A reminder that someone caused you pain."

"But then . . . don't you ever forgive someone?"

She frowned at him. "I don't know if I can. I just know I want to yell at her more and that I'm not going to give up being angry until I'm good and done being angry."

They fell silent for a while. A woodpecker knocked against a tree in the distance. Poppy listened to the sound of their breathing as they hurried toward her house.

Mack nose-sighed, next to her. "Well, it looks like

there's a storm rolling in, and at least there will be something in your pantry besides berries, tentaculars, and stale bread."

She rubbed her hands together. "We'll eat. And then we'll make a plan to get my parents. For real this time."

CHAPTER TWENTY-THREE

Poppy wasn't sure what she'd been expecting when they first opened the front door—using the spare key hidden in the toad hole under the edge of the house—but she had been expecting *something*. Leaving home and breaking her blood ward to wander the Grimwood should have made her different. Really different. The kind of different you could see all over the place.

Maybe she had expected to feel stronger. Or perhaps she had expected to be bigger than she used to be . . . though bigger in what way, she wasn't sure. At least she had expected to be bigger than all the things that she had always needed but never had.

She was a lot more sad and angry, but Poppy didn't *feel* any different—not really. She had pushed open the door to her house and stepped through into the hall— looked at the wall full of all her lonely portraits and . . . just felt like herself.

She *knew* more. That was certain. And she'd lost more too. But she was still just Poppy.

The quiet of the house was salt in a fresh wound. There was no Dog to greet her with great galumphing leaps. Jute had promised he would return, but she didn't know when, and without him worrying over her, the homecoming didn't feel real. And—though she should have been used to it by now—there were no parents puttering in the lab up on the third floor or slinking up the stairs from the kitchen with bed head and snacks.

It was home, but at the same time it wasn't. And she was Poppy . . . but at the same time she wasn't. She was something in between who she used to be, and who she was supposed to become—the Poppy she had expected. It made her head spin.

Everything was still and empty, except for the dust motes floating through sunbeams, and the creak of the floor. Those were familiar. Her portraits stared back at her, and they all looked younger than she remembered. That was different. She had only been gone a few days, but she felt older.

"Are you okay?" Mack asked.

She was about to answer him with a shrug and a nod, but she paused, the truth springing to her lips before her brain could hide the words. "I'm not sure," she said.

They stood, looking at her portraits, until at last Poppy asked, "Do I . . . *seem* different to you?"

Mack scratched his head. "Different—how?"

"I don't know . . . just . . . different."

"You mean, from going into the Grimwood?"

"Yeah. I mean, shouldn't I be like—" She grimaced. "I don't know. Shouldn't I be different, or—just—bigger or something?"

"Bigger? Humans don't usually grow that fast . . . do they? I mean elves have big unexpected growth surges, and so do giants. Actually, lots of the wood folk—"

"That's not what I meant."

"Well, do you *feel* different?" Mack asked.

"No. Maybe. I don't know."

Mack shrugged. "Well, when I first started coming to your house—"

"Yeah. Did you feel different when you left the wood?"

"Sort of. I did, but—it wasn't really that I felt different in myself. It was weirder than that. It was more like a door that I didn't know was there suddenly opened."

"A door . . . *in* you?"

"Yeah. Maybe. Or in the world."

"I mean, a door did open. Our door."

"Ha. Ha. Very funny. But—it really was like that, Poppy. It was like there was a door I didn't know was there, and it opened, and there was more for me . . . and more *of* me . . . than I had imagined."

"More . . . What do you mean more? Like what?"

He grimaced. "Like, for me it was that you're my friend, and you're a human, and you know—"

"And you have a human grandfather, that you never got to meet."

"Yeah, so getting to know you was like getting to know part of myself too. Plus, there was mac and cheese. I didn't expect to like it, but then I did—a lot. And it made me wonder if my grandpa liked it too, you know?"

Poppy pondered this for a minute until it started to make her head ache almost as much as her heart. "Let's eat," she said at last, and Mack was halfway across the hall before she'd finished the sentence.

The kitchen was dark and still. It set Poppy's teeth on edge. The house had always felt lonely to her, but she hadn't realized just how full it had truly been—with Jute's fussing and Dog's galumphing around. Even her parents had held space somehow. They had a presence in the house despite their frequent absence. She just hadn't realized it.

Now the house felt cold, as though it was a forgotten creature crouching in a dark corner waiting for something. But at least it was dry inside, while out in the meadow, a storm had rolled in. The day had gone dark. Rain poured out of the sky as if it would flood the world. It drummed against the porch and the roof, as thunder rolled over the Hollows.

Poppy packed their backpacks full of whatever food they could find left, and a few more supplies—mostly salt and iron, just in case, while Mack lit the stove and made hot chocolate.

Poppy pulled the front door open to let a little more light and fresh air into the gloom, and they sat on the floor looking out as they held their steaming cups and watched the storm roll across the meadow.

Despite the chill at her back, there was something comfortable about it that made Poppy think again of Jute. She wondered when he would be home. He'd said he would stay to talk with the Oak before he returned, but surely he would be back soon.

She remembered too what Jute had told her after he'd saved their lives from the kelpies—that contentment is just a place that you pass through, but that it would grow as familiar as an old friend. She still wasn't exactly sure what he meant, but watching the rain pass with Mack at her side sipping his cocoa, she thought maybe she might get it a little. She tried not to laugh as Mack tried to suck the steam off the top of his cup and blow it out again.

She had never been more grateful for Jute's well-stocked pantry. He had left a lovely loaf of fresh homemade bread and a hunk of cheese. Poppy put out some olives, black walnuts, fresh tomato slices, and some smoked fish. It was a veritable feast.

The food made her body feel better, but it couldn't take the ache from her heart, or the sting from her pride. Not only had she still not found her parents, she'd lost her Dog—and a friend. Her heart just ached and ached, like a tide, ebbing and flowing with every breath. *Like pieces of me got carved out.*

The rain had slowed to heavy drops by the time they had stuffed themselves full. Poppy leaned back with a sigh.

"Now what?" Mack asked.

"Now we find the governor and ask him what he knows."

"Will he talk to you?"

"It's a market day," she began. "There's a good chance he'll be there somewhere. That's where we'll start."

Mack stepped closer. "I'm coming with you."

"Mack . . . you can't."

Mack licked his lips. "Listen, Poppy. It's true I don't want you to go by yourself. But mostly I just want to see it. I want to see a human town, even if it's nothing like the cities outside the fog." He paused and lifted his copper eyes to hers. "I'm tired of waiting too."

His ears began to redden. "I want to see how different other humans are from . . . from you."

Poppy felt her own cheeks get warm. "But Mack, you could get caught."

He grinned. "I'll go in disguise."

Her mouth fell open. "Disguised as what?"

"An old lady." Mack rose from the kitchen table and grabbed Dog's old blanket that lay folded neatly on the bench along the wall, wrapping it over his head and shoulders, hunching over. He stooped low and mimed holding a walking stick, hobbling across the kitchen. Poppy tried not to laugh, but couldn't help herself. Even at the worst of times, Mack could make her smile.

"Wait there," she managed to say and ran for the stairs, climbing two at a time. At the very back of her mother's closet was a dress that had belonged to her grandmother—hand sewn. It was dark brown, with light blue flowers all over it, and giant patches for pockets. She nearly fell down the stairs, running back down to give it to Mack. "Put this on," she panted.

He squinted a little, but didn't argue, disappearing into the living room for a little privacy. When he returned, Poppy barked a laugh, and circled him.

"You'll have to wear shoes. No respectable old woman would walk through the market barefoot."

He pulled a face. "Fine."

"These might work." She ran to the front hall and reached into the shadows under the bench to pull out Jute's dark green ankle-high galoshes.

Mack pulled a face, reaching for them uncertainly. Poppy held her breath as he worked to jam his feet inside.

"How can you hear anything with these things on?" he asked, gazing around as if he needed to get his bearings.

"Well . . . humans don't hear the way elves do. We can't feel sounds."

"So weird." He stood up and shot her a grin. "Hope I

can walk." He took a few tentative steps, rocking back and forth like a tipping ship.

"They're perfect!" Poppy couldn't remember when she'd seen Mack looking so happy.

"You'll have to keep your eyes down. You know that."

He nodded. "Yeah. I'll try."

"And tuck your hands into your sleeves. They don't look old."

He followed her instructions as Poppy jammed more food into her backpack—including some of Jute's elderberry jam that she found at the very back of the pantry. Then they filled their canteens at the pump over the sink and checked the supply cupboard for anything else useful. The only thing in there was a dusty cartridge of nets. She took it, but for all she knew the nets were full of holes.

"Ready?" she asked, wishing again that Dog was by her side—or even that Jute was there to argue with.

"As I'm going to get," Mack proclaimed with a smile that could have lit a room.

"What are you so smiley about?"

His grin widened. "I can't believe I finally get to see Strange Hollow."

Poppy laughed. "Hope you're not disappointed." Her expression grew serious. "We're going to head straight down into the market. I'll keep watch for the governor, but we head for Beth at the far edge of the square."

"I'll follow you." Mack grinned.

They dragged an old dead branch out from under one of the little apple trees at the side of the house, and broke it into a reasonable walking stick for Mack.

"With Jute's galoshes on, I'm going to need it for real by the time we get down the hill," he griped.

"You'll be fine." Poppy patted his back. "Just keep your head down, and don't say anything. You'll just be my little granny, visiting from . . ."

"Trader's Hollow."

"Yeah, from Trader's Hollow, way on the other side of the Grimwood."

The rainstorm had passed and they walked in companionable silence, each drawn into their own thoughts. Bees buzzed carefully through the wet wildflowers as they walked. The sky still harbored a few clouds, but the blue was bright and gaining strength. Even the standing stones gleamed in the storm light.

It was a beautiful day—a beautiful afternoon for a rescue.

"Mack?"

"Hmmm?"

"You don't think anyone would hurt them—my parents, do you?"

His brows furrowed. "I don't know, Pop. I think it depends on who did the catching. People make bad choices when they're scared."

She swallowed. "Yeah."

Poppy listened to the swish of the tall grass and the warm beat of their feet on the soil, and tried not to think about what that might mean. They were almost at the edge of town when she turned to Mack. "Time to get into your character," she teased.

He snorted and pulled the blanket tighter over his head, stooping lower. His steps slowed.

Poppy watched him walk down the hill. The overall effect wasn't bad. He didn't exactly look like the average granny . . . but if you didn't look too closely, he could pass. She had never seen Mack wear shoes, and etched the image in her mind to think about later, but decided to keep her mouth shut. There was nothing to be gained from pointing out that he was walking like a duck with a backache. She just hoped it would be good enough.

CHAPTER TWENTY-FOUR

S trange Hollow was quiet. All the doors were shut. The whole town felt abandoned, as though the breeze had picked up all the people and blown them away.

There were even more ward carvings than the last time she was in town. Several tall ones had been lifted onto roofs to look out over the town. And there were signs posted that announced a dusk curfew. No one was to be out after dark.

"Whoa," Mack said, his eyes wide. "Is it always like this . . . empty? Is this . . . a human thing?"

The hair along Poppy's neck slowly rose. "No," she admitted with a shiver. "It isn't."

"Listen," Mack hissed and leaned forward on his staff. Voices—no—*a* voice, drifted over the houses and through the alleys from the market square.

They quickened their steps and turned the corner.

To find the whole town.

The crowd was packed into the square, shoulder to shoulder, listening.

Governor Gale stood on a makeshift platform made of crates, flanked by a handful of men that Poppy didn't recognize.

"The Hollows are the future! The fog will shelter us from the outside, but for too long we have shared this air and the sacred waters of the Veena with monsters!"

A roar went up.

Poppy and Mack edged their way around the outside of the crowd. Mr. Talon, the innkeeper, was standing in the door of the inn. His eyes narrowed at them as they passed. "Keep moving," he said under his breath. "We don't need your kind here."

Poppy's heart skipped a beat. Was he talking to Mack?

"My kind?" Mack repeated, raising his voice and adding a quaver. "What do you mean? I'm just an old woman."

"We don't need *spies* for the wood." His gaze sharpened on Poppy.

"Heavens." Mack spun to look over first one shoulder, then the other. "Spies! Where?"

Poppy elbowed him. "We're not spies, Mr. Talon. We're just—"

"I know about your parents, little miss—going in and out the Grimwood like it's nothing." He looked down his nose at her.

"Have you seen them recently? My parents, I mean."

"Maybe the wood finally took them. Claimed them as its own."

Poppy stood a little taller. "They're not in the wood, Mr. Talon."

"And how would a little girl like you know a thing like that?"

"I just know, that's all. Now have you seen them, or haven't you?"

"What business would they have out here, among good folk?"

Poppy swallowed. "They *are* good folks! They keep you safe. They—"

He snorted. "Some imagination. Next you'll be telling me the maledictions are harmless. Or perhaps you have some magic beans you'd like to sell me?"

"But Prudence Barebone—"

He folded his arms across his chest. "Wherever your parents are . . . if they're smart, they'll stay gone. And if *you're* smart." He leaned forward into her face, so she had to take a step back or be nose to nose with him. "If *you're* smart . . . you and your . . . granny will keep moving till you're out the other side."

Mack hunched over harder and grabbed Poppy's arm. "Come along, dear. Come along. Let's not provoke the nice man."

"Yeah," Mr. Talon snorted. "Don't provoke me."

Mack dragged her away, while Poppy shot one last venomous look at Mr. Talon. They moved around the edges of the crowd toward the front row, where the governor stood above the gathered crowd. The tall stone clock tower loomed above him. Its enormous pendulum cast a shadow that moved like a blade across the crowd with each swing, like they were all running out of time—speeding toward something that could be sensed, but never truly measured.

Mack stopped walking. "Hey, Poppy, I don't feel so good," he said with a groan.

"Why? What's the matter?" Poppy looked around, checking that no one was watching. Mack lifted his copper eyes to meet hers.

"I don't know. I feel . . . kinda sick . . . and, I don't know—funny. Maybe it's because I'm wearing shoes. My . . . my whole body keeps cramping up."

"It's . . . it's probably just nerves, Mack," Poppy said, trying to shift her concentration away from her parents. Her heart pounded just thinking of them. Were they here somewhere? Could they see her? Would they hear her if she shouted their names?

Mack grabbed her hand and held tight.

She gave it a sympathetic squeeze. "We just have to stick it out a little longer—till we get something—a clue, about where my parents are. You'll be all right . . . you've just never been around so many people, that's all."

"I . . . I don't think so, Pop."

"This is our world!" Governor Gale yelled into the air, distracting her. He was practically frothing at the mouth, shaking his fists in front of him—first one, and then the other. An angry red vein throbbed in his forehead. "Yet we're prisoners in it!"

Poppy's skin went clammy. "We'll go soon," she assured Mack. "There's no way we'll get the governor alone in this crowd anyway. I just want to hear what he's saying."

Next to her, Mack grunted and gave her a nod.

"Our security is an illusion! People can live in peace—but for how long? How long before the wood starts taking *more* people? How long until sneak attacks turn into full-fledged battles? I say, we beat them to it! I say, we start this war on our own terms! Cleanse the forest! Purify it! Master the wood, and rid ourselves of all the monsters once and for all. The time has come—and if that means a battle must be fought, so be it!"

Another roar of approval, but smaller this time. Poppy leaned against a stack of crates behind her, knocking one of the lids loose. An acrid smell filled the air.

Mack's chin shot up. "What's that smell?"

Poppy peered into the crate. "It's coming from these bottles, I think. It looks like beer or something." Poppy put a steadying hand on his arm.

Mack gave a grunt and seemed to double up, his arms shifting to wrap around his stomach.

"Are you okay?" Poppy asked. "We can go. Are you going to puke?"

"Soon!" the governor yelled. "Soon we will take the fight to the trees—and purify the wood once and for all!"

Purify—what did he mean?

"I call all of you to arms! Be here at this same time on—"

Mack let out a bellow that would have gotten the attention of the soundest sleeper.

Poppy spun to him.

He had thrown off the blanket and stretched out his arms as if welcoming a hug from the sky but his eyes were wild, and his face contorted with pain.

Poppy tried to block the crowd's view, but it was no use. Silence fell around them, everyone staring, pale and wide-eyed.

Mack cried out again, and this time, he grew.

He shot up a foot in an instant. His legs—his arms—all of him. He collapsed to the ground, out of breath and shaking his head like it was full of buzzing insects.

Poppy was at his side in seconds, but in that instant, the words "wood folk" whipped through the crowd, first soft and disbelieving, and then louder, more indignant—angry.

Without a word, Poppy wrapped Mack's arm around her shoulders and helped heft him to his feet—which were bare again. She hadn't seen what happened to Jute's garden shoes. "Get up, Mack. We've got to go. Come on. Hurry!"

Mack stumbled to his feet and they began to move out of the crowd toward the far end of town.

Behind them, voices gathered, growing louder.

They were only a few steps out of the square when they passed a dark alleyway, and a small girl with light brown skin stepped out of the shadows. A little boy with her same dark curls joined her.

"Come on." She waved them over. "This way! Follow us."

CHAPTER
TWENTY-FIVE

The children zigzagged through alleys and behind buildings, leading Poppy and Mack in a dance all around Strange Hollow, in and out of alleyways, through two deserted houses, and at last, into the edge of the meadow.

The whole time, the boy—Peter—regaled them with questions: Was Mack really an elf? What was it like? Could he hear people's thoughts? What did he eat? Were there other elves in the Grimwood? What about the pickers . . . had he ever seen one?

Poppy tried to answer, as Mack was in no condition to do so. He hadn't been kidding about wood folk having unexpected growth surges. She half dragged him along as he bumped into corners and tripped over the cobbles and his own feet. He nearly knocked her over twice, just trying to adjust to his new size.

The questions went on and on, and the girl, who introduced herself as Mags, hung on every word, watching them with sharp eyes as she turned corners and climbed over the short fences that separated people's homes.

By the time they reached the relative safety of the meadow outside Strange Hollow, Mack was a greenish shade, and Poppy was gasping for air.

She held up her hands. "Just a minute. Just a minute."

Mags stopped, placing one hand on her hip as though to say, we can stop, but I really don't see why it's necessary.

"Mack . . . are you okay?"

He gave her a little nod and took her canteen when she held it out, draining the water. "I didn't think it would be like that," he said apologetically.

"Your growth surge? Yeah. Me either."

"Sorry, Poppy."

"Don't be sorry. It wasn't your fault." She put one hand on his arm. His shoulder was a lot higher. He was taller than her now—by a lot. She looked up to meet his eyes and smirked. "Did you see their faces?"

His mouth twitched. "I imagine they were hard to miss . . . but to be honest, I didn't see much of anything."

Her smile faded and she lowered her voice. "Did you hear anything they were saying, Mack? They're planning something. The governor wants to . . . to purify the wood. That's—"

Mack's eyes had widened. "That's not good. When? How long do we have?"

A bitter taste rose in Poppy's mouth. "I don't know,"

she whispered, fighting back a thread of panic. "He didn't say. But . . . not long."

Peter, who had been hopping from one foot to the other the entire time they were standing there, suddenly launched into another round of questions.

Poppy held up her hand. "Wait. I—not that we don't appreciate your help, but . . . why are you doing this?"

Mags moved past her brother and Mack to stand right in front of Poppy. Both hands were on her hips now, and her brown eyes flashed. "You heard my brother. We have questions. Questions no one will answer."

"Questions no one *can* answer," Peter grumbled.

"Right. We know who you are. You're that Poppy girl that goes into the Grimwood."

"Are your parents really in league with the wood?" Peter's voice quavered.

"No! Of course not. It's not like that."

Mags sent Peter a smug look. "Told you. She's just a girl—like me."

Poppy had a hard time believing that Mags was *just* anything.

Mags pinned Poppy with her eyes. "When we saw your friend was sick . . ." She tipped her chin at Mack. "We knew this was our chance." She shrugged. "I don't like to miss chances."

"I see," Poppy said, liking Mags more and more. Somehow, despite everything that had happened, she trusted these two kids. She understood them—their curiosity. It was their driving force, and as familiar as a friend.

"Where are you taking us?" Mack asked, his words slurred with exhaustion.

"Just up here, out of sight of the Hollow." Mags led them up the sloping hill along the edge of the trees, and they tried to answer Peter's questions along the way. Yes, Poppy had met Mack in the forest. Yes, there were monsters in the wood. What kinds? Well, banshees and witches and faeries. Were there other kinds too—that would eat you alive and kill you dead? Yes. There were.

"Have you ever seen a Mogwen?" Poppy asked, trying to turn the conversation around.

Peter shrugged, looking at her curiously.

She explained the Mogwen and was pleased to see Mags's eyes get a faraway look. "We saw a herd of unicorns just a couple days ago," she added, her cheeks heating.

Mags stopped in her tracks. "You did not."

Mack stretched. His face had gone back to its normal color. "We did."

"Tell us," Peter breathed.

Poppy shook her head. "No. I mean . . . not now. Listen. Something bad is coming. The governor's going to . . . *do something* to the Grimwood. Attack it somehow. And I need to find my parents."

"Find them? What do you mean?"

Poppy hesitated. "They've been taken. We think someone in the town has them."

Mags chewed her lip, processing the new information. She crossed her arms on her chest. "Fine. We'll find out," Mags proclaimed. "Meet us back here at the edge of town in two hours." Poppy and Mack exchanged a look.

"I'm not sure that's a good idea," Mack began.

"Fiddlesticks," Mags insisted in a tone Poppy was certain came from the girl's mother. "I know a few people who will help. And anyway," she continued. "You can't go back into town now. You need to wait until dark. Once the sun sets there's the curfew, and then we can all creep around all we want. And we know the town better than you do—we live there."

Mack laughed out loud. "She has a point," he said.

Poppy studied Mags, then Peter, who was back to hopping from one foot to the other. She didn't want to wait until dark. She wanted to find her parents *now* . . . but she understood the logic. "I have a feeling Mags always has a point," she muttered, and lifted her own hand to her hip. "What's the catch?"

Mags's eyes flashed. "Well, we won't do it for free."

Poppy scoffed. "Well, I haven't got any money."

Peter had blanched and was staring at his sister.

"We don't want your money," Mags scoffed back. "What we want . . . is answers."

304

Mack smiled. "Answers."

"Yes, answers. What's so funny about that?"

Poppy's heart gave a familiar twang. "Not a single thing," she said softly. "I know just how you feel."

Mack gave her a funny look. He must have seen acceptance in Poppy's face because he stopped objecting.

"We're not even sure they're in Strange Hollow," Poppy admitted. "But with whatever the governor is planning, we don't have a lot of ti—"

Mags pulled a face. "Don't worry. We're not going to waste your time. Fair trades only. Anyone who helps can ask questions."

Poppy considered. It would take her and Mack a long time to search the entire town, and it was true she wasn't nearly as familiar with it as the local kids. On the other hand—she thought of all the angry townspeople. She wasn't sure she wanted to drag more people into it, especially not kids. "How do you know you can trust them . . . the people you want to ask for help?"

This time it was Peter and Mags who exchanged a look. "Oh, I know it," Mags breathed, lifting her chin and folding her arms over her chest.

Peter's voice was the firmest Poppy had ever heard it. "Mags keeps all her promises. Everyone knows better than to break their word to her."

Hope stung her heart. With Mags and Peter's help they could find her parents faster . . . and Poppy knew what it was like to have questions. If that was their price, she would gladly pay it. *Knowledge is the enemy of fear.* Her father had written those words in the margins of his journal—more than once—as if it were a prayer, or a reminder.

Poppy held out her hand to Mags. "We'll see you here in two hours when Strange Hollow has settled for the night. But keep it quiet. If anyone follows you that shouldn't, we might have to run again, and then our deal is off."

Mags nodded solemnly. "I promise."

Mack leaned forward. "If you're lucky, our other friend will come too. She's a pooka."

Peter's jaw dropped and Mags dragged him away at a run.

Poppy glared at him. "Why did you say that? Nula's not here anymore—and we don't need her."

"Oh come on, Poppy. We need all the help we can get. And Nula wants to make up for what she's done."

"But—"

"Anyway," Mack insisted. "When I talked to Nula before . . . I told her not to give up. I told her she should stay close. She said she'd camp out just past the standing stone at the edge of the Grimwood."

"You did *what*?"

Mack's cheeks flushed. "She's our friend, Poppy. It's not like we have dozens of those lying around—that we can just stay angry at when they make a mistake."

"A mistake that cost me Dog."

His hand dropped onto her shoulder. "I miss them too, but in the end, it was your bargain . . . not Nula's."

Poppy's stomach turned. "Are you saying it's *my* fault the Faery Queen took Dog?"

"I'm saying it's not anyone's fault but the Faery Queen's." He paused. "Mistakes were made. All that means is that we need each other more than ever."

Poppy chewed the inside of her cheek. When she tasted blood, she relented. "Fine. Let's go get her."

Mack's smile almost made the decision worthwhile. His whole face lit up. "Good," he said.

Poppy gave him a look, but followed it with an eye roll, so Mack knew she wasn't really angry. She hated to admit it, but she missed Nula. The pain of losing Dog hadn't made her miss Nula less. Plus, the pooka was crafty, and she *could* use her help. Especially now. Whatever the governor had up his sleeve, she didn't think he would wait long. They had to find her parents *now*.

Dusk was falling and the Grimwood was shifting into shadow, but Poppy could make out Nula's silhouette beyond the tall stone that marked the wood's boundary. If she turned a little more and looked up the sloping hills of the meadow, she could see the lines of her house, the sun golden in the small front windows, and across the windows of her tower. She blinked and looked away. Hopefully Jute would get back soon. It wasn't home without him.

Mack lifted his hand, and Nula stepped out of the shadows, smiling. Poppy and Mack stepped past the stone and into the forest to join her.

There was a strange spinning sensation, and the temperature dropped. Goose bumps broke out all over Poppy's skin. She tried to make sense of what she was seeing as she looked around, and the goose bumps broke out a second time. They were in a wide clearing that hadn't been there a moment before. Nula was nowhere to be found.

Poppy spun around to stare at Mack, but he looked as perplexed as she felt. "Where are we?" she asked. There was no sign of the meadow, no flower-covered hillside, no hint of her house.

Mack looked around wildly, then froze.

Poppy followed his gaze. He was staring at the standing stone. It was the only thing vaguely familiar about their surroundings.

"The stone," she breathed. "So . . . was Nula . . . Nula was right! The stones really can take you to other parts of the forest."

The carvings on this stone were different. It had spirals, while the other was covered in small concave circles.

Mack reached out one hand as if he would touch it, but pulled back at the last moment. "But where are we?" He looked around, trying to get his bearings. "Where did it take us? And why?"

His words echoed in Poppy's head. She could see the

whites of his eyes, and seeing Mack look frightened raised the hair on the back of her neck. There must be a reason they'd ended up here, but the chances of it being a *good* reason . . . well, they weren't high.

Dusk was over, and darkness had fallen in this place—as if they had moved not just through the wood, but through time too. The glowing silhouettes of tall white birches surrounded the clearing. Fireflies filled the gloom. Their flickers filled the air with a soft glow and unexpected brightness.

Mack took a few steps ahead and looked back again. "Do you have anything with you? Any salt? Anything to form a barrier."

Poppy shook her head. "My pack is in the meadow." She swallowed. "You?"

"We should go. Now. Head toward the outer edge of the Grimwood and whatever Hollow is on the other side."

Poppy shivered. The idea that Mack didn't know where they were made her brain hurt. It was like trying to imagine the sea wasn't wet, and suddenly all she wanted was to get out of the wood.

They hurried into the trees beyond the clearing, back toward where they should have been all along. Poppy trusted Mack's instincts to lead them toward home.

"Don't go!" a soft voice cried out, drifting over the boggy grass. "Please! Wait!"

Poppy spun.

"No! Just leave it, Poppy. It's dark. You can't trust anything now."

"Help me, child. I beg you. Help me!"

"Mack, someone needs our help. We can't just leave."

"We can," he said, but Poppy was already drifting across the clearing in the direction the voice had come from.

The fireflies gathered, dancing in front of her, shifting and blinking, lighting her way, and leading her toward the voice.

"Please, help. Follow my voice! I need you."

Mack was suddenly behind her. "Poppy, I thought these were fireflies, but they're not. They're wisps."

She stopped walking. "Those nasty little things that lead people into swamps? They can't be. These are just fireflies."

"The ground is wet, Poppy . . . I think we're at the edge of a swamp now. And come here—look!" He held up his hand, a soft glow sifting from between his fingers. He uncurled them as Poppy leaned in. The creature in his hand was small and delicate—a soft neon green with lacy wings and tiny features that blurred in and out with the light.

"It's a . . . a tiny person, with wings."

"Poppy, *please*. Listen to me. This is a wisp. The will of the wisp is to lead people into traps. You *can't* follow them."

Poppy paused to let his words sink in. He was asking her to trust him. "Okay. I won't—"

A whistling sound whipped the air, and a thorny black tendril wrapped around Mack's arm, yanking him back.

"Mack!" Poppy cried. *Where had it even come from?*

She searched the glade desperately as Mack tugged at the whip, but she couldn't see any thorn trees. A second whip struck, wrapping around his calf. He cried out.

Poppy pulled her knife from her boot and lifted it to slice the whip around his arm, but when the voice sounded again, it was as though an arrow pierced her heart. "Pleeeease!"

She should be running toward the voice. What was she even doing here—trying to help this person who was obviously somewhere he didn't belong?

"Child! I need you!"

Poppy stood frozen, staring at the boy stuck in the whips for long seconds—trying to figure out who he was. He looked familiar, but she couldn't place him.

"Child!"

Another whip struck the strange boy, and he snatched the knife from her hand, slicing through one of the whips. She spun away and began to walk toward the sound of the voice.

"Poppy!" the boy's voice rang out. "NO! Don't listen! Put your fingers in your ears. Sing! Anything!"

Mack! The sound of his voice brought Poppy back to

her senses, but she couldn't seem to make her feet stop walking. Her stomach lurched. "I can't stop!"

"Plug your ears," he called. "Sing! Loud!"

Poppy shoved her fingers in her ears.

"Come here! Come here!" the voice called over and over like an echo.

Her fingers dulled the voice, and Poppy's steps slowed, but it wasn't enough.

She began to sing a song from the Hollows at the top of her lungs—something about dark nights and bountiful harvests. Her feet slowed more, but still she inched forward, as behind her, Mack struggled to get loose.

CHAPTER
TWENTY-SIX

In front of her, out of the shadows of the trees, a form emerged, tall and willowy. As the shape grew closer, Poppy saw it was a woman. Everything about her was pale and cold. Blue veins ran up her forearms. Her eyes, the color of ice, gave off a faint glow. White-blond hair floated around her, as if she moved in water.

Poppy tried to step back, but her feet wouldn't listen. They inched her closer, then closer again. Behind her she could hear Mack shouting and struggling to get free, but she couldn't stay focused. She kept forgetting who he was . . . what she was doing, her attention drawn back to the stranger.

Mack was yelling something, but she couldn't make it out, his voice fading in and out as the woman drew nearer. The wisps hovered around Poppy like a swarm, their light shaking and shifting.

The ground grew wetter, squelching under her feet. When she was just beyond an arm's reach, the woman shivered with excitement. She reached out a long finger and touched Poppy's cheek.

Poppy jerked.

She was in her kitchen. Jute was there, making cookies. Her mother and father were there, laughing and looking . . . at her. She tried to speak but couldn't. The scene went on as though she was part of it—warm, happy, and together. Everything she had ever wanted. "Come with me." The cold voice tickled her ear. "Come with me, and all of it can be yours. I can give it to you."

Poppy trembled. Her mother reached out and took her hand. Her father gazed at her with pride in his eyes. Her heart turned over.

"Just follow. Follow the sound of my voice."

Poppy took a step forward.

"That's it. Come on."

Another step.

A cry behind her startled her out of the reverie. She shook her head and opened her eyes. When had they drifted shut?

In front of her the woman had changed. Her icy eyes blazed and her wide smile had grown even wider, sharp teeth gleaming.

Poppy pulled away, just as Mack appeared at her side, his arm and opposite leg bleeding badly. He snatched her up, and instantly Poppy's head cleared.

The woman screeched, reaching out her arms to grab Poppy, but Mack was too fast.

"Mack! Are you all right?"

"I'll live," he breathed, running with her across the clearing toward the edge of the birch trees. Poppy looked back over his shoulder. The strange woman stood where she was—not chasing them.

Why? "Mack?"

Mack launched them into the trees—away from the clearing.

And they reentered the same clearing again, behind the woman.

Mack spun, confused.

"Put me down," Poppy said.

He put her down, and they turned as one to hurry back into the wood.

And reappeared on the far side of the clearing, looking toward the woman. Poppy grabbed his hand and they turned again, running this time.

And nearly ran into her. The woman had stepped closer to the edge of the trees, her eyes glowing.

Mack handed her knife back and pulled his own. "We're trapped."

The woman's slow smile grew as she crept closer. It reached from one ear to the other.

The wisps filled the air around them, jiggling and dancing until Poppy began to feel seasick.

The woman reached out a finger—

And a roar filled the clearing.

A tiger—huge and dark brown with blue stripes—threw

itself onto the woman, knocking her to the ground and putting out her light.

The clearing vanished, leaving nothing but tall dark pines and a few thorn trees tucked into the shadows among them.

"Nula?" Poppy breathed.

"Come on!" Nula was up and running, and they didn't ask questions. The three of them ran through the trees together, into the darkness, away from the monster and her wisps. Poppy noticed that Nula stayed with them as herself while they ran, like they were a team. She wasn't shifting into another form.

"What *was* that?" Poppy gasped.

Nula panted. "It might have been a bog witch, but I think it was a lamia. I didn't even know we had one of those in the wood."

Mack was limping. The thorn tree had left huge gashes on his leg. "I've heard of them," he said. "They're the ones that eat people?"

"Children," Nula clarified. "They eat children."

"Gross." Poppy shuddered.

Nula followed Poppy's shiver with her own. "Yeah. They do it out of loneliness."

Poppy's breath was raw in her throat, but they kept running. Anything to put distance between themselves and the bog.

Finally, Poppy got a stitch in her side and had to stop.

Mack was limping so badly he might as well have been hopping. "That's enough," she declared. "I can't run anymore."

Nula looked at Mack. "Think we're safe?"

He looked around at the dark Grimwood. "Well, no. But I think we're safe from whatever that was."

"Where do you think we are?" Poppy asked.

"Oh, I can tell you that," Nula said. "We're about three miles west of your house . . . and two miles toward the center of the wood."

Poppy stared at her. "How did you find us?"

Nula lifted her chin, her gold eyes bright. "I tracked you."

After a moment Poppy reached out to take Nula's hand. "Thank you."

Tears filled Nula's eyes. Her bottom lip quivered. "I'm . . . I'm so sorry, Poppy. About what I did. About Dog." A blue tear rolled down her cheek. "I can't even tell you how sorry I am—about everything."

Poppy whisked away a tear of her own with the back of her hand. "I know." She couldn't bring herself to say more.

"So," Mack interrupted. "A tiger, eh?"

Nula broke into a shy smile. "Wanna see?"

Poppy and Mack both nodded, and a tiger paced in front of them—its back as tall as Poppy's waist. Nula's stripes remained, and the gold of her eyes. Poppy could see her looking out through them. Nula let out a roar that shook the trees and set Poppy's knees quaking. She laughed.

Then the pooka stood in front of them again, her cheeks flushed. "It's my form, I think," she confided. "It feels different from the others. I feel—strong."

Mack clapped her on the back. Nula turned to look up at him, her eyes widening slightly. "You're taller."

He grinned. "I had a growth surge."

"Right in the middle of Strange Hollow," Poppy finished.

"No!"

"Yes." He snorted. "Couldn't have been worse."

Nula grimaced. "I bet. The humans must have pitched a fork."

Mack smiled. "A fit, you mean."

Poppy laughed. "Let's get back. We have a date to keep, and I don't know about you two, but I'd rather not hang around."

Nula frowned. "A date?"

"We'll fill you in on the way," Poppy replied, hurrying to keep up with Mack's long strides as they headed east toward home.

"Start at the beginning," Nula said, pushing ahead to get in front of Mack.

They filled Nula in on all that had happened—and on the children's promise to help.

The Grimwood stayed quiet—almost peaceful as they trudged along, exhaustion heavy around them. Poppy took a deep breath. The air was full of the scent of pine. The Grimwood's spike frogs thrummed from high branches, quieting as Poppy and her friends passed beneath them. Tentaculars along the tree trunks and on fallen limbs waved their colorful tentacles through the air. An owl called in the distance.

Poppy thought about the vision the lamia had shown her. She had known, even while it was happening, that it wasn't real. Maybe she could recognize it as false because what she wanted now, more than anything, was something that felt real. She didn't want a dream. She wanted something that felt like her own life—something that matched her and was meant for her—even if it wasn't what she had hoped for when she was smaller.

Before—before she'd entered the Grimwood—it was as if her questions and her yearning was all of who she was. But that had fallen away, a little bit at a time. It wasn't that all her questions had been answered. It was just that she knew she and her friends could find the answers she needed—and that they would be there by her side. Warmth rushed through her, despite the chill lacing the night air.

At last they reached the edge of the Grimwood and toppled into the meadow. The clearing in the forest had been dark, but out of the wood, dusk was just falling. Her house stood in deepening shadow, the windows dark. It almost hurt to look at it, knowing all its rooms were empty and uncertain. The evening was warm, and the moon was rising, bright and friendly.

Mack threw himself down on the ground. "The curfew must be in effect by now. The kids will be here soon. We should try and rest a little."

Poppy's thoughts spun out like webs, sticky and relentless. They had to find her parents—and find out what the governor was planning to do to the wood. There was no time to waste. It was torture to sit here and just . . . wait. "Yeah." She pinched the bridge of her nose. "Pretty sure rest is not going to be a thing for me." She turned to Nula. "Could I . . . maybe have another look at that book?"

"Of course!" Nula fished the small leather-bound book from her tunic, handing it over. She held out her herb knife in her other hand.

Poppy opened to the center page. The inklings were asleep again in their strange little blobs. As her blood dripped onto the page, they scattered, then gathered into words.

> Stay away from the Grimwood, child.
> Stay away from the fog.
> Stay away from the thorn trees, child.
> Stay away from the bog.
> Tooth for tooth.

Blood or bone.

Promises are made of stone.

Know your place, and

Watch the weather.

Wood and home must rise together.

Poppy ran her fingers over the last line. "All magic has a cost," she recalled under her breath. Mack and Nula settled in close to her. "I've been thinking about this," Poppy said under her breath. "We already know the maledictions are the cost for humans' long lives, right?"

Nula nodded. "That was Prudence Barebone's bargain to keep the peace. And to get something out of it for herself as well," she added.

Mack brushed his hair out of his face. "And the maledictions grow in the soil of the thorn trees—so the Holly Oak knows they're the cost, but couldn't say anything to anyone who didn't already know. That was Prudence too."

"But this . . ." Poppy traced the last line of the rhyme again. "'Wood and home must rise together.' To keep the promise intact, we both have to keep the peace. The woods can't attack the Hollows, and the Hollows—"

Mack's eyes widened. "The fires! It's him, isn't it— the governor? It's been humans all along! And that's why there have been more maledictions in Strange Hollow lately!"

"That's what I think too. Mack, do you remember that

strange smell in the square?" The image of the crate, filled with bottles of amber liquid flashed in her mind. "It was just before you grew . . ."

"I remember—"

"Well, I don't," Nula grumped. "So, explain."

Poppy forced herself to slow down. "The governor said he wants to purify the wood. He said . . . something about how the time has come, and there's a battle to be fought." She paused. "They have these bottles . . . I think they're setting them on fire and throwing them into the wood."

"Like that day the trees exploded around us," Nula recalled.

"Right. And then the thorn trees grew around us. I think it's been humans setting the fires in the wood all along. I think—I think the governor wants to burn the Grimwood down. That's his plan. That's what he wants the town to do."

Nula's ears lay flat, disappearing into her cropped hair. "How can he do that? Why?"

"Easy," Mack said, his eyes flashing. "He wants to get rid of the forest, and everything in it."

Nula paled, her tail whisking forward. She clutched it in her hands, brushing her chin with the tuft. "But the rhyme says rise together . . . so what's that mean, then?"

"Rise together," Mack muttered. "We rise *together*— you know, help each other out . . ."

Poppy gave a slow nod. "But then, it stands to reason that if we rise together . . ."

Nula's tail whipped the air. "Everything has to balance. If we rise together, then we fall together."

Mack grimaced. "If the Grimwood attacks the Hollows, then the wood falls too . . . but if humans attack the wood . . ."

Poppy gave him a dark look. "Go on."

"Then the Grimwood can openly attack the Hollows. Tooth for tooth. Blood or bone."

Nula lay down on the other side of Poppy and let out a long breath. "I bet the Faery Queen would love that."

"Other things too," Poppy agreed.

"I hope that governor guy is willing to listen," Mack grumbled as he stretched out on the other side of Poppy.

Poppy's throat was dry. "I hope he believes us." She lay down next to her friends and tried to push the worry out of her head, but it only filled up with all the things she missed. She missed the warmth of Dog's body lying next to her—missed Eta watching her until she fell asleep, and even Brutus's bad breath. She missed the sounds of her parents puttering in their lab late at night, their voices drifting up her tower stairs. She even missed, a little bit, the longing she had before she went into the wood— because it meant she had known exactly what she wanted.

She wasn't sure how, but Nula and Mack both dozed off. She watched the stars come out instead of sleeping.

Faint music drifted up the hill from Strange Hollow. Poppy tried to listen, but she could barely hear the strange melody over the tumult of her thoughts and the rushing of her blood. It took every ounce of her self-control not to race toward Strange Hollow and search.

Bad things were coming. The governor had a plan to burn the Grimwood, and the Holly Oak would never let it happen. Not without a fight. She needed to get to her parents—find them, and get them out of the Hollow. Instead, she was stuck here, waiting for the children to come. *Waiting a little is worth it*, she reminded herself. More people searching will save time.

She recognized the melody then. It was the townsfolk's warding song, weaving itself through the air, rising and falling in the warm breeze. It trembled in the air like rainfall.

Nula's feet twitched in her sleep as though she was running, but her face was peaceful. Mack wore a scowl, but soon let out a snore that made Poppy giggle.

She gave up on even trying to sleep and sat up to watch the pale twilight moon as it slowly rose above the horizon. Her thoughts drifted, and it seemed like only moments before a small silhouette was climbing the hillside in the moonlight. Other shadows followed, clustered close for warmth or confidence.

Mags stopped her march at Poppy's feet. Her brother— Peter, was it?—stood by her side, and at her back was a group of six or seven other children. One girl at the back looked just a year or two younger than Poppy. Poppy yanked her ponytail tight. Mags wore a pale blue dress with a delicate floral pattern that belied the absolute power she clearly wielded over the other children. Her brother, dressed in tidy gray with his arms crossed, looked for all the world like a guard ready to keep back the adoring masses. Poppy's heart warmed. She nudged Mack and then Nula.

"Who are we looking for exactly?" Mags asked.

"We're looking for my parents," Poppy explained, and she pulled their locket pictures from the little pocket in her backpack where she had stored them. She handed them to Mags to pass around.

"If we can't find them . . . then we're looking for any signs that might lead us to them. Locked doors that aren't normally locked. Signs of someone being kept hidden. People sneaking around or acting strange. Anything. And we need to hurry. Governor Gale is going to . . . do something bad. We don't think there's much time."

Mags and Peter exchanged a look. Then Peter dipped his head, mumbling at his shoes. "You're right," he said. "We heard our parents talking. They're planning to do it soon—tomorrow morning."

"What?!" Poppy snapped.

Mags pushed past her brother. "Don't get any ideas though. You promised us answers. You have to—"

"We'll keep our promise." Poppy scowled, and any other person would have been intimidated, but Mags just scowled back.

Mack rose to his feet, and half the children cowered behind Mags. Several were staring at Nula, who gave them a sassy grin and turned herself into a falcon, a weasel, and then a lynx in short order. When she *poofed* back into herself, all the children were staring at her with wide eyes, including Peter. Mags's cheeks had reddened, but she kept her eyes on Poppy with great strength of purpose. "I've thought about it, and seeing as you're in a hurry, I've decided we'll ask questions on the way. Once we get into town, we'll split up. The kids will report back to me." She lifted an eyebrow as if expecting a fight. "It will save time," she added.

Poppy let out a breath. "Thank you."

Mags lifted her chin and nodded—and as they all marched down the hill, the assault began. Mags chose who could ask the questions, and she got to go first. She asked about blood wards—and wards in general, and Poppy and Mack took turns filling in the details. Nula jumped in to tell the kids how to break a blood ward.

Mags's hierarchy was unquestioned. Every third question belonged to her brother.

Nula was brilliant. She put Poppy and Mack to shame, playing to the crowd like she was born to it. It wasn't long before all the questions were whether she could turn into this creature, or that creature.

And she obliged them all. She even turned into a crocodile—as described by one of the girls who had seen a picture in a book from outside the fog. The girl screamed when she saw it, which earned her a demotion. Mags didn't pick her again.

"This is awe-ful," Mack said with a chuckle.

Poppy cocked a brow at him. "You mean awe*some*?"

"Right. Awesome."

She grinned. "It is, isn't it?" Despite everything, her chest felt warm, as if some little crack in her heart had healed up, sealing itself as the children asked their questions, and *got* their answers.

"Maybe this time you'll actually *see* Strange Hollow . . . even though it won't be quite the same with the whole town in bed," Poppy smirked at Mack.

He gave her a playful shove.

They were just reaching the first houses of Strange Hollow when Mags turned to face her, and Poppy found herself standing a little straighter.

"*I* have a question," Mags said as the crowd of children quieted around her.

Poppy stepped forward. "Ask. I'll answer it if I can."

"Part one. What do *you* think about the Grimwood—do you think it's evil? Part two. What should we know about it . . . that we don't?"

Mack let out a low whistle, and Nula threw up her hands.

Poppy swallowed, and considered her answer. "Okay. Part one. No, I don't think it's evil. I just don't think it's good either." She paused and thought about the forest—about the Veena river as it ran over the rocks, and the Boatman. She thought about how Nula had come back again and again, even when she was scared. She thought about the song of the Mogwen, and the tentaculars, and the unicorns. "It's the most beautiful, mysterious place in the world," she breathed at last, watching Mags's eyes light up. "And it's the most dangerous and slippery one as well."

"Slippery?"

Poppy lifted one shoulder. "You never know what you're going to learn . . . and it isn't always simple . . . or comfortable."

"That's obvious," Mags scoffed.

"Okay, well, I think the Grimwood is . . . I think there's a lot we still don't know, and even more that we don't understand, but I also believe that knowledge is the enemy of fear." Poppy's heart squeezed. Her father had said this so many times, she could almost hear his voice.

"So, you're saying we should learn more."

"Yes." She glanced at Mack. "But we have to do that and still be cautious. Fear has its place, and so do rules . . . and respect."

Mags thought about this. "What about the second part of my answer?"

Poppy shifted her weight. Next to her, a little boy was

reaching up to touch Nula's arm. The pooka gave her tail a mighty swish that forced him to jump back a step.

"That's easy," Poppy said. "Prudence Barebone."

Mags scowled. "Who?"

Nula, understanding, handed Poppy the book along with her small silver knife.

Poppy opened to the woodcut of Prudence making the bargain with the Holly Oak where the inklings still slept. She made a small poke on the pad of her pinkie finger. Mags paled.

As her blood dripped onto the page, the inklings scattered, and the children pressed in.

"Let her through," Peter called out, and the sea of children parted to let Mags and him to the front.

"What does it mean?" Mags asked, and for the first time, Poppy saw fear in her eyes.

Poppy didn't answer, but she turned to the rhyme next.

"It's not the same as the rhyme we say," Peter noted.

"No," Poppy agreed somberly. "It isn't. *This* is Prudence Barebone's promise. And it means we *have to* keep the peace with the wood."

"The woods take people," Peter said, his voice grave.

"The maledictions trick people out—that's true," Poppy agreed, noting that they were still very close to the village now. The dark windows of the houses caught the moonlight and gleamed like eyes. "But no monsters have ever attacked us—nothing has left the Grimwood to attack the Hollows. And the maledictions are the cost we pay for our very long lives. That was part of the promise too."

Outrage flew across Mags's face as she lifted her eyes from the book. "So, you're saying this Prudence lady just went and tied us together, is that it? She asked for long lives—which was nice and stuff, but she just *ignored* the cost—maybe didn't even *ask* about it?"

"We'll never know *exactly* what happened. But . . . yes." The girl was sharp. Maybe even sharper than Poppy herself—though Poppy hated to admit it. Mags was easily three or four years younger.

"Hmph." Mags shook her tight curls and crossed her arms. "That's a terrible promise—that's a promise that *should* be broken!"

Poppy startled. She hadn't thought about it quite like that, but Mags's words rang true. Prudence's promise was wrong from the start. "But . . . we can't," she realized out loud. "We can't break it. Our ancestors agreed. They sealed the promise with their blood—and they're all dead. None of them can take it back."

"We're tied together," Mack added. "It's done."

Mags made a huff of breath through her nose that reminded Poppy so much of Mack she almost laughed. "So," Mags huffed again. "If the Grimwood attacks us, it falls too? And if we attack it?"

Poppy finished her thought. "Then anything in the

Grimwood can attack the Hollows . . . for real. Tooth for tooth. Blood or bone."

"Sheesh," said Peter. "That oak-lady meant business."

Poppy gave him a sad smile. "I'm not sure she had much choice, or at least, she didn't think she did."

"Why didn't anybody tell us?" Mags folded her arms.

Nula's tail whipped the other direction. "Because humans have incredibly short memories. You would forget your own names if they weren't written on your hands during childhood."

Mags pulled a face, and Peter studied his hands with a perplexed expression.

Poppy leaned in to whisper in Nula's ear. "Humans don't write their children's names on their hands."

"What? Really?"

Poppy shook her head.

"Well, anyway, you have terrible memories."

"So." Mack cracked his knuckles as they approached the town. "Questions answered. Promise kept. Now, let's go find Poppy's parents."

Mags frowned and reached out to grab Poppy's arm. "When can we do it again?"

Nula laughed. "No fair! That's a question! Time's up, Mack said."

Poppy rolled her eyes. "We're not the faeries, Nula." She turned to Mags. "I don't know. Right now I need to find my parents. Ask me after that."

Mags held out her hand, and after Poppy shook it, she reached into her pocket and pulled out a pretty little wooden whistle. She handed it to Poppy. "Take my extra whistle," she said, casting a dark look around at her gathering of friends and compatriots. "If things go sideways, use it." She met Poppy's eyes. "You blow that whistle, and we'll come."

CHAPTER TWENTY-SEVEN

Strange Hollow was peaceful with everyone in sleep's gentle care. Poppy's footsteps echoed off the sides of the houses. There were signs posted about the curfew at every corner ward. People were to be inside with their doors locked and their wards set by dark. She stopped to look at one. There was a really bad sketch of Mack on it that made him look terrifying.

As soon as they entered the town, Poppy found herself watching Mack. The last time he had walked through Strange Hollow it had been broad daylight. He'd had to hunch over and keep his eyes down to maintain his disguise. *Until things went sideways*, Poppy thought, wrapping her hand around Mags's wooden whistle.

Now, despite the dark, Mack tried to take in everything they passed. His eyes were wide, his gaze shooting from one thing to another like spring birds gathering seeds. They paused at one of the low fences and he looked at Poppy expectantly. "Is fencing your house a human thing?" His steps faltered. "Elves only fence pigs."

"I guess," Poppy answered. "I think they like to keep everything separate."

"You don't have a fence around your house . . ."

Poppy shrugged.

"Maybe it's just because they're all pushed together," he suggested.

A few more steps and Mack opened his mouth to ask another question. Mags turned around and gave them a scathing look. "Come on," she hissed. "We have a lot of ground to cover. Mack, you come with me and Peter. There are some empty buildings just to the east." She pointed at a tall blond boy. "Silas, you take Reva and Thomas and check those outbuildings on the south end of town by the blacksmith's forge. The rest of you go west. Check the grain silo, and the barns between here and the fog. But hurry, and don't get caught. We'll meet back in the square in two hours."

Mack raised both eyebrows at Poppy as if to say, "Glad she's on our side," then did as he was told and moved ahead with Mags.

"Where should Poppy and I look?" Nula called softly.

Mags narrowed her eyes at her. "Check the square, and the marketplace. Don't go too far."

Poppy and Nula watched the children scatter, sneaking off to see what they could discover. Moonlight spilled across the cobblestone streets.

Poppy allowed herself the luxury of walking down the

middle of the main road as they moved through the center of town. Nula crept along in the shadow of the houses next to Poppy. The road led through the square and toward the market on the far side.

Once they got past the stone clock tower in the center of the square, the road twisted past the brickmakers's and the herbalist's, through darkened side streets. Poppy passed house after house, and all, without fail, had their warding bells hung at the top of the doorframes, and a line of salt and iron at the footboard. Most also had lines of salt along their windowsills.

A horrible thought struck Poppy. "Nula? What if . . . What if my parents aren't in Strange Hollow? What if they're on the other side of the wood?"

"In one of the other Hollows?" Nula's voice hissed from the shadows. "They could be. I don't know." She twitched an ear. "But we've got packs ready back in the meadow. We can keep going if we have to."

Poppy frowned. "I don't even know how far Trader's Hollow is, but it's on the other side of the wood . . . so it's days, at least." Anxiety squirmed in her gut. What if they didn't have days? What if she was too late?

"We'll just have to do our best. We've got each other . . ."

Poppy bit her lip. "You're right. We'll search here, and if they aren't in Strange Hollow, then we'll have to find them the old-fashioned way."

Nula's gold eyes shone out of the darkness under the eaves. "What's the old-fashioned way?"

Poppy grimaced. "Keep looking."

They moved to the edge of town. The air smelled of petrichor and tomato leaves and night. Poppy inhaled deeply as they moved between the houses, staying close together and moving fast. Nothing seemed out of place or strange. There were no locks . . . or chains across a door to give away her parents' location.

The town was quiet. They touched base with Mags twice as the night ticked past. Each time the girl shook her head, and each time, Poppy's hope waned a little thinner.

Nula skirted a fancy two-story house with a newly thatched roof and three windows facing the street. She stopped at the edge of the house. "It's time to turn back toward the square, Poppy."

"Already? So soon?"

"Yeah," Nula said in a low voice, but her eyes were pinned to the ground.

Mack and Mags, along with her brother and several of the other children were waiting. They looked exhausted. One girl had her shoes off and sat on the cobbles rubbing her feet.

"Anything?" Poppy asked.

Mack shook his head. Mags folded her arms, but her expression was apologetic. "We tried. We searched all the outbuildings and storehouses. There are a few abandoned houses that some of the kids checked too. There's no sign that anyone's being kept there." She scowled. "I—I'm sorry. We did our best, but there's nowhere else to look."

Poppy felt her shoulders slump. They weren't going to find her parents this way. "Thanks for trying." She started to hand back Mags's little whistle.

"Listen, Peter and I will make one more round and I'll come to you in the square if we find anything. You . . . keep the whistle," Mags added, giving them another apologetic look as Peter tugged her toward the other side of town. "We can't stay out too much longer. We've got to get back before dawn."

Poppy watched them go. The girl was fierce, kind, and clever—everything a girl should aspire to be. There was no telling what she would accomplish, but Poppy was glad Mags was on her side.

When the kids had gone, Mack turned to Poppy. "East or west?"

Poppy sighed. "Either. I guess. We'll check around once more too . . . then we'll get our packs and try to come up with a way to stop the governor." She tried to ignore the feeling of despair that seeped into her heart like bog water. "After that—I guess we'll see. Maybe my parents are in Golden Hollow."

Somewhere in the square a door banged. Poppy, Mack, and Nula pressed themselves against the wall of a heavily roofed house. The thatch hung low, casting thick shadows over them. They all held their breath as a dark-haired woman hurried across the square with a basket on her arm. She jumped when a bird fluttered nearby collecting bugs from the cobbles in the dim light.

The woman glanced over her shoulder, as if she was afraid someone had seen her.

Poppy scowled. There were plenty of ways for people to be up to no good. There was no guarantee that the woman had anything to do with Poppy's parents. But there was something about it that put Poppy's teeth on edge—something that told her to trace the woman's path.

Mack and Nula followed as Poppy slipped slowly around the back side of the clock tower, but there was no sign of the woman. She spun to stare back across the square.

Nothing. She was gone.

The sky was just beginning to glow in the east with the first hints of dawn. The cobbles gleamed wetly.

Poppy raced around the edge of the square with Mack and Nula on her heels. She checked down each side street, but all of them were empty and cold, still draped in the night's shadows. Behind them a door slammed again and Poppy turned to see the woman disappear, this time into the shadows on the far side of the square.

Nula gave a low snarl.

"She could have come from anywhere," Mack admitted.

"Except she didn't," Nula said, sniffing the air. She dashed toward the clock tower in the middle of the square with Poppy and Mack right behind her. When they reached the backside of the clock tower, which still lay in shadow, Poppy held her breath while Nula studied the stones. After a moment, the pooka cocked her head, reaching out to trace her fingertips over a thin line of shadow that stretched up the clock tower wall. "Here," she said, her voice hushed.

Poppy let her breath out, shifting closer to see. A crack ran across the top. "A door!" She couldn't hide. There was no handle, but the seal wasn't tight enough to keep it completely hidden from view.

"There's probably a lever or something," Poppy said, sliding her hands over the stones.

"Too slow," Nula grunted and levered her clawlike nails into the crack of the door. Nula pulled hard, and after a moment, Poppy slipped her fingertips into the cracks next to Nula's so they could pull together. Mack stood behind them as they hauled back on the edge. As soon as the crack was big enough for his fingers, he took hold of it and yanked.

The door flew open, scraping against the cobbles with a terrible noise.

Across the square, shutters banged shut, someone closing their window. Whether against the noise or the chill, Poppy couldn't be sure.

A lantern hung just inside the clock tower door—still warm. Someone had just been here. Poppy's heart began to pound a heavy drumbeat in her chest. She looked at Mack . . . then Nula. "Do you think . . ."

Mack stared into the black, his face fierce.

"There's only one way to find out," Nula growled, disappearing into the dark.

Poppy fumbled with a match, trying to light the lantern with shaking hands.

"There are stairs back here," Nula called softly.

At last the match flared to life and Poppy lit the lantern, holding it high. She and Mack moved to look up the narrow stair that twisted up into the tower.

The steps looked rickety, and the first one Poppy stepped on creaked as though it feared for its life. Nula stepped aside to let Poppy pass, she and Mack following behind.

The whole scaffold shivered and rocked from side to side as though it hadn't been used in an age. Poppy could see in the glow of the lamplight that the stairs weren't dusty, even though everything else was thick with cobwebs. *Someone* was using them. She moved faster.

A family of bats flapped past, and Nula muttered a curse that made Mack blush. They got higher and higher, following the creaking steps as they curled around the inside walls of the tower. At the top was a platform, and there they found another narrow door, its curling black iron handle the only decoration.

Poppy took a breath and gave it a yank that echoed through the tower. "Locked."

Nula crouched low to look beneath the handle. She rose with a grin. "They never learn." Then she was gone, and the tail of a thin green snake vanished under the handle.

Mack bent to look. "She went through the keyhole," he confirmed.

The door swung open a moment later, and Nula swept them in.

Poppy froze. She couldn't take a breath against the weight on her chest. Across the room, tied into two cushioned chairs, were her parents. Their eyes were closed, and they were both gagged.

Were they dead? Her stomach lurched. A scatter of dirty dishes had been pushed to the side. *No. Not dead. Nobody fed dead people . . . and they don't gag them either,* her brain supplied a moment later. She gave a sharp inhale as her mother opened her eyes.

Poppy crept forward, her heart in her throat, each of them staring wide-eyed at one another—then tears sprang into her mother's eyes, and Poppy was wrapping her arms around her.

A grunt from the other chair spun her around. Her father, staring at her with amazement—and, love? She laughed in relief, and moved to hug him. Mack was busy taking the cloth off her mother's mouth as Nula untied her father's wrists.

"Poppy," her mother gasped. "What are you doing here?"

"Rescuing you," Poppy laughed again as she took the cloth from her father's mouth.

"But how did you find us?" he asked with wonder in his voice.

Nula piped up from behind him. "Poppy's an amazing human."

Poppy's cheeks heated. "I had a lot of help." She smiled.

Mack rose from untying her mother and came to her side. "Who did this to you?"

"It was the governor," her father said through gritted teeth. "Him and his pack of zealots."

"He wanted us to tell him how to destroy the Grimwood," her mother added, rushing to throw off the ropes on her father's ankles. "To help him do it! As if we could tell them anything they don't already know." Her face darkened. "As if we would."

"We should leave," Mack said, his voice low.

"Are you all right?" Poppy asked them. "Can you walk?"

"Yes," her mother started, "but Poppy . . ."

"There's lots to tell you, but it will have to wait. We need to get out of here before they catch us."

Her father rose from the chair, bending to rub the cramps out of his legs. "I think we should listen to Poppy, love. I think she knows what she's doing."

"Well, she's her father's daughter," her mother agreed. "Lead the way, Poppy Sunshine."

They moved as fast as they could, but with so many of them on the delicate scaffolding, the stairs had begun to sway in earnest, creaking and cracking in a way that made everyone jumpy.

Poppy reached the bottom and gathered them all together to check that the coast was clear before heading out into the dusky dawn to make their way home.

As they turned a corner, though, Poppy came face-to-face with a crowd of angry looking men and women—all waiting for her and her family with torches in their hands. She spotted the woman she had seen crossing the square, and standing next to her, his face pale and full of shadows, was Governor Gale. His expression contorted into a mask more frightening than any monster's. "Going somewhere?" he asked.

CHAPTER TWENTY-EIGHT

Before Poppy could say a word, Nula had reached into Poppy's pocket, pulled out the whistle, and blown a loud, shrill blast across the square.

For a split second everyone froze. Poppy stared at her. "What?" Nula said. "Better too soon than too late."

An instant later, the townsfolk had them.

"You think you're beyond justice," Governor Gale snarled, as one of his burly followers grabbed Poppy's arm in a grip that was sure to leave bruises. "You think, because your family serves the Grimwood, that you're safe—never mind what happens to the rest of us. Well, the tide has turned. We humans are coming to our senses. It's time to make our world safe and clean at last. And you're just in time to watch it all burn."

"You can't do that," Poppy said. "You don't understand—"

"Oh, I understand, little girl. I understand that you and your family are in league with *monsters*."

"Leave Poppy out of this," her father shouted, and she

looked over her shoulder to see that he had shaken off one of his captors. "She has nothing to do with the Grimwood. It's her mother and I that hunt maledictions."

"So, you admit it. You search for these maledictions—for our benefit, you say. But *I* say you bring them to our doorstep. *I* say you help the wood capture our people! You have been given free rein for too long. No more! Now it ends! Now the Grimwood ends . . . and *you* end with it!"

"We hunt them to save you!" her mother cried.

"You don't keep us safe," someone shouted.

The adults broke out in a chorus of yells around them. Poppy tried to break free from the two townspeople holding her arms, but she couldn't escape their grip. She tried to shout over the din.

"Burn it down!" they shouted. "Liars! Murderers!"

"That's not true!" Poppy yelled.

No one even turned their heads.

"Throw them to the thorn trees!"

"Stop! Please! You can't break the promise! Please, you have to listen to me!" Poppy struggled. "The Hollows made a promise! They were led by Prudence Barebone. They made a promise with the Holly Oak for all generations . . ."

But the townsfolk weren't listening—they were too busy shouting insults and angry words as they dragged Poppy, her friends, and her parents back toward the tower door. Mack or Nula could easily have overpowered them, but some of them held knives, and she could see from the pleading expression Mack wore that he didn't want anyone to get hurt.

Nula had no such qualms. She turned herself into a tiger and people screamed and fell back. She roared and threatened, swiping at them with her claws outstretched. Poppy could tell she had no intention of attacking, but it was a good distraction. Poppy took advantage of it by stomping on the toes of the man who held her right arm, and elbowing the man who gripped her left arm in his stomach. She twisted herself out of their grasp.

Two men still held Mack, but Nula had distracted the rest, and he shook them off. Poppy drew her knife and, back-to-back, she and Mack made their way through the crowd toward her parents. Nula, still in tiger form, followed, parting the crowd around her.

Poppy met her father's eyes as they passed and let them fill with a question—"Are you ready?"

He gave a tiny nod.

"Now, Nula!" Poppy cried, and her friend lunged at the men who held Poppy's parents.

They let go.

"Come on!" Mack bellowed, following Nula's lead and lunging at the crowd. Nula let out another roar and the crowd scattered.

Poppy yelled, "Run!"

They all ran—back through the town as if monsters were at their heels.

And they were.

The townsfolk gathered again behind them, their torchlights flickering against the alleys and cobbled streets as they followed. Angry voices rang against the stones as the crowd chased Poppy, her family, and friends through the early dawn streets.

"Poppy, where are we going?" her father called.

"We're going home!"

Mack slowed, falling to the back to let her parents move ahead. "It's high ground at least, and maybe they'll get tired of chasing us once we're out of the Hollow."

But they didn't.

The townsfolk followed, calling insults and promising violence.

"Burn it down!" the governor's voice rose above the crowd. "It ends today! Burn it all down!"

Poppy wove through the standing stones across the meadow, the breath harsh in her throat. They all ran up the hillside, beating down the dawn-lit wildflowers, but still the mob came.

Her house—her beautiful, strange home, was lit and welcoming. She could see a tall figure on the porch.

"Jute!" she screamed.

He flew off the porch, racing for them with his knees lifting high. "Come!" He waved them ahead. "Hurry. Get inside."

They were all tired, and her parents were struggling

up the hill, their legs dull from days of captivity. Mack grabbed Poppy's father, and Jute took her mother in his arms—stumbling for the house. Behind them the glow of torches moved forward with the threatening rumble of angry voices.

When the door to their house was shut and locked behind them, they all collapsed to the hall floor, panting and heaving. Inside, it was warm and quiet, the voices outside fading. "Now what," Poppy gasped. "Will we have to fight them?"

Her father rose to his feet. "I hope not, Poppy. I hope we can talk sense into them. But we can't take any chances. Jasmine, get the net guns from storage. Jute, go to the lab. There's a jar of stonebrew on the shelf. Get as many small jars filled as you can. Poppy? There's a room in the cellar . . ."

"We're not hiding. Don't even ask."

He paused, a small smile playing across his face. "No. I don't suppose you would."

Poppy took the net gun her father offered her. She secured her knife in her boot. "What's stonebrew?"

Her mother let out a bark of laughter, and lifted one hand to touch Poppy's cheek. "Oh, Poppy Sunshine. I missed your questions."

"It's something your mother and I cooked up," her father said. "It freezes most creatures—but only for a few seconds."

"Seconds can help," Mack confirmed.

Nula touched Poppy's arm, then Mack's, before shifting herself back into a tiger.

"Everything's locked upstairs," Jute said, hurrying down the stairs to join them in the hall. He held a basket of thumb-size jars, and everyone shoved a few into their pockets.

Her heart racing, Poppy took the memory of them, all together, into her mind. She wanted to remember it forever. She would do whatever it took to keep them all safe. She knew it with every cell in her body. Everyone moved closer to one another and waited, watching the door. Only a minute had passed before someone pounded on it.

"Come out and face justice!" the governor's voice rose. "Come out and face us, monsters! We all saw them! You can't pretend anymore! We saw your elf spying in town— and your shape changer! We saw the creatures you're hiding in there!" His voice dropped. "Send them out . . . turn them over . . . and we'll leave you in peace."

Her mother pushed to the door, fury contorting her features. "These *monsters* are better *people* than any of you! You don't deserve—"

"Burn it down!" the governor cried, drowning out her words.

The sound of glass smashing against the front of the house was followed by the rushing heat of flame.

"No!" Poppy screamed.

The house caught fire at once, the hall filling with orange light.

Another smash, and fire burst into the living room.

"Out the back," Jute said. "Quickly."

They raced out the back door, into the small meadow that was the only buffer between Poppy's house and the wood. A flaming bottle flew end over end, spilling fire and smashing above them against Poppy's tower bedroom.

Poppy stared at the flames, her heart in her throat.

"What should we do?" Mack called.

"They're back here," a voice called, and suddenly there were people everywhere, swarming toward them.

Poppy cried out.

Nula dropped into a crouch and let out a roar that stopped their pursuers in their tracks. Her parents began firing their net guns.

Several men and women headed for Mack. Poppy aimed her net gun at one man and fired, knocking him to the ground. She hurried toward him, but caught sight of Jute and stopped. He was by the house, grabbing handfuls of dirt and throwing it at the flames as if there were the slightest chance he could put them out.

A shout spun her around. More people surrounded Mack, and Poppy broke into a run. She aimed her net gun again and was about to fire it, when from the corner of her eye she saw the governor stride around the side of the house—saw the moment when he spotted Jute. She lurched to a stop, her feet rooting to the ground. *Who should she help first? Which way should she go?* Mack had thrown two of the men off, but more were coming.

She looked back at Jute. He didn't see the governor at all. "Jute!" Poppy cried. "Jute! Look out!" She raced toward him, but the governor was too quick. He stabbed the end of his torch toward Jute. The hob screamed.

Suddenly her father was there, lunging at the governor and hauling him backward. The governor slashed at him with a knife, freeing himself and opening a cut on her father's arm.

Everything around Poppy slowed. Jute had fallen back to his knees, still trying to throw dirt on the fire, his burned arm clutched to his chest.

Mack had gotten loose and stood with Poppy's mother, throwing the small bottles of stonebrew at the attacking men, but it only slowed them a little. They were driving Mack and her mother back toward the edge of the wood.

Her father, blood running down his arm, rolled on the ground with the governor, neither able to get the upper hand.

Poppy stood, frozen. She didn't know which way to turn. Everyone she loved was in danger.

More people came around the sides of the house. A big woman's black eyes glittered at her as she closed in.

To her right, Nula was surrounded by torches, her fierce tiger eyes reflecting their light.

They were losing.

They were losing.

Strange Hollow wouldn't listen—and they wouldn't remember.

There was a crash as part of her home's roof caved in and the flames licked higher. The whole house was burning now.

"Look out!" Mack yelled from behind her somewhere.

The ground began to shake.

For a second, Poppy thought it was just her imagination, but then, around her, people lost their footing, stumbling. Some dropped their torches as they looked at one another, trying to get their balance and figure out what was happening.

From under the flaming husk of Poppy's house, glittering black trees rose from the ground. The fires sizzled and hissed, and began to go out.

Jute stood, watching with a horrified expression as a thorn tree pushed its way out of the ground.

One after another the thorn trees rushed toward the sky.

"Home and wood must rise together," Poppy mouthed the words as a black tree rose a few feet in front of her, blocking her view of Jute and the dawn-lit sky.

As the sunlight reached out to sparkle over its black bark, one whip lashed out and tore a gash across her cheek. Poppy lifted her fingers to touch it.

They came away covered in blood. *Blood.* She flashed to a memory of Nula at the Grimwood's edge with her knife in her hand. "Blood for blood," the pooka had said. "It's the only way in the Grimwood."

The promise of Prudence Barebone had been made with blood—just like blood wards were. Maledictions too, she realized, thinking of the Faery Queen. Maledictions could be undone . . . or changed, with blood. *Maybe they are all just different kinds of promises*, Poppy thought. *Blood can make a promise in the Grimwood. And maybe blood can break a promise too— remake it.*

Poppy gave herself one moment—one moment to reconsider. But she knew what she had to do. If the people wouldn't listen, then maybe the Holly Oak would. *Isn't the house hers? Aren't the thorn trees?*

Time quickened again as she took a breath and threw herself forward *into* the thorn tree, gripping its trunk. She had to get the Holly Oak's attention—had to call her somehow.

"Poppy, no!" Mack cried from far behind her, and she turned her head in time to see the desperate look of terror that crossed her best friend's face as she rode the tree upward.

She screamed. She couldn't help it. Whips wrapped each leg. One threaded itself around her waist and tightened, piercing her abdomen. Blood ran down her arms and legs. She tried to steel herself for what she still had to do.

Below her the ground was chaos. Her loved ones fought against capture, while every soul, cursing and crying, scattered out of reach of the thorn trees. They were everywhere now, filling in the half-crumbled house until the flames were nothing but hissing embers. Whips flew through the air, crashing into the ground and one another as they reached to try to snatch people. A few brave souls had knives in their hands and slashed at the whips.

"Stop!" she called down. "Stop fighting!"

Below, she could see Mack struggling to make his way to the tree.

And then—there were children everywhere.

They ran into the crowd to hang on to their parents' arms, some crying, others yelling.

Poppy stilled, listening through the sharp agony of the thorns. "Listen to her," she heard one kid yell, and thought she recognized Peter's voice.

"Stop fighting! They're nice! They're good!" another voice called.

Some of the kids were yanking on the adults' torch arms, while others skipped the arms and jumped onto their backs.

Torches and weapons fell as parents desperately tried to get the situation under control.

Poppy caught sight of Mags, just as the girl looked up and saw her. The girl's warm brown face turned the color of ash.

Across the distance, Poppy met her eyes and forced herself to shout, "I have to make a new promise! They have to listen!"

There was a pause. Then Mags pulled a whistle from her pocket and blew it so loud that even Poppy's ears rang. Silence fell. Mags pointed up at Poppy, and the other children took her cue like soldiers, pointing up at the girl in the thorn tree, pleading with their parents to wait . . . to listen.

Poppy's father caught sight of her and yelled her name. She tried to smile down at him reassuringly as her mother slowly sank to her knees, staring up.

"Listen to me," she called. "Please! That's all I ask."

"You're well and truly caught, girl." Governor Gale pushed his way forward as Nula let out a low snarl. "Looks like you'll have to talk fast." His lip curled. "I don't know how you won over our children, but if you—"

"We made our own choices," Mags insisted.

"Put down your torches," Poppy called. "Put down your knives. My friends . . . my family won't hurt you. I promise you. If what I say doesn't persuade you, they'll leave the Hollow. They'll go quietly."

Nula roared, and Poppy shot her a look.

"Poppy," Mack cried, his voice breaking. "What are you doing?"

"What has to be done, Mack."

"One wrong move from anyone," the governor hissed, "and we'll feed you all to the thorn trees."

Poppy's throat had gone dry. She cried out as one of the whips tightened again. "A few minutes—that's all I ask. I need to tell you about Prudence Barebone."

And she did.

She mustered all her strength and spoke loudly. She left no room for confusion and told them everything she knew about Prudence's promise. Some of the older people in the crowd conferred with one another—a few nodding. An old man tugged the governor down to whisper in his ear.

The governor sneered. "Suppose we believe you about this promise," he called up. "Suppose we believe that the fate of the Hollows is tied in some way to the fate of the Grimwood. How do we know this isn't all your doing? Why shouldn't we cleanse this place and destroy the wood forever?"

"You can see for yourself what it would mean to the

Hollows! You set fires—the forest makes thorn trees."
Her body was beginning to feel heavy. She forced words
past her lips. "Prudence wanted to have long life and
was willing to pay for it . . . and now you pay the same
with maledictions. The woods has to defend itself, but
the Holly Oak is still keeping her promise . . . and if you
destroy the Grimwood, you'll destroy the Hollows too." A
wave of dizziness rolled over her. "Tooth for tooth. Blood
or bone."

Alarmed expressions followed this pronouncement.
The old man began to tug on the governor's arm again.
The governor shook him off.

Poppy narrowed her eyes at him. He wasn't interested
in what was best for the Hollows—not now, maybe not
ever. He was too full of fear, and anger.

She had to strike now, while she still had the strength.
"Holly Oak," she cried. "Holly Oak, I want to make a new
promise!"

Everything stilled. Her father's voice echoed in
her head. *"Nothing more powerful than blood in the
Grimwood."*

"Holly Oak!" Poppy cried. "I know you're rooted
in the Grimwood deep, but you told us that the thorn
trees were a part of you—here to protect and defend
the wood. I know you can sense me. I hope you can
hear me."

Her head lolled as she tried to stay conscious.

"Poppy, hang on," Mack cried, lurching toward the tree.

Nula appeared at his side, and took his arm, pulling him back. She whispered in his ear, tipping her chin toward the wood. Mack looked past her in the same direction and stood a little taller. He wiped his arm across his eyes and nodded.

"Knowledge is the enemy of fear," Poppy called down, fighting against the heaviness of her limbs. "I'm offering a new promise and all the people of the Hollows have to do is make their pledge."

She took an agonizing breath. She could feel the drips of her blood as they fell from the tips of her fingers.

Poppy lifted her voice. "I offer peace! I offer a new peace between the Hollows and the woods. The woods gives us fertile soil, and clean water, and strong harvests, but from this day forward, we will no longer buy extra years with the lives of our loved ones. There will be no more need for maledictions—no more cost to be paid. We say goodbye to Prudence's greed and fear." The world began to spin, but Poppy forced the words through her lips.

"Humans in the Hollows will live their normal lives. We will take from the forest only what we need . . . we will respect your home, as you will respect ours. And . . . attacks without cause will not be permitted. All living beings will keep this promise, or be forced to go—forced to take their chances in the fog. The Holly Oak—the being whose magic built this place will be our judge."

The governor went pale. Around him the crowd had fallen silent. Faces turned to him as something heavy scrambled onto Poppy's shoulders.

She grunted, but her eyes had drifted shut. She couldn't see what it was.

She peeled them open again. Mags was below, just outside the reach of the thorn trees, holding up a tiny knife. "I'll keep the promise," she shouted, and before her parents could stop her she'd touched the tip of the knife to her hand, and pressed it to the earth.

The other children gathered around her, following her lead, and soon the adults too were dropping to their knees.

Something nudged Poppy's shoulder again. She turned her head. A weasel with golden eyes was biting through the whips, loosening her binds. "Nula?" Poppy breathed. The weasel nudged her with its cold, wet nose. Poppy tried to smile, but everything was heavy.

"Poppy!" Mack's voice called from somewhere below as her eyes drifted shut again. "Hold on! Help is coming."

The rest came in hazy flashes.

There was a scrabbling of limbs.

A sense of falling, then of floating.

Poppy opened her eyes to find herself in the grasp

of a picker. It carried her gently against its abdomen, down the tree to join its herd where they waited at the bottom.

The other pickers parted as it made its way across the meadow with Poppy. From the picker's embrace, Poppy caught the gleam of golden light against the crushed meadow grasses as the sun crested the hillside. She saw townsfolk watching, some kneeling to join their pledges to the new promise, pressing their hands—their life-blood—to the soil.

The picker let her down, slowly backing away to join its herd. Then Poppy's family was around her. Her mother pulled her into her lap, rocking her. "You're all right," she said. "You're all right."

Mack and Nula pressed close, each holding one of Poppy's hands.

The herd of pickers crept back into the wood, and with their departure, the last of the fear and loathing seemed to leave the humans of Strange Hollow. People trickled off to their own homes, their arms around their children.

Mack leaned over, staring into Poppy's face, his copper-brown eyes sharp. "Don't ever do that again," he said.

Poppy coughed a laugh. "No problem," she managed to say.

She stared past him to where the thorn trees loomed

over the ruins of her home. The scent of smoke hung thick, making her eyes burn and water.

Mack held her hand tighter as her eyes began to drift shut. She fought them open long enough to see her parents shifting to join more of the people of the Hollows as they knelt to make their promise.

CHAPTER THIRTY

It took Poppy two days to wake up, but when she did, there was an entire pot of mac and cheese and an enormous cup of hot chocolate waiting. Memories flooded her system as she ate, studying the bright, round room to figure out where she was.

Her home had burned. She remembered that well enough, and tears pricked at the back of her eyes. But this room was made of roots too. She could see the coils in the walls and across the floor. A branch held the lamp over her bed.

She shifted and spotted Mack, asleep in a chair across the room. There was no sign of Nula.

The door creaked open, and Jute poked his head in, his quail-egg eyes blinking in the bright sunlight. He glanced at Mack and back at her. "How are you feeling, child?" he whispered, coming to perch on a small three-legged stool by her bedside.

Poppy considered. "All right, I think. It's . . . hard to tell, actually."

He smiled. "I'm not surprised. We took forty-nine thorns out of your body, sweetling." His bushy brows furrowed. "What possessed you to do such a thing?"

Poppy picked up Jute's hand and held his warm palm to her cheek. She closed her eyes and inhaled his green smoky scent. "It was all I could think of to do," she said.

He stroked her hair. "Well. You're alive. And *everything* has changed."

Poppy's eyes flew open. "Really? Tell me!" She paused. "And *where* are we?"

Jute looked around the room. "We're home. South of the new thorn tree grove, farther down the meadow. Still at the edge of Strange Hollow."

"But—"

"The Holly Oak. It was built by the time we left the ashes of the old one. It's smaller." He dropped his hands back in his lap with a wink. "But you still have the tower."

"And the Hollow?"

"Has been remarkably quiet." His nose wrinkled. "But I must tell you, there has been the most perplexing number of children banging on the door and demanding to see you."

Poppy laughed.

"They're quite persistent. I imagine they'll be back before long."

"Where are Mom and Dad?"

"Ah." Jute's smile widened. "They've gone to the Holly

Oak. She requested that they come and tell her the story of the battle, and of your sacrifice. And—" He held up a finger to keep her from interrupting. "Your parents both said you should join them there when you're feeling well enough." His eyes grew sappy. "They said they hope you'll tell them your story . . . and that you'll let them help you with *your* next project." He held out his hand for her empty mug. "More?"

Poppy's throat worked as she struggled to find words. At last she just nodded, and Jute gave her a knowing look and took the mug from her hand.

As the door closed behind him, Mack stirred. He did a double take when he saw she was awake and sitting up.

He shot to his feet, swaying slightly. His tight copper-brown curls lay flat on one side where he had slept on them. "Poppy!" he croaked. "You're awake! You're okay? How are you?"

She gave a tight laugh and held up her bandaged arms. "Well. I've been better . . . but aside from feeling like a pincushion, I think I'll live."

Mack moved to the stool. His face was drawn, as serious as she had ever seen him. "When I saw you up there . . . Pop." His voice caught. "I thought for sure . . . you were . . ."

Poppy's throat tightened. She took his hand, her own disappearing underneath. "I know. I'm sorry."

Mack looked down at his lap, and Poppy saw a tear drop.

"Mack—"

"I'm really proud of you, Poppy."

Loud barking cut him off, followed by the sound of feet—like a herd of something—pounding up the stairs. Poppy leaned forward as the door flew open and a tiger careened into the room. She was followed by a three-headed dog.

"Eta!" Poppy wailed, lurching to her knees on the bed. "Two! Brutus!"

Dog launched onto the bed, threatening to trample Poppy with their love before they had finished greeting her.

"Down, Dog." Mack took their collar and pulled them off, letting Poppy catch her breath.

"Nula," Poppy gasped in between the licks of all three of Dog's heads. "How?!"

Nula reappeared and nudged Mack with her elbow. She grinned down at Poppy. "Glad to see you're feeling better. Told you," she added to Mack under her breath.

"When you said you were going to run an errand, I didn't realize you had *this* in mind," Mack laughed. He paused, a slight frown twisting his features. "How did you do it? I didn't think the Faery Queen would let Dog go for any reason."

A slight blue flush colored Nula's cheeks. She

shrugged, but Poppy noticed she wasn't meeting their eyes. "Nula?"

Nula shrugged again. "What can I say? I'm extremely clever."

Mack and Poppy exchanged glances. Mack sank to sit on the stool again, pulling Dog close. "And . . ."

"And I am a first-class shape-shifter."

Poppy tipped her chin. "Go on."

Mack cleared his throat. "Nula, did you *steal* Dog from the Faery Queen?"

Nula met his eyes. "Are you sure you want to know, elf?"

Mack dropped his face into his hands.

Poppy swallowed. "She'll come for them."

"Nonsense," Nula scoffed. "She's already lost interest. I told you, it's all about owning rare things with them. Now that she thinks she has them, she'll forget all about them. And even if she doesn't, she'll just think they've run off."

Poppy rubbed her forehead against Eta's. "I hope you're right . . . but thank you. Thank you for bringing Dog home." Poppy caught her and held on. "You're a good friend, Nula."

When she finally let go, she leaned back to study her friends. Mack stood rocking back and forth on the balls of his bare feet. Nula was looking all around the room and swatting Dog on the rump with her tail.

In that moment, Poppy knew—in a way she couldn't quite explain—that her path had carried her somewhere new, and that she wanted to see where it would go next. And she knew that wherever the path went, she wanted to go there with Mack. And with Nula.

"You know," she said in a voice that turned both her friends' faces toward her. "We make a pretty good team."

Mack's eyebrows rose, and Nula put one hand on her hip.

"I . . . I think we should maybe go into business."

Mack's eyebrows got even higher.

Poppy let out her most mischievous grin. "I think we should be ambassadors."

Nula whipped her tail. "What's an ambassador? Is that like . . . those little animals that have armor and roll up in a ball?"

"No. No, it's not."

Mack blew out his breath. "An ambassador is like a peacekeeper, right? Someone who listens and learns and shares what they know with others."

"Think of it as being a professional friend."

Mack nose-sighed. "I'm in . . . but do you think it will be enough . . . I mean, can it keep the peace?"

"I don't know. But I want to try. And . . ."

"And?" Mack smiled and shook his head. "Of course, there's more."

Poppy wrapped her bandaged hands together in

front of her as if she were going to say a prayer. "I was thinking . . ."

Mack froze. "Thinking . . . about what?"

Poppy smirked. "I was thinking about the passage stones."

"Oooooo," Nula purred, her gold eyes sparking. "Now *that* sounds interesting."

EPILOGUE

Poppy dropped into a chair with two small gargoyles carved on the back to wait. Sun poured in through the small round windows Jute had added to the front hall. It had taken a while for Poppy's injuries to heal. She still tired easily. But . . . it was also true that she smirked less, and was prone to smiling in an easy, casual sort of way that was new. Poppy Sunshine was sunnier than she had ever been before, which is to say, she was a little bit sunny.

She had been into Strange Hollow several times, and just last week had a fascinating conversation with Beth, who she was expecting to knock on the door at any moment.

The Battle of Strange Hollow, and Poppy's Pact, as they had come to be called, had changed almost everything. Though the people of Strange Hollow were still wary of Poppy and her family, now it was as much from awe as fear. They would raise their cups toward her if she passed, as if toasting her good health. They'd leave flowers on her doorstep. Some days she'd come out of the house to find a small group of people gathered outside as if they'd come on a pilgrimage.

To her great embarrassment, she'd even heard some kids practicing a new skip-rope rhyme in her honor. It went like this:

> At the Battle, it is said,
> Poppy Sunshine lost her head
> Thank your lucky stars she bled
> If she hadn't, we'd all be dead
> How many drops of blood she shed . . .
> One, two, three . . .

Not everyone was so appreciative, of course. The governor hated them more than ever, and though it was a small group of people, he wasn't alone. He did like being in charge, however, and since he didn't want people to turn on him, he stayed quiet and bided his time. At least, that's what Poppy's father told her.

Still, the whole thing had worked out better, and weirder, than she could ever have expected. She'd promised Mack the next time she went into the Hollow, he could come too. He had heard from her parents that the tavern had something new to eat called *fish fingers*, and he was dying to learn all about them.

The Holly Oak had tasked her parents with arranging for a small group of townsfolk to visit each of the other six

Hollows and spread the word of the new promise. They would offer a choice—people could agree to pledge themselves to the new pact, or they could leave on the next solstice through the fog.

It would be Poppy's first visit to the other Hollows. Mack and Nula were coming too, of course, but they all had something they had to do first. Poppy peered out the window. *Where was Beth?*

Her father came into the hall wearing his best black shirt and jeans. Her mother followed. She had on a deep gray dress that drifted at her shins as she moved. Poppy stood and brushed off her own dress—dark blue with a belt that looked like stars. "How do I look?" she asked.

Her mother beamed at her. "Like a hero," she said. "Like the girl who saved us all from ourselves."

Poppy felt her cheeks heat. She smiled. "Thanks, Mom."

Her father leaned down and kissed the top of her head. "We are so proud of you, Pandora." He pulled the three of them into a hug. "We are a family of strong, stubborn, independent people . . . but we need one another." He squeezed. "Thank you for reminding us."

"You're welcome," Poppy gave a muffled laugh into his chest.

She was going to have to tell them sometime, of course . . . about her plans. Maybe after they got back from the other Hollows. For now, Poppy hadn't even told

Mack and Nula *exactly* what she had in mind. She had some details to work out, but she knew some stuff. She knew she wanted them to track down and map all the passage stones—cartography it was called. They would figure out which stones were magical leaps to other parts of the wood, and which stones were just . . . stones. They'd have to figure out how they worked too, of course.

Really, she wondered if perhaps her true calling was to map the whole Grimwood—if she could. *A cartographer and an adventurer.* She rolled the words over in her mind and smiled.

There was a knock at the door, and Jute hustled past to answer, casting a fond look at the three of them huddled together. He swung it open.

Beth, grinning in her usual market dress, startled at the sight of him. "My—you're quite something, aren't you?"

Jute chuckled. "Won't you come in?"

Mack and Fionnula came in on Beth's heels, and she cast Nula a nervous look. "So much to learn." She hesitated, then moved to Poppy's side.

Poppy threw her arms around the old woman. "I'm so glad you're here, Beth. I'm glad you get to finally meet my family."

Beth's wrinkled face broke into a smile. "And a fine family they are, lightning bug."

Mack raised an eyebrow.

Beth patted Poppy's hand. "Let's take the picture outside, all right? The light is better, and we have to see all your faces if the statue in the square is going to be right."

Nula snorted. "I still can't believe they're making a statue of us," she laughed.

"A fountain, they decided," Beth corrected. "Bringing someone through the fog specially this solstice."

Mack gave her shoulder a gentle pat. "It was nice of the folks in Strange Hollow to insist like they did."

Beth laughed. "It was that little girl Mags's idea, of course. She is a firecracker! I haven't seen one like her since . . ." Her eyes drifted to Poppy.

Nula and Mack both laughed. Poppy's cheeks grew hot again.

Beth's smile faded. "I *am* sorry about my son's attempt to keep them from honoring you all. He cannot understand what his anger has cost him. I'm afraid he's governor in name only . . . and even that won't last much longer." She leaned down to whisper in Poppy's ear. "There are rumors that your father's name has been put forward for the job."

"Well, let's get on with it, then," her father said, cutting off Beth's whispers and hurrying them outside. "Mack, can you grab Dog?"

"Yes," Poppy called back, steering her father out into the meadow. "We're not a family without Dog! Now,

Jute—you come stand by Mom. Mack, you'll have to be at the back and hold Dog. No, over there. Nula, you're up front here. Mom, Dad with me by Jute."

Beth lifted the black box that her father used to take pictures.

"Say Fae!" the old woman cried.

"Fae!" They all grinned diligently. Eta barked.

Beth lowered the box and smiled. "One for the ages—and I lived to see it."

"Now." Her father took the box back from Beth. "We'll develop the picture in the lab and be sure to get one to you, Beth."

Beth thanked them. "I'll have to give it to the sculptor when they bring them through."

"You'll have it," her father promised.

"Can you make another one?" Poppy asked. "One just for us?"

His face softened. "Of course I can, Poppy Sunshine."

"What a lovely idea, Poppy," her mother chimed in.

"Yes," said Beth. "You should have a record of this day and your beautiful family."

Poppy moved to stand next to Mack and Nula, more excited about the future than she had ever thought possible. "We can hang it in the hall." She smiled.

ACKNOWLEDGMENTS

◆◆◆

hat a time 2020 has been—for all of us—this whole past year. I am so very grateful for all of my readers, and for the opportunity to share this new story with you. There aren't enough exclamation points in the world to capture how emphatically blessed I feel!!! I'm especially thankful for my editor—Nicole Otto. You are a unicorn—rare and amazing. This wild little world of mine became so much more powerful through your care and expertise. Thank you to my agent, Catherine Drayton, at Inkwell Management. You are as stalwart and true as any knight! Thanks also to Claire Friedman at Inkwell for her insights and support. I'm beyond grateful to everyone at Imprint/Macmillan—Erin Stein, Weslie Turner, Raymond Ernesto Colon, Dawn Ryan, John Morgan, Natalie Sousa, Jessica Chung, Elynn Cohen, Carolyn Bull, Katie Halata, and Madison Furr. Thank you to Brandon Dorman for my absolutely stunning cover art. What a treat it was to *see* my story for the first time. Thank you to Grace Kendall and to everyone at FSG for your kind enthusiasm, and for jumping in to support this book. I appreciate it more than I can say.

I'm so incredibly lucky to have the support and friendship of a wonderful writing community. I want to especially thank Heather Kassner, and Gita Trelease, who gave this story (and this author) love at every opportunity. I so look forward to sharing cocktails and "vats" in person—and to laughing over velcros past and present, among endless other things. Thank you to my longtime friends and writing partners, Julie Artz and Jessica Vitalis, who read and gave input on EoSH, and to Sara Faring, Rebecca Petruck, and Mark Holtzen for their kind words and support. Speaking of kind words . . . thank you to Fran Wilde and Quinn Sosna-Spear for their lovely quotes on the cover of *EoSH*.

Thank you to my amazing group of Pitch Wars writer-friends—the PNW Mentors on the Sound, and especially to Joy McCullough for her ongoing friendship. It is so lovely to have such a wonderful group of people with whom to write, build friendships, and make change. I'm looking forward to the time when we can meet up in person again!

All books are built with an author's blood, sweat, and tears. We need a lot of support, and I've had the advantage of caring friends and family who have believed in me from the beginning. I'm thankful to my lifelong friends for their constancy and shine: Meryl McQueen, Katrina Alcorn, Erin Mooney, Hannah Field, and Heather Ostle.

I want to thank my parents, Sally W. Kirouac and George J. Kirouac for their endless and unequivocal support. Mom, I love you—and am so grateful you get to hold my stories in your hands and see what your unpredictable child has wrought. Dad—I miss you. I'm sending you a campfire song, a coffee (black) and some cackling, wherever you are. Thank you to my sister, Martha, and my brother, Ian. You two are my bookends—you keep me upright. I love you. Thank you to my aunt, Mary Lou Hurley, and to Bernie Pilichowski for a lifetime of support and love, and to author Barbara Hazen for being an early inspiration. Last, but never least, thanks to the enormous (in numbers and in heart) Torras/Byrne clan, and to the Wilson/Reeder, and Wolter clans for all of their love and support.

Thank you to my daughters for putting up with me, and for their ongoing inspiration. I am so proud of who you are both becoming. And finally I want to say thank you to my husband and best friend, Daeg. For twenty years, through thick and thin, I've counted on your love and support, your thoughtful input, your soothsaying, your amazing coffee, and most of all your true presence. You are my north star, and I love you.

Thank you, readers. Thank you, universe. Keep going. I love you.